BEYOND A HIGHLAND WHISPER

LATHARN'S STORY

A MACKAY CLAN LEGEND
BOOK TWO

MAEVE GREYSON

MAEVEGREYSON.COM
Magical Romance Sifting Through Time

Contact Information: maeve@maevegreyson.com

Author Maeve Greyson LLC

55 W. 14th Street

Suite 101

Helena, MT 59601

https://maevegreyson.com/

Second Edition – July 2023

Published in the United States of America

Tonight, Latharn was different.

He didn't go any further than the hungry possession of her mouth or his desperate, crushing embrace. Nessa sensed he needed this night to be different. His body tensed beneath her touch, and he restrained his caress as if he wanted her to reason rather than just shatter into mindless bliss.

He raised his head and gazed into her eyes. Nessa flinched at the depths of pain and frustration etched in his face. He struggled, trying to communicate, to connect with her deepest emotions without the use of words. He took his palm, flattened it against his heart then placed it upon her chest. His brows drew together in a questioning frown, as he tilted his head and waited for a sign she understood.

Her lower lip quivered at the very obvious gesture. Nessa whispered, covering his hand with hers, "Are you telling me you love me?" The words almost caught in her throat.

A corner of his mouth pulled up into a relieved smile as Latharn nodded and brushed his lips across hers. He took a deep breath as though steeling himself against his deepest fears. He took her hand and repeated the heart touching gesture from her chest to his. Then he raised a brow and awaited her answer, anxiety filling his eyes.

A lone tear escaped down her cheek as Nessa stared at her hand splayed upon his broad chest. "You know I love you," she murmured with a moan. "I just wish you were real."

He squeezed his eyes shut and pulled her into his arms to cradle her against his chest. Holding her close, he stroked her hair as she gave way to tears.

His arms tightened around her and he gently swayed as she softly wept in his arms.

CHAPTER
ONE

M acKay Keep
Scotland
1410

"Latharn, are ye sure ye never touched the lass?" His father's scowl burned across the room mere seconds ahead of the words.

The reproach in Laird Caelan MacKay's voice stung Latharn like a physical blow. Tension knotted his muscles and his body stiffened with the bitterness pounding through his veins. Only years of respect for his father held his tongue. How could his sire treat him this way? He wasn't an irresponsible boy anymore. How dare he be treated like a lust-crazed lad!

The great hall of the MacKay Keep spanned the largest part of the castle and housed every important gathering of the clan. Flexing his shoulders, Latharn inhaled a deep breath. From where he stood, the room shrank by the moment. He couldn't believe his father had chosen the monthly clan meeting as a means for resolving this matter. How dare he try to shame Latharn into a confession by confronting him in front of his kinsmen. This ploy had worked well enough when Latharn was a lad. His father had used it often whenever he or his brothers had gotten into mischief. Latharn involuntarily flexed his buttocks in remembrance of punishment received after a confession ousted in just such a manner. However, he wasn't a mischievous boy anymore. This was private; they could handle it between themselves.

Every man, woman, and child strained to hear Latharn's reply. His father's closest warriors leaned forward upon the benches. The servants peeped around the corners of the arches, their serving platters clenched to their chests. Latharn rubbed the back of his neck; his skin tingled from their piercing stares.

His father's face flushed a decided shade of purple. Apparently, he'd delayed his answer long enough. Clipping his words just short of blatant disrespect, Latharn growled through a tight-lipped scowl. "How many times must I swear to ye, Father? I have never laid eyes on the MacKinnett lass. I canna bring her face to mind and I havena planted a child in her womb!"

The hall remained silent. Even the dogs sprawling beneath the tables ceased in their endless scuffling for scraps. The only sound breaking the tense silence was the pop of the wood just thrown upon the fires.

With his hands curled into shaking fists, The MacKay pounded the arm of his chair centered at the head of the great hall. Laird MacKay raised his voice to a throaty growl as he edged forward in his chair. "The MacKinnett clan has always been allied with ours. Their lands join our southernmost borders. Must I tell ye how serious these allegations are to our families? The treaty between our clans has been solid for years. God's beard, son! If ye've dishonored their family, there will be no more peace. This lass is the only daughter of their laird!"

His knuckles whitened on the arms of his chair as he continued his tirade. Laird MacKay tensed on the edge of his seat as though he was about to spring upon his prey. His hair heavily streaked with gray, Laird MacKay's once-golden mane gave him the appearance of a battle-weary lion. Though his body showed subtle signs of an aging Highlander, his eyes still blazed as his roar echoed throughout the great hall.

"Always, ye've been one to skirt danger, Latharn! I will admit...'twas usually for the greater good. However, you yourself must also agree, there have been times when ye have yanked the tail of the sleeping dragon just to see if it would breathe fire. So far, your quick wit has kept ye safe from whatever troubles ye have stirred. But this time, I must know the absolute truth: did ye lie with The MacKinnett's daughter?"

How many times was he going to ask him? Did he think he was going to change his answer? Anger surged through Latharn's veins. Rage flashed through him like a cruel, biting wind. He crossed his arms as a barrier across his chest and curled his mouth into a challenging sneer. They didn't believe him. No matter what he said, they didn't believe his words. He read it in their eyes. He spat his words as though their bitter taste soured on his tongue. "I swear to ye upon all I hold sacred, I don't even know the lass's name!"

A brooding man the size of a mountain stood at Laird MacKay's side. Stepping forward, he thrust an accusing finger toward Latharn's chest as though aiming a lance for the killing throw. "Since when did not knowing a lass's name keep ye from tumbling her in your bed?" Latharn's brother, Faolan, stalked forward upon the dais, shaking his head at his brother's latest scandal. Faolan was the eldest of the MacKay sons, next in line to be laird. The look on his face plainly told Latharn he deemed his brother guilty on all charges as stated.

Latharn snarled. "Stay out of this, Faolan. Ye may have beat the rest of us out of Mother's womb, but ye're no' the laird, yet." Latharn met his brother's glare, squaring his shoulders as he stalked forward to answer Faolan's challenge.

How dare Faolan pass judgment against him? Latharn didn't deny he'd enjoyed many a maid since he'd grown to be a man.

However, that didn't mean he'd ever treated them unkindly or shown them any disrespect. He'd sated them fully and when their time was done, he'd taken care to spare their feelings as best he could. Never once had Latharn been inclined to give of his heart...nor had he pretended to do so just to lure a pretty maiden to his bed.

"The lady's name is Leanna and you will speak of her with respect." The clear voice rang out through the archway of the hall, causing everyone's heads to turn. Latharn's mother, Rachel, emerged from an offset alcove, her eyes flashing in irritation toward her youngest son. "Her clan says she has named you as the father of her child. If she carries your child, Latharn, you will do right by her."

Latharn winced as thunder rumbled in the distance. Whenever his mother's emotions were in an upheaval, the weather's stability always suffered. Rachel's powers directly connected with the ebb and flow of the forces of nature. Her emotions meshed with the energies coursing through the physical realm. Thunder, while Mother was clearly upset, was never a promising sign.

Latharn's heart sank as he heard the ring of doubt echo in his mother's voice. She had always been his greatest champion. Whenever the rest of the family rushed to deem him guilty when trouble was in their midst, Rachel always kept an open mind until she'd heard his side of the story. If his mother already believed him guilty this time, how would he convince the rest of them he didn't even know this lass existed?

Latharn had emerged as the youngest of the MacKay triplets. His name was Gaelic for "the fox" and it had served him well. Little did his parents know how aptly the title would fit when they had chosen it for the innocent babe. Whenever mischief occurred, the wily young Latharn had always been the first to be accused. But that same charm and cunning that was the source of all the mayhem also bailed him out of any trouble he'd caused. That is until now, until this latest uproar that had the entire family in such a stir.

Casting a furtive glance at his mother, Latharn wondered why he was to blame for the women always chasing him. It wasn't as if he went a-whoring all over the country for just anyone to warm his bed. Since he had reached manhood, there didn't seem to be a lass in the Highlands who could resist him. He didn't know why they always sought him out. He didn't do anything special. He was just nice to them...and they followed him to his bed. In fact, sometimes they didn't follow him. Sometimes, he'd find them waiting for him when he arrived in his chambers. Latharn shifted in place and adjusted his kilt. A lass probably lurked in his private hallways this very minute. It had become somewhat of a problem escaping them.

Latharn had grown restless. Now that he was older, he'd grown weary of their freely given charms. A quick tumble with a lass was once an incomparable elation. Now the euphoria had dimmed. The satisfaction had dulled to basic physical release. Even while lying spent in erotic exhaustion with a sated lass cooing by his side, Latharn knew there had to be more.

Of late, he'd found a night spent in a luscious maiden's arms left his heart troubled, as though a question nagged at the tip of his tongue, and the answer danced just beyond his reach. No matter her beauty, no matter her sweetness, they all left him empty and cold. Loneliness settled over him like a weight crushing on his chest.

There had to be more than the mere physical pleasure of losing himself in a woman's embrace. He knew there was more to be found. The security of his parents' love for each other had strengthened their family as far back as he could remember. He sought that glow of contentment he'd seen in his parents' eyes when their gazes met across a room. No matter how many years had passed between them, the look they shared never changed. He ached for the connection his parents had found. He longed to lose himself in another's eyes and speak volumes without saying a word. It was time he cradled his newborn child in his arms, with his loving wife nestled at his side.

Latharn stifled a shudder; the tension gnawed at his gut. The expressions on their faces told him so much more than words. They'd never believe the things he'd done to avoid the women vying for his embrace. His emptiness ached like a festering wound that refused to heal. He had decided to search for the elusive answer by honing his mystical powers. He'd hoped by refining and perfecting his magical gifts, he might solve the mystery of his untouchable heart.

Of late, he'd been so engrossed in sharpening his goddess-given powers, he'd not even walked with a woman in the gardens for several months. He'd been holed up in the northern tower of the keep. There was no way he fathered the MacKinnett woman's child. By Amergin's beard, it had to have been at least five full moons since he'd been outside the castle skirting walls!

The air of the keep closed in around him; the sweltering heat of too many bodies shoved in one room added to his discomfort. Latharn raked his hands through his hair and tore himself from his tortured musings. His mother glared at him, her foot tapping. Perhaps it was the fire that flashed in her eyes bringing the heat to his skin.

"I know of no Leanna MacKinnett!" he ground out through clenched teeth. Latharn braced himself for his family's damning replies. His gut was already wrenched with the unspoken accusations springing from their eyes.

Raking his own hands through his graying hair, Laird MacKay expelled a heavy sigh. Fixing his gaze on his son with a disappointed glower, he dropped his hands to the arms of his chair. "Their *bana-buidhseach* will arrive at any moment. Their clan will not be satisfied with your denials until their seer has had a chance to speak with ye and weigh the truth of your words."

Latharn turned to his mother. There was one more thing he had to say in his defense. He didn't care if the rest of the MacKay clan didn't believe him. His mother would believe his innocence.

"Mother! As many abandoned bairns as I've rescued while on my travels, as many waifs as I've brought home to this clan, do ye honestly think I would be able to deny a child of my own blood, a child I had sired? Do ye truly think I would turn my back on a bairn of my very own?"

Latharn towered over his mother, peering down into her eyes and opening his soul to her senses. She had to believe him. He trusted his mother's intuition to see the truth in his heart. His voice fell to a defeated whisper as he groaned and repeated his earlier words.

"I swear to ye, Mother. I am not the father of the woman's child. I know of no Leanna MacKinnett!"

Rachel's hand fluttered to her throat, and she slowly nodded. "I believe you, Latharn. Moreover, I will do what I can to shield you from their *bana-buidhseach*. I hear this woman's powers are amazing, perhaps even stronger than mine. But I'll do whatever I can to protect you from any evil that may be traveling upon the mists."

With a heaviness in his chest and a catch in his voice, Latharn embraced his mother and whispered, "Your belief in me is all I've ever needed, Mother. Ye know I would never bring dishonor to our family or shame upon our clan."

He brushed his lips across his mother's cheek just as chaos erupted at the archway of the hall.

Her shrill cry echoed through the keep as the MacKinnett *bana-buidhseach* screeched like an enraged crow. "I demand retribution for Clan MacKinnett. That heartless cur has sullied Leanna MacKinnett's good name!"

The bent old woman rocked to and fro at the entrance to the hall, brandishing her gnarled walking stick overhead like a weapon.

Her white hair hung in tangled shocks across her stooped shoulders. Her black eyes glittered in her shriveled face, like a rat's beady eyes from a darkened corner. Her somber robes swept the rush-covered floor with every dragging step. Even the brawniest Highlander in the crowd faded back as she hitched her way to the front of the cavernous room.

Drawing a deep breath, Latharn's muscles tensed as the old crone edged her way toward him. Tangible power emanated from her swirling aura as he studied her twisted form. This seer's energies rivaled those of his time-traveling mother. The battering rush of the crone's malicious emotional onslaught threatened to slam him against the farthest wall.

His mother's powers had been refined through several generations to her in the twenty-first century. However, her aura had never emitted such waves of energy, not even after magnification through the portals of time.

Immense anger emanated from deep within this old woman, reaching out toward Latharn like a deadly claw. The crone's soul overflowed with touchable hatred.

Latharn braced himself as a rising sense of dread curled its icy fingers around his spine. He shuddered, swallowing hard against bitter bile as he noticed something else. The *bana-buidhseach's* aura seethed with an underlying layer of evil his mother could never possess. The witch's pulsating energy roiled with a menacing thread of darkness he'd never seen the likes of before.

Cocking her head to one side, a malicious glint shone in her eyes. Her mouth curled into a grimace as she croaked, "What say ye, MacKay cur? Do ye deny robbing my laird's daughter of her precious maidenhead? Do ye deny ruining her for any other man?"

With a single stamp of her crooked staff upon the floor, enraged lightning responded outside, the flash splintering throughout the room. Everyone in the hall cowered against the walls, shielding their faces from the narrow windows high overhead. The acrid tang of sulfur hung heavy in the air from the burn of the splitting energy.

Theatrics to get her point across. This did not bode well. His hands tensing into clenched fists, Latharn took a deep breath before he spoke. "I fear there has been a grave misunderstanding. I have not been outside the walls of Castle MacKay in the passing of the last five moons."

"Exactly!" she spat, jabbing her bony finger from deep within her ragged sleeve. The *bana-buidhseach* hitched sideways closer to Latharn and shook a threatening fist in his face. "Ye appeared to the lass while she lay in her bed. Your vile essence washed over her silken body by the light of the swollen moon. As your spirit swirled upon the mist of the bittersweet night, ye violated her ripe nest and filled her with your seed."

Eyes flashing with a mother's protective rage, Rachel shoved her way between Latharn and the snarling hag. Resting her hand on Latharn's chest, Rachel stood nose to nose with the crone. "Surely, you don't believe in such an outlandish tale? The girl could not possibly find herself pregnant in the way you just described."

The crone hitched her way even closer to Rachel, her dark eyes narrowed into calculating slits. Hissing her reply, her foul breath nearly colored the air around her as she spat through rotted teeth with every word. "Do ye call me a liar, Lady MacKay? Do ye slur the name of Leanna MacKinnett and the honored MacKinnett clan?"

The hall crackled with the conflicting forces of emotional energy as lightning once again splintered the electrified air. Thunder roared, shaking the walls until debris rained down from the rafters.

Rachel circled the wizened old hag. "I've nothing to say about Leanna MacKinnett or the good name of the MacKinnett clan. I defend my son's honor against your lies. I challenge your slander against an honorable MacKay son!"

With a wave of her hand and a narrowed eye, the hag halted Rachel where she stood. The spell she cast silenced Rachel's voice and paralyzed her body. Sliding around Rachel, she stabbed a gnarled finger into the middle of Latharn's chest. A demonic smile curled across her face as she sidled her body closer. With a flourish of one hand, she withdrew a ball of swirling glass from the folds of her tattered robe. Her cackling voice rose to a maniacal shriek as she lifted the ball for all to see. "Do ye deny lying with every maiden whose head ye happened to turn? Do ye deny withholding your heart from every woman in which ye've ever planted your cock?"

Latharn's voice fell to a low, guttural whisper as dread gripped him in his gut. "Who are ye, woman? What is it ye seek from me?" An icy premonition, fear of what was to come, stole the very breath from his lungs. Latharn knew in the very depths of his soul there had never been a Leanna MacKinnett. This wasn't judgment for ruining some woman or the name of her clan. The stench of something much more sinister hung in the air. It rankled with every breath he took.

With a crazed laugh, the shriveled old woman transformed before his eyes. Her dry, tangled hair lengthened into flowing black tresses. Her sallow, wrinkled skin smoothed into creamy silk. Her bent frame straightened, blossoming into a shapely woman, breasts full, hips round and firm.

Her eyes remained black as the darkest obsidian, and her full red lips curled into a seductive, malicious smile. Her voice became a throaty, honey-laced melody, deadly in its hypnotic tone. "Do ye remember me now, my beautiful Highlander? We were together once, you and I. We were lovers, but now I come here as your judge and jailer. And I have found ye guilty of withholding your heart from the only one who truly deserves your love."

"Deardha?" Latharn recoiled from the seductress bearing down upon him.

As she thrust the deep violet globe into his face, Deardha's voice echoed across the hall. "Aye, Latharn. Ye remember me now? Listen closely to my words. I condemn ye to this eternal prison. I banish ye to this crystal hell. Ye are far too powerful a charmer of magic to be toying with women's hearts. No longer will I allow ye to sow your seed with any poor fool who warms your bed. If ye willna pledge your heart to me, then ye shall wish ye were dead." As Deardha uttered the spell, blinding white energy swirled from the tips of her long pale fingers. The shimmering tendrils flowed and curled, constricting around Latharn's body.

With an enraged scream, Rachel broke free of Deardha's binding spell. Forcing her way between Latharn and the witch, she clawed at Deardha's face.

"Mother, no!" Latharn roared, fighting against the tightening bands of the curse meshed about his body. "Ye must get away from her. Save yourself!" He couldn't breathe. His heartbeat slowed and the room darkened around him. This must be what it felt like to die. Latharn struggled to focus his eyes.

The conflicting forces threw Rachel across the room as Deardha's field of malevolence blasted against the walls. The winds howled and roared as the demonic chaos ripped through the castle. Then all fell silent just as swiftly as the storm had risen and a fog of sorrow settled over the room. Latharn shuddered awake to an icy smoothness pressed against his spine. Finding his arms freed, he flexed his hands, wincing as he rolled his bruised and battered shoulders. Where was he? He lifted his head, staring about in disbelief at the see-through globe enclosed around his body.

Everyone eased their way out from where they'd taken cover: they crawled out from under tables, from behind overturned benches. Eyes wide with fear, they glanced about the room to see if the attack was over.

Latharn spread his hands on the curved, cold glass. What were they doing? Why did they mill around him like he wasn't there? It was as though he sat among their feet on the floor. What the hell were they doing?

The serving lads rushed to re-light the torches lining the walls. The scattered clansmen and villagers rose from the floor, checking each other for injuries. Tables and benches lay about the room like scattered rushes strewn across the floor. Tapestries and tartans hung in tattered strips, nothing left on the standards but bits of colored shreds.

Laird MacKay shoved his way through the wreckage to his wife. Rachel lay in a crumpled heap beside the hearth, her weakened breath barely moving her chest.

"Mother!" Latharn shouted against the glass. If she was dead, it would be no one's fault but his own. Standing, Latharn stretched to see if Rachel would move.

Laird MacKay cradled her against his chest, pressing his lips to her forehead until she opened her eyes.

Rachel struggled to lift her head, her eyes widening with disbelief as she looked across the room directly toward Latharn. Lifting her hand, her voice cracked with pain as she keened her sorrow to all who remained in the great hall. "My baby!" she sobbed. Waving her trembling hand toward her son, she buried her face in Caelan's chest.

Latharn closed his eyes against the sight of his mother rocking herself against her pain. As her wails grew louder, he covered his ears and roared to drown out the sound.

CHAPTER
TWO

**ashington University
St. Louis, MO
2010**

"Professor Buchanan, do I get extra credit for fixing you up with him? You know, the fine piece of man we met? That guy we met at last month's conference?"

Nessa Buchanan peered over the top of her laptop, scowling from behind the pair of reading glasses perched on the end of her nose. "If you were one of my students, Ms. Sullivan, you would've just failed the semester for hooking me up with that so-called fine piece of man."

"Oh, come on, Nessa. He couldn't have been that bad." Trish sank her teeth into the apple she'd been juggling as she sauntered around Nessa's office.

After she tossed her glasses onto the desk, Nessa steepled her fingers beneath her chin.

"Trish, do you remember his lecture on the existence of different realities and their definitions as determined by any one individual's perceptions?"

"Vaguely." Trish nodded as she munched another bite of the apple and thumbed through the exams on Nessa's desk.

"Well, it appears that his perception of all night long is my reality of maybe—and I'm really stressing the maybe part—of about, oh, maybe ten minutes."

Nessa stretched across the desk and slammed her hand down on top of the pile of exams. "And after the questionable ten minutes of all night long, he started snoring!" Snoring didn't begin to describe it. He'd practically rattled the windows out of her apartment.

With a grimace, Trish shuddered and tossed her half-eaten apple into the trash. Wiping her hands on the tight seat of her jeans, Trish shrugged. "Come on, Nessa. Was he really all that bad? He seemed kind of nice at the conference."

"He farts in his sleep." Not looking up, Nessa shoved folders of exams into her backpack in a futile attempt at unearthing her disappearing desk. The guy had been a veritable methane gas factory.

"I see," Trish observed with a sigh. "Well, that settles it since we both know you never fart." Trish groaned out loud, as Nessa handed her another stack of exams that wouldn't fit in her already overstuffed backpack.

"And he sucks his teeth," Nessa continued, holding out two more piles of papers toward Trish.

"Before or after he farts?" Trish asked as she juggled the packets of oversized files.

Nessa grunted. "After he eats." Dragging her backpack over into her chair, she huffed as she kneed it shut and wrestled the straining zipper.

Trish backed away from the desk with a defeated shrug. "Okay! I get the message. No more fixups. I'll just leave you to your fantasies about your nocturnal Highlander."

Nessa stopped grappling with her overstuffed backpack long

enough to point her finger at Trish. "I will have you know my dreams of my ancient Scotsman have made me what I am today."

The youngest Ph.D. in Archeology at Washington University, Nessa prided herself on the position she'd attained in her field. She'd worked long and hard to get this far, untold hours of solitude, sweat, and tears. She also knew the reason she'd achieved such a lofty position. Nessa owed it all to the inexplicable dreams she'd had since the summer she turned eighteen.

She'd never forget that horrible summer or the catastrophe of her eighteenth birthday. She'd spent summer vacation mooning over the muscle-bound exchange student staying with her mother's best friend.

Nessa realized now she had grown up an insecure child. And no wonder, the way her thoughtless parents had always maligned her with constant criticism.

"Develop what little mind you've got, Nessa. As plain as you are that's all you're ever going to have." Those words had been their constant mantra for as long as she could remember.

However, her mother had noticed Nessa's infatuation with Victor and had plotted a little birthday surprise. The night of Nessa's party, Victor attended her every move. Everywhere she turned, Victor was there. Nessa was delirious. She was thrilled by his touch. She couldn't believe he really liked her. But at the end of the party, the delightful fantasy shattered when Nessa saw her mother hand Victor a check. Her mother then bestowed a pitying smile upon her and told her, "Happy birthday".

Nessa sobbed herself to sleep that night, the night she'd had the first dream. He had appeared as though in answer to her silent cry of despair, this man, this great, hulking warrior the size of a mountain. Soul-piercing eyes glimmered so green and haunting Nessa felt adrift in a sea of pines. High cheekbones, aquiline nose. She sighed. His features had struck her breathless. He had the reddish blond hair that bespoke of Viking ancestry, the strong Norse genetics forged when the marauding invaders overtook weaker villages and sowed their ancestral seeds. At eighteen years of age, Nessa didn't know much about men. But she knew enough to realize this one was pure perfection.

He'd never spoken to her, not a single time. The first time he'd appeared, he'd stood a few steps away as though he didn't wish to frighten her. His gaze had swept across her body, while the faintest of smiles had pulled at one corner of his mouth. The understanding in his eyes had pushed the loneliness from her heart. He'd reached out to her with the barest touch, brushing the back of his fingers across her arm. The trust had telegraphed like electricity across her skin. At last, she'd found someone who wouldn't humiliate her.

As she'd grown older, his repeated visits had changed and evolved into something much more. The dreams had become a subtle courting, a gentle winning of her heart. He'd found clever ways to draw her close, pursue her with a sensitive glance. Always intuitive, he appeared when she needed him. He never pushed her but never failed to respond whenever her subconscious called out. Her Highlander soothed her with his silent caress. He strengthened her with his touch.

She didn't realize her nocturnal visitor was a true Highlander by birth until one of her history classes touched upon the turbulence of Scotland. She'd always loved his unusual garb but had never placed it until one day when she'd opened to a particular chapter in her history book. His kilted plaid fit snugly about his narrow hips as though it were part of his body. His ancient claymore hung at his side as a silent warning. His hand often rested on the hilt as though he found comfort in its touch.

When he'd taken her hand and guided it over the ancient crest pinned at his shoulder, Nessa had fallen hopelessly in love with the man and all things relating to the Scot.

After that, she had been a soul possessed to find out everything she could about Scotland's past. She'd spent months trying to find the elusive crest, in the hopes of identifying her Highlander's clan. She'd found some that were close, but to her dismay, she'd never located an identical match. That's when she'd decided he was just her fantasy. At least if he was only in her head, it meant he could never leave her. Her Highlander would always be hers.

Even though she'd accepted deep in her heart her Highlander couldn't be real, Scotland remained the first love of her life. She studied its history with relentless passion, from its bloody past to its determined people, and how it had changed the course of civilization through the ages. The only drawback of her single-minded obsession, and a rather annoying side effect of her dreams, was the fact that any male met during her waking hours didn't quite measure up against her perfect nocturnal Highlander.

Nessa blamed her continued solitude on the fact that apparently, her parents had been right all along. She must be too homely for any man to consider taking home to meet the folks. That is, any man worth having. Any man like the one in her dreams. There were plenty of them out there ready and willing to participate in messing up the sheets. If you weren't too picky and had approximately ten minutes you didn't mind donating to a total waste of time.

"Nessa! You're doing it again!" Trish dropped a stack of books on the floor.

Nessa jumped, jolted from her reverie.

"I mention dream dude and there you go, off into Nessa-land again."

Fixing Trish with a threatening glare, Nessa tucked her reading glasses into the neck of her shirt. "You drop my textbooks like that again, and I'm gonna recommend you for the Research Department! I haven't forgotten how much you just love disappearing into the archives for days—and nights—at a time."

An opened letter on the desk caught her attention and Nessa's irritation with Trish vanished. "You have to see this! Look! Are you up for an extended trip to Scotland?" Scooping up the paper, she pushed it under Trish's nose, then slung the groaning bag over her shoulder. That multi-folded piece of paper held her magic genie. Her wishes were finally granted.

Trish shook her head as she unfolded the paper. "Come on, Nessa. You know I can't afford airfare to Scotland right now. I'm still up to my eyeballs in student loans from getting my master's degree."

Scanning over the well-worn letter, Trish wrinkled her nose as she read. Pinching the page where her reading had stopped, Trish's face grew thoughtful with what she'd just digested. "Where exactly is Durness?"

Excitement bubbled inside Nessa as though she was a can of carbonated cola. All of her studying and long hours of solitude had led her to the land of her dreams. "Northwestern tip of Scotland. The Highlands. It's finally happened, Trish! I finally got the grant!"

Trish's grin spread into an excited smile as she glanced up again from farther down the page. "This is it? You finally got the grant from the University of Glasgow? This is the one you've applied for three years in a row?"

Snatching the letter out of Trish's hands, Nessa waved it in the air. "You got it, my friend. I finally got the grant. I've received the funding to go on an extended archeological study of the Durness sites and the surrounding areas of Balnakiel. All I have to do is register all of my findings with the University of Glasgow. Anything I find will be tagged by their history department for use in further studies. And since you're my assistant, your expenses are just as fully paid as mine."

"Well then, woo hoo!" Trish hooted at the top of her lungs with a jab of her fist in the air. "That's fantastic! You've been trying to get this grant forever. And Scotland...what is it you call it after you've had about half a beer? The land of your heart's desire? Hey! Maybe you'll meet the great-great-grandson of the guy in your dreams and finally have a sex life worth talking about."

Great. She could always count on Trish to put things in perspective. Nessa laughed as she folded the well-worn letter and forced it into the outside pocket of the backpack. "Tell me, Trish. Why is it you can remember things like that but you can never remember what we've named our database files? And is sex all you think about? I think you're the one who needs to find a guy worth taking to bed."

With a wicked wink, Trish patted her shapely rump before she scooped up an armload of folders off the desk. "I'm not the one who has a problem with snoring, farting, ten-minute teeth suckers taking up space between my sheets."

THREE

Finally. Almost six hundred years in this accursed prison. Some would call it an eternity. The reward for his infinite patience was about to be received. He had turned her in the direction of the sphere and she was bound for the land of his birth. His freedom, the wife, and the children he'd always dreamed of having, all were within his grasp.

Latharn stripped to the waist. His kilt hung low about his hips as he worked with his ancient sword. The massive claymore swung like an extension of his arms. The hilt as good as melded to the palms of his hands. Latharn smoothed his fingers across the cold, hard steel with the gentleness of a lover's caress. The blade had been his ever since his father had presented it when he had become a man. Slashing through the air with tireless rhythm, his body and soul tingled with the heat of the ancient dance.

The steel sang, whispered through the wind of the sphere, consoling Latharn in his isolation. Faster, harder, it severed the air, whistling a lonesome tune.

Hours of dueling unseen enemies had staved off the madness of centuries. The madness of isolation from the rest of humanity, but still being forced to watch their every move. No one could see within the crystal cell, but Latharn watched everything around him. The one-way walls showed his friends, his family, and all the orphaned children he'd ever saved. They'd lived their lives within his sight and also faced their deaths.

Before his mother had discovered the way to break the curse, Latharn decided to end his hell. He couldn't accept an eternity of unjust punishment within the crystal ball. He'd rather take his life and take his chances at losing his soul to the abyss. At least there, he wouldn't be isolated and his family would find closure with his death. In their own time, they'd also find their peace.

However, the malicious sorceress had foreseen such a possibility and taken care to prevent such an easy escape. Latharn couldn't count the times he'd slashed open his body, just to watch the wound heal before a single drop of blood spilled.

Therefore, he'd accepted his fate and turned his mind inward to find a way to survive. The chief druid, Emrys MacKay, had once told him meditation was the key to finding his strengths. All the mysteries of the universe waited inside him. All he needed was the patience and the discipline to find them.

As he crouched, then sprang to whip the blade through the air, the song of the steel echoed through the chamber. Its strength pulsated through his veins, the energy coursing through his mind. The power of the dance grew frenzied, his body tensed as he lunged for his unseen prey. His heart pounded; he barely breathed. His unblinking eyes stared straight ahead. Once again, Latharn's mind escaped the stifling realms of his prison; he traveled through the mists of time.

His consciousness journeyed through untold planes of existence. He explored universes of energy, discovering levels of enlightenment he'd never hoped to attain. It was during these travels through the veils that he'd found a fascinating form of energy he couldn't resist.

An aura of light pulsated with such an intensity of compassion it drew him like steel to a magnet. He'd touched it with his consciousness, to discover it flowed through him and connected to his soul. Shocked at the joining, he pulled away from the energy. He'd never experienced such an intimate melding on any of the planes he'd explored. Intrigued, he touched the energy again, locking with it as though it were a piece of a missing puzzle. The two auras danced and swirled upon the plane, discovering the universe together.

He'd followed the light for an untold amount of time, since on the current plane, time didn't exist. The playful energy teased and danced with him, first touching his mind before jumping back like a puppy pouncing on an enticing toy.

It took him eons to realize this comforting presence was the life force he was destined to love. However, this realization confused him more. Before his mother died, she had discovered how the curse of the witch's ball could be broken. The one woman capable of winning Latharn's heart must call out for his release. If this presence was the consciousness of the woman he was to love, where was her physical body?

As it turned out, it was more like when was her physical body. Latharn had known the moment she was born. He'd become so adept at meditating through the planes, he'd watched over her as she'd grown. He'd suffered in silence as her parents belittled her. He'd watched them treat her as though they'd wished she'd never been born. His soul raged within his crystal prison as he watched the tear-filled life of the emotionally battered child. How could anyone be so cruel to a bairn of their own? Their words pained and damaged the lass more surely than if they'd beaten her with a club.

When at last he'd found the pathway to her dreams, he'd been determined to do his best to comfort her. He would ensure she knew she was a precious gift. She would know her inner beauty was even greater than the loveliness of her physical body. It didn't matter if he ever escaped his hell. All that mattered to Latharn was that he delivered Nessa from hers.

He'd been proud as he'd watched her grow into a talented young woman. He wished she could see her own beauty but she was more sure of herself than he'd ever hoped she would be. When she'd started relationship exploration with the opposite sex, it was almost more than he could bear.

It was then he decided to shape destiny with his own hands. If he'd consoled her subconscious while in her dreams, then he should be able to guide her to the location of the globe.

And now she was on her way to Scotland. He'd even managed to fixate her upon the area of Durness. Once upon his homeland and in the exact proximity of the globe, Latharn knew he'd be even stronger at manifesting his powers around her.

It was time he took a different path in her dreams. As her lover.

CHAPTER
FOUR

Deardha couldn't believe he had never cried out to her. Damn, that hard-headed Highlander. She had figured for certain he would drop to his knees and beg to hear her terms. She would've wagered her finest athame Latharn would plead for his release within weeks of his imprisonment. She had watched the man his entire life. Latharn MacKay thrived best when surrounded by those he loved. The man needed the touch of his clan more than he needed the touch of his damnable Highland plaid. And yet even when he'd watched his mother jump to her death, the stubborn fool had just stood there within the bauble, silent as a stone cairn.

"I shouldha' just destroyed him rather than imprison him!"

With an irritated hiss, Deardha traced her fingertips across varying sizes of globes as she worried about the darkened room. The shelves flickered with crystal orbs glimmering in every spectrum of the rainbow. Over the past six hundred years, she had collected souls much as a child collects fireflies on a summer's eve. She smiled with pride at her varied collection. It wasn't easy tending so many fools. A few scattered orbs along the shelves had gone dark. She'd allowed their lights to flicker away. Some of the occupants became such simpering bores. No matter. Bright, shining replacements abounded.

Turning from her beloved collection of souls, she focused on the largest orb of her assortment. Her scrying globe rested upon a massive stone pedestal in the center of the room.

"Show me the bitch," she commanded with a wave of her hand as she stormed across her chambers.

The center orb filled with a blue-white haze as though someone had just exhaled a puff of smoke and blown it inside the glass. Mist swirled inside the globe as Deardha tapped her nails upon the surface. "Focus now! I know she's far but Latharn has succeeded in guiding her to our shores and we must prepare for her arrival."

Nessa's laughing face appeared in the vision, chattering into her cell phone as she packed for her trip. A shiver of revulsion swept over her body as Deardha stroked the cool smooth glass between her hands. "I still do not understand what he sees in that bit of fluff. There's not enough woman there for a good night's ride!"

Deardha dispersed the vision with a wave of disgust, spitting her disapproval on the floor. Smoothing her hands over the frigid glass, she inhaled a deep, cleansing breath, and lowered her voice to an evil purr. "Now, on to more pleasant things. Show me the weak one we found the other day, the one who shows such promise for destroying the scrawny bitch."

The crystal didn't falter but shifted to show the image of a surly, dark-haired man as he towered over a cringing young woman. Excitement surged through Deardha's body. Oh, this was wondrous. Perfect timing. She watched the scene play out within the crystal: the man stormed in a fit of rage and the woman cowered before him, terrified. Deardha rubbed her hands together as she hissed into the glass. "Oh, go on, you know you want to hit her. You know she really deserves it."

A resounding slap echoed from the depths of the globe, followed by the sound of the woman's sobs.

Deardha nodded with a satisfied chuckle. This one would serve her purpose well. She controlled his weak soul without even taking over his body. He was her puppet, his mind so open to her suggestions, she need but whisper to him across the mists.

Of course, she should get out more. It had been centuries since she'd been out in the world. She could stir up so much more mischief if she possessed the man. It wouldn't take much to take him over. After all, the simpleton had already forfeited his soul when he read the ancient mantra backward during the dark of the moon.

"Ye should figure out what those Latin words mean before ye start dabbling in my world, fool."

She idly tapped a fingernail on the glowing crystal before her. With a sigh, Deardha decided to wait and see how it all unwound. After all, she hadn't survived over six hundred years by tossing caution to the wind.

CHAPTER
FIVE

"Of all the languages I've been able to learn, why is it I can't seem to grasp Gaelic?" Trish worried the earbud from her ear and leaned forward to peer out the window of the plane.

"Trish." Nessa sighed in her most motherly tone. "You know they speak English in Scotland, right?" Thumbing through the pile of archeological journals in her lap, she continued making notes without glancing up from the pages. They went through this on the way to every dig. How many languages did Trish think she had to learn?

As she pulled a map out of her carry-on, Trish stabbed the paper in emphasis of each of her words. "Look at some of these place names! Are you trying to tell me if I didn't know Gaelic it wouldn't be easier for me to get us around?"

Ignoring the map as she highlighted an entry in her journal, Nessa placated Trish with an absentminded nod. "You always do a wonderful job of getting us around, Trish, no matter what country we find ourselves exploring." Maybe Trish would take a nap once the engines settled into their regular flight pattern drone.

Nessa pulled the journal closer as a particular article caught her attention and she adjusted her reading glasses for a better view. "MacKay? Why does that name seem so familiar? Is that the name of any of the contacts we've been given to get in touch with once we reach Balnakiel?"

Pulling her BlackBerry out of her pocket, Trish studied the screen as she rolled the wheel with her thumb. "Hmm. No. I don't have any MacKays on my list. Why? What's it say?"

Nessa pinched the bridge of her nose, then stuffed her glasses into the neck of her shirt. Leaning her head back against the seat, she squinted her eyes, struggling to place the name. With a shrug, she hid a yawn behind her hand as she stretched her legs as far as the seat would allow. "Nothing really." She yawned again and nodded toward Trish's BlackBerry as she struggled to stay awake. "You better put that thing away. You're not supposed to have it on. The journal just mentioned something about how MacKay Castle had been restored at Balnakiel Bay."

Trish shrugged in obvious dismissal of Nessa's words. "Lots of castles have been restored. Scotland's National Trust restores a lot of the castles as well as a lot of privately funded landmarks. I was reading about it on the Internet the other night. Scotland is proud of its past." Trish shoved her BlackBerry back in her pocket and fiddled with her iPod. Stuffing her earbud back into place, she closed her eyes as the lesson began.

With a tired sigh, Nessa pushed all the journals back inside her carry-on and shoved it under the seat. With a glance at Trish, she realized she needn't bother answering by the faraway look on Trish's face.

Maybe the reason the name MacKay sounded so familiar was that it cropped up every time she turned around. The closer they got to Scotland, the more the name appeared. It was as though someone were trying to lead her toward some unknown goal. Trying to guide her to...what? What could be so important for her to find out about the MacKay clan? What awaited her arrival in Scotland and how did it link to the MacKay family? Could it be some sort of career-making find, mystically fueling the excitement in her blood?

Serendipity? Fate? Destiny? Karma? For some reason, Nessa couldn't seem to get these ideologies out of her mind either. She was a fervent follower of archeological history and fact. She believed what she could see and touch. Why did these mystically directed belief systems keep cropping up in her head?

Could part of it be because her fantasy Highlander had become increasingly more seductive in her dreams? Once she'd planned her trip to Scotland, the man had a single-minded purpose. The Scot was determined to have some sort of active part in her waking life and not just in her subconscious mind. Her Highlander ramped up his visits each night to ensure he maintained a place in her constant awareness. Her undivided attention during her dreams was no longer enough. He now wanted her mind during her daylight hours as well.

Although he still never spoke, it was obvious he led Nessa down a path with single-minded determination The seduction level of her dreams served to deepen their relationship even more.

With an amused huff, Nessa closed her eyes and settled deeper into her seat. Thank goodness the man was in her dreams and didn't exist in her waking reality. In real life, what in the world would a hunk like that want with a homely little bookworm like her?

He cradled her chin in his hand and lifted her face to meet his smoldering gaze. Lowering his head, he brushed his lips across hers and traced his fingers along her cheek. With a velvet touch, he tasted her upturned mouth, lingering as though she were a tempting treat to be savored.

She never tired of the scent of him, a luscious combination of the essence of pine, the sea, and aroused male. Nessa inhaled deeper as she released herself to him.

Leaning into his arms, she molded herself against him. She relished the heat of his hardened body. She starved for his touch, every nerve ending heightened, waiting for his exploration. From his rippling muscles to his velvety skin, she ached to devour him, to enfold him with all of her senses.

He deepened his kiss, his unrelenting mouth opened hers, demanding complete possession. He closed his embrace, then slid his hands down her back, pulling her body hard against his erection, rock hard and straining against her belly. There was no doubt of what was to come.

His lips seared a trail down her throat and suckled her tingling breasts. Her knees grew weak. Her mind wasn't interested in maintaining her balance but in the delights caressing her body. Nessa's knees buckled; she would've collapsed had he not caught her up in his arms and lowered her to the ground.

Her breath caught in her throat, lips parted with expectation as his body loomed above her. With painstaking care, he ran his hands up her thighs and gently splayed her legs. As he blew against the dark curls at the vee of her thighs, he fixed her with a heavy-lidded gaze. A smile of satisfaction curled his lips as he watched her breathing quicken. Imprisoning her eyes with his own sultry stare, he traced his fingertips down her inner thighs. As he lowered his mouth, he purred with pleasure and introduced her to the other uses of his skillful tongue. His mouth was pure, unadulterated rapture.

How was it possible for him to ignite so many nerve endings with his inquisitive tongue? Head to the side, she arched her back in ecstasy, burying her hands in his hair. Pulling him tighter into her welcoming heat, she moaned with abandon as he exquisitely tortured her until she thought she would die. Her heart risked exploding from her chest, pounding against her ribs. He suckled her nub into his mouth as he buried his fingers into her greedy depths. Caressing and teasing, he drove her past reason. She was beyond anything but pure sensation.

Nessa shrieked as her body exploded into delightful shards of bliss.

"Nessa! Wake up!"

Nessa grunted as Trish elbowed her in the ribs. Trish glanced around the cabin of the plane before she settled back into her seat.

"Dammit!" Nessa blew her short curls out of her face and struggled to catch her breath. She needed some air. What a dream. Fanning her shirt, she squirmed in her seat. Now she needed to change her clothes.

Trish stretched over Nessa and clicked on the overhead fan. "'Dammit' is right. I'm not going to ask what you were dreaming about because me as well as everybody else sitting in coach, and maybe even first class, already knows."

With a wicked grin as she adjusted the tray table, Trish caught the eye of the flight attendant and motioned for two glasses of water.

Pulling a tissue out of her pocket, Nessa dabbed at the sweat on her face. She accepted the water from the winking attendant and gulped at the welcomed drink.

She glanced around the cabin at all the smiling faces then edged up to Trish with a breathless whisper, "I think I just had my first mind-blowing orgasm."

CHAPTER
SIX

At least they had placed his shelf so he had a decent view of the streets. Latharn's humorless laugh echoed off the glass walls of his prison. His shelf. After six hundred years, he'd reduced himself to referring to his prison as though he were a child's bauble in the nursery.

"Brodie, my love, what did ye do with the crate of hand painted-dishes Moira brought round yesterday eve?" Fiona MacKay's voice lilted from the stockroom at the back of the store.

Latharn heaved a bored sigh as he leaned up against the clear, curved wall. This century's guardians—his descendants, Brodie and his wife, Fiona—were decent enough, but he failed to see their interest in this little shop they'd decided to set up in Balnakiel. Fiona should be home having babies and Brodie should be caring for the MacKay estate while they waited for Nessa's arrival in Scotland. Yet there the man stood in the corner with a dust rag in his hand as though he were some sort of chambermaid. And if Brodie bent over one more time and gave Latharn a clear view of his arse in that kilt, Latharn was going to pelt him with an object from the other side of

32

the shop. His distant cousin's hairy backside was not the view he preferred in all of Scotland.

"I've already brought them in here, my love. I thought they'd best be displayed on the shelves in this bay window facing the street." Brodie ran his cleaning rag around the edges of the newly installed windows. He'd polished the panes clean and clear in the dawning light of the day.

"They'd be better displayed in the garbage bin." Latharn snorted as he leaned closer to the walls of his cell. "Those things are hideous. I wouldn't use them to feed the swine."

Fiona emerged from the chaos of the stockroom, pushing her damp hair back from her face. She nodded at Brodie's results with the sparkling panes. She shoved up her sleeves and bent to pull the plates from their bubble wrap and stack them on the shelves. She paused with a plate held in midair as a flickering purple light cast a haze across her apron.

"Did ye notice your cousin over there appears to be more active these days since we've placed him in the shop?" Fiona nodded toward Latharn on the high shelf behind the counter, where he stood inside the glowing glass sphere perched on a hand-carved wooden stand.

A surge of pride swelled through Latharn's chest. Ah yes, there was a job well done indeed. It had taken him quite a while to guide Brodie to Fiona. The hardest part was getting the hardheaded fool to propose. A few subconscious suggestions here and there and now the lad had finally settled down. Little did Brodie know that Latharn had scared away all his other girlfriends. Latharn didn't like those modern girls. Brodie needed a woman who loved tradition and would watch over him. Fiona was all of that. Latharn had watched her. He had chosen her for his descendent. Everyone needed a little guidance now and then.

Tossing the rag on the counter, Brodie studied the pulsating globe. "Aye, I've noticed. I wonder if we'll be the generation to see Cousin Latharn released from his wee crystal tomb."

Latharn tensed at Brodie's words. There would be no wondering about this subject. Nessa was on her way to Scotland right now. He had brought her this close. Latharn would not consider the fact that Nessa would draw this close to him and then fail to break the curse.

Fiona stretched and lifted the violet ball from the shelf. She eased it to the counter between them for its daily polishing.

"Can ye imagine being imprisoned for nearly six hundred years inside a witch's ball?"

"Ye could never imagine," Latharn whispered hoarsely as he turned away from the swirling rag upon the glass.

Brodie leaned closer to the globe as he spoke, squinting as he peered into the prison. "I wonder if he's gone mad in there? Latharn MacKay's been imprisoned for all those years; he's watched all the people he knew and loved grow old and pass away. He's witnessed them all pass from this life to the next, leaving him behind. The stories say that even though we canna see within, there's nothing to keep him from seeing outside of his curved glass walls into the world beyond."

Latharn covered his ears, squeezing his eyes shut, trying to block their words as well as six hundred years of memories. All their faces, all their laughter, it all tormented him—and he remembered each and every one.

Fiona polished the ancient stand, where for centuries the MacKay generations had rested the globe. "At least his mother discovered how to break the curse before she jumped to her death."

Brodie scowled as he helped Fiona clean the stand. "Aye, Rachel MacKay found how to break the curse. But I still don't understand how it will ever come about. If the one woman Latharn MacKay could ever love is supposed to whisper the breaking of the curse..., wouldn't she have existed back in his time? Wouldn't she have lived in 1410? The legends said he wouldn't give his heart to any of the women he'd ever met. But how's he to meet this one woman he's supposed to love if he's imprisoned within the globe?"

Latharn waved his hand to seal his words within the sphere.

Pacing back and forth within the globe, Latharn roared at them from his side of the walls. "I have already met her! It will happen, Brodie. She comes to us as we speak." The time wasn't right to communicate with his descendants even though his frustration level neared explosion. In the past, when he'd spoken to his guardians, they'd sometimes had difficulty trusting their sanity. He had to wait until the proper moment. For now, it was better they think of him as the family legend, the bauble on the shelf requiring a daily dusting.

Fiona shrugged as she returned the orb to its shelf. "I don't understand it either, Brodie. I've heard the stories ever since I was a lass toddling along beside my grandmam's skirts. She told me how a chosen member of the clan must guard the globe until Latharn found his release. But I never understood how he was supposed to find the love of his life if he was imprisoned inside a tiny crystal cell."

Latharn nodded his approval. Fiona was a traditional girl; her lullabies had been the family legends. She would understand in time.

Brodie dusted the countertop as he mused on his ancient cousin's fate. "They say he was a powerful sorcerer, trained by his gifted mother and the clan druid. They say he'd only begun to discover just how powerful he was when the dark *bana-buidhseach* entrapped him within the ball. They say Cousin Latharn scorned the woman after taking her to his bed."

"That is not what happened at all." Latharn groaned. "Why can they never get it right? Every century it gets worse with the telling. At least this century, they got the part about the sorcery right." Three hundred years ago, they had said that he was some sort of mythical ogre.

Fiona tucked her arms around her husband's waist and rested her cheek upon his back. "Well, if Cousin Latharn was as good a lover as a certain MacKay lad I know, then I can understand how the woman could be upset and determined for a bit of revenge."

With a nod toward the back room, Brodie waggled a suggestive brow. "Ye know, we've yet to hang the open sign on the door just yet.

And there is a bench in the back room that looks verra promising by the way it is designed."

As a pang of loneliness tore through his chest. Latharn heaved a weary sigh. This was the part he hated the most, the utter seclusion. The isolation tormented him. Down through the centuries, he had agonized while watching his guardians with their loved ones. The solitude was the gaping wound that never healed. He wanted his life back. He wanted his Nessa. Dammit. He wanted to live.

Fiona smiled, easing her way toward the back room. With a toss of her head, she beckoned for Brodie to follow. "Why, Brodie MacKay. That bench is for sale as an authentic midwife's labor chair. I canna believe ye would suggest such a thing. Ye should be ashamed of yourself."

As they turned in unison toward the back room, the bell above the outer door jangled. Someone had chosen that inopportune moment to enter the main room of the shop.

Latharn stared across the room, flattening his hands against the frigid walls of his prison. It was her. She had arrived at last. His Nessa stood in Scotland, sharing the same room as the accursed globe. She was beautiful. The sight of her stole the breath from his lungs. He clawed his fingers against the glass, itching to touch the silk of her hair. He yearned to caress her, to take her into his arms. She was so close. She was almost within his reach.

"Nessa," he whispered.

"Excuse me. I was wondering if you could give us some directions? I must've gotten an out-of-date map at the airport."

A flustered redhead stood tapping her fingers on the counter where she'd already spread out a several-times refolded map. Her face was dark as a storm cloud; it was obvious she and her companion had been having a heated discussion. The elfin brunette stood just behind her. The brunette was not happy. She leaned against the counter glaring at the redhead. A disgruntled look upon her face, she rested her head on her hand as though she'd rather be anywhere but standing beside the redhead.

Latharn tore his eyes away from Nessa long enough to sneak a glance at Brodie. "God's teeth, Brodie." The man's cock stood at full attention making a pup tent in the front of his kilt. If they were outside, Latharn would call up an icy rainstorm to help the man bring things under control. Scrubbing his face, Latharn chuckled to himself and leaned against the crystal wall. Well, the lad was on his own, he'd just have to keep his randy arse behind the counter.

Brodie coughed and adjusted the front of his kilt as he edged closer behind the waist-high counter. His voice a bit strained, he cleared his throat and smiled at the two young women.

"Where might ye be headed? I've not seen ye here in town before. And from your accent, I don't believe ye're from anywhere near Balnakiel."

The tiny brunette grinned, her face lighting up with a victorious smirk as she nudged the redhead in the shoulder. "I told you we overshot Durness an hour ago and you should've turned right at the last burial cairn!"

"That's my girl," Latharn purred. He loved it when Nessa showed her fire. She looked tired. What he wouldn't give to massage all the aches and pains from her body. She worked too hard. Well, that would soon be over. When he was free of the globe, she would work no more. He would take care of her. She wouldn't have a care in the world. Her life and her happiness would be in his hands. He would take care of her every need.

"Don't start with me, Nessa," the redhead hissed in irritation. "We always end up where we're headed." Her voice softened as she turned to face the politely smiling MacKays. With a nod toward the map, she added with a tight-lipped smile, "We just sometimes take the scenic route. Besides. I didn't realize this was a race."

"Hmm...that one there is going to be the undoing of some poor man," Latharn noted with a grin. He had been watching Trish's friendship with Nessa for years. Latharn missed the camaraderie he'd once had with his clan whenever he watched the two women together. It reminded him of just how isolated he was. He swallowed hard as he pushed the memories of his clan aside. Enough of this senseless bickering. It was time to put on a little show.

With a polite smile forced across her face, Trish elbowed Nessa in the ribs. Just as she opened her mouth and started to speak, Latharn jostled the witch's ball across the shelf. If Brodie hadn't caught it when it reached the edge, it would've vibrated off into the floor.

Tiptoeing to get a better view across the polished counter, a look of wonder crossed Nessa's face. "What made it rattle off the shelf like that? I didn't feel a tremor or anything. Did you?"

Nessa leaned closer and studied the crystal ball Brodie held between his hands. The lights from the sparkling orb pulsated and danced, reflecting up into her face.

"Hello at last, my precious love," Latharn whispered up into her eyes. He waved his hand across the sphere, increasing the rhythm of the lights to match the pulse of his heart.

Brodie's face paled. He swallowed hard as he risked a glance at his wide-eyed wife. His voice cracked as he coughed and slid the globe to a safer spot on the counter. "It must've been the vibration of the slamming door. I've needed to level that shelf and tighten it for some time now. The slightest movement always sets this thing to dancing. Ye never know when it's going to come flying off the shelf and try to go crashing to the floor."

Fiona rapped her knuckles on the counter and raised the map to Nessa's face. "Ye need to go back this way but a few kilometers. Here's the turn ye must've missed."

Nessa poked Trish on the shoulder again and waggled a teasing brow. She held the marked map just inches beneath Trish's upturned nose and goaded her with a know-it-all voice. "See? I told you! What good does it do for you to buy all these maps if you're not going to listen to me when I'm telling you what they say?"

Latharn chuckled, leaning harder against the infernal glass wall separating him from his love. If only he could touch her, she stood so close. The heat of her filled his senses.

"Fine," Trish muttered through clenched teeth. Nodding to the

MacKays, she snatched the map from Nessa's hands and stuffed it under her arm. "Thank you for all your help. Once you get your shop set up, we'll stop back in and have a look around. If the rest of your items are as unusual as that crystal, your business should really do well."

Fiona cleared her throat and glanced at her speechless husband who stood with the globe clenched between his hands. "Why, thank ye for your kind words. That'll just be grand." Fiona twitched her head in gratitude as she spared a glance at the animated witch's ball.

"Nessa, no!" Latharn pounded his fists against the glass as Nessa moved away from him toward the door. Now that he had her so close, he couldn't bear to see her go. The scent of her perfume wafted through the glass, a delicate orchid scent. Latharn grasped at the sweet essence as though he could pull her into the crystal by inhaling the fragrance that had once surrounded her body. *By all that is holy, please don't let her leave.* He flattened his palms against the frigid walls, his heart falling the farther she moved away.

When the two women had argued their way out of the shop, Fiona locked the door and pulled the blinds. "What was that about?" Fiona hissed, eying the dwindling light flickering from within the glass ball.

With a puzzled look, Brodie handled the sphere with a ginger touch and eased it over onto the counter. "For some reason, Cousin Latharn seems verra interested with one or both of those foreign lasses."

Fiona pursed her lips, her brow creased as she studied the pulsating light. "Was it the fiery redhead with the well-endowed chest and the tiny, upturned nose?" As she turned the ball, she leaned in closer, watching the globe as she named Trish's most obvious attributes. "Well, that brought no reaction. Then it could only have been the tiny curly-haired lass with the striking blue eyes."

It was about time they got to the point. Latharn responded with the entire spectrum of his emotions. Now he would give them a light show. It was time Brodie and Fiona met their ancestor. He illuminated the entire room in a play of iridescent lasers. The energized light electrified everything it touched. Every surface in the room rainbowed with a prismatic glow.

His brows arched to his hairline; Brodie splayed his hands across the countertop as he stared at Latharn's prison. Leaning in closer, his breath fogged the glass as he matter-of-factly spoke to the ball. "Well then. That was a definite choice. So ye like the dark-haired lass?"

Latharn laughed so hard the globe shook. Brodie was the master of the understatement. This century must have diluted the lad. Latharn vibrated the globe again, sending it scooting across the counter.

As he captured the vibrating base between his hands, Brodie gaped into the pulsating depths of the crystal. "What do ye think we should do now, Fiona?"

"Ye go after her, ye blessed fool!" Latharn's deep voice rumbled out of the core of the orb and echoed off the walls of the shop. As his thundering voice dissipated and faded away, so did the lasers dancing about the thrumming globe.

Brodie's face drained of color. He pushed away the crystal and steadied himself against the edge of the counter, his hands shaking, knuckles white. He opened his mouth as though about to speak, closed it, then opened it again. Visibly swallowing as though about to choke, he finally found his voice. "Ye can make yourself heard! Is this the spirit of Latharn MacKay? And if it is, why have ye not spoken to us before now?"

The light of the orb diminished in strength as the crystal reduced to a subtle glow. Latharn blew out a weary breath as he paced the circumference of his prison. His voice grew quieter as he tersely replied, "Aye, I am Latharn MacKay. As for allowing ye to hear my voice? Up until now, I had nothing to say."

Brodie's jaw dropped. "Ye had nothing to say?" He spun on his heel and jerked his chin toward Fiona. "Fiona and I have been your caretakers for nigh on six years now. I have been around ye since I was but a gleam in my Da's wandering eye. And ye mean to tell me in all those years, ye didna' have one small thing ye might have wanted to say to us? Not one word?"

The tension in his chest eased a bit and Latharn chuckled with relief. Brodie had fire. Good for the lad. At least, he'd not considered himself mad when Latharn had spoken aloud. The MacKay power was strong in this one. He swirled the energy just beneath the surface of the crystal and shimmered it at Brodie's growling reprimand. "If it makes ye feel any better, Cousin, I havena spoken to anyone in several hundred years. I've no' uttered a word to the outside world since my mother took her life and traveled to the next plane."

Fiona covered Brodie's hand with hers and silenced her husband with a shake of her head. "Forgive him, Cousin Latharn. It's just that Brodie has always defended ye and felt a particular sorrow for all ye have suffered."

With a curt nod, Brodie cleared his throat as he stared down at Fiona's hand over his. "Aye, please forgive me, Cousin. My words were thoughtless but I meant ye no ill will. I just thought ye would have spoken to us before now. It might have helped us in your search for the woman who was the one to set ye free."

Latharn deepened the color of the globe by allowing his emotions to fuse into its aura. The force of the light intensified as his voice echoed through the room.

"I've watched ye since before your soul decided to leave the cosmos and join us on this plane. I know your heart is pure, Brodie MacKay. Hear me when I say I am proud to know ye will be the one to aide me when I rejoin the world."

Brodie propped his elbows on the counter, his face reddened as he strained to see even deeper into the orb. "The legend says the one woman ye could ever love must whisper for ye to join her and be her lover. Is that true? Is that the secret to breaking the curse and setting ye free?"

Latharn caused the witch's ball to shimmer with his response. It flared brighter than the light from the farthest window. "From everything my mother could find that appears to be the way of it. Ye see, my fine cousin, the dark sorceress, Deardha, thought me quite incapable of ever losing my heart to another. And to tell ye the absolute truth of it, I had often doubted it myself."

Latharn pulsed the glowing aura with each word he spoke. He ensured the energy kept a perfect tempo with his words. "When she first cast me inside this crystal hell, I meditated upon the mysteries for the first hundred years. With my mind, I searched through many planes of existence to find the melody that resonated with my own. It was during my meditations that I found her spirit's existence. Her essence called out to me from far across time and space. Her song came to me from deep within the mystical winds. It echoed into the depths of these crystal walls. When her soul decided it was time to choose a physical form, she was born. Ye canna imagine my relief when I found she existed on this plane. In the summer of her eighteenth year, an act of cruelty revealed the pathway to her dreams. Her heartache called out to me. It weakened the void. It enabled me to connect with her...to contact her subconscious mind. Through her dreams, I've been able to form a bond with her even though I've never been able to speak. Ye have no idea how difficult it is to attempt to guide someone to ye without ever saying a word."

Scratching his jaw, Brodie paced back and forth in front of the counter. "Why can ye not speak to her? Why can ye not talk with her while ye walk among her dreams? As your guardians, they warned us never to speak of the curse. Your glass tomb would be shattered and your soul splintered into the depths of the eternal abyss. Are ye telling me the same thing could happen if ye tried speaking to the lass whilst ye walked in her dreams?"

Brodie's innocence amazed him. It must be the century. Latharn's rumbling chuckle boiled up through his belly and rippled through the glass, spilling out across the room. "If I was able to speak to the lass, then I'd be able to tell her how to break the spell.

Your heart is too pure, Brodie, m'lad. Ye would make a terrible wielder of dark magic."

Fiona shoved her face closer to the globe as she pushed Brodie aside. "Are ye trying to tell us ye've turned evil, Latharn MacKay? If that be the case, we'll not be helping ye break free of your prison in any way! We'll have no evil walking among us. We'll leave ye to your crystal hell!"

Fiona had no idea. What a dear sweet lass. Latharn struggled to remember his descendants couldn't fully understand. How could they? They had never walked his path. He inhaled a deep, cleansing breath, and forced himself to rein in his temper. With a jerk of his hand, the room swelled with a pulsating flash of energy. The shock-wave blasted out of the ball and shoved them both away from the counter.

"I am not evil, Fiona, my lass. However, I will warn ye of this. After six hundred years of imprisonment inside this globe, my patience is no what it used to be."

CHAPTER
SEVEN

He lit the candles. This time, the ritual would be right. She had spoken to him and shown him the error of his ways. He had the book now. She had given him strength and taught him the meaning of the words. The moon was waxing, and he had a bit of the woman's hair. With this spell, he would have his revenge. Thick, sputtering candles lit the darkened room. It reeked of the incense he'd used to cleanse the space. He'd copied the diagram on the floor with the stone he'd dug from the graveyard.

He'd cleansed his body then ritually fasted and bathed to honor the Dark One. He had stripped naked, shaving his torso to be marked with the symbols for the spell. The preparations were complete. This time, she would be honored and impressed.

He traced his finger down the page. His lips moved as he repeated the words to himself. Over and over, he repeated the curse until he was certain he'd get the rhythm correct. He must be perfect. She must be pleased. He must not disappoint her.

Hand shaking, he took the athame and ran the blade across his palm. He didn't flinch as the razor sharp steel of the ritual knife sliced into his flesh. Unblinking, he stood mesmerized as blood drizzled down the tips of his fingers and dripped into the awaiting chalice.

He brought a neatly tied bundle of reddish blonde hair to his lips for a kiss before adding it to the cup of blood. Then he sprinkled some powder from a brown, folded packet, smiling as the contents bubbled and hissed. After tucking the cup beneath one arm, he walked in a counterclockwise circle around the table full of sputtering candles. The choking incense filled the room. Fists pounded the inside of his head. The smoke from the candles stung his eyes; he blinked as his sweat also blinded him. He breathed in more smoke. She would strengthen him. If he remained steady, she would return to his dreams.

He dipped his fingers in the murky concoction and smeared the symbols on his torso. He muttered the curse under his breath as he circled about the table. Nine circuits he made around the table, chanting the ancient curse. Nine times, he called out to the darkest power to give him the magic he desired. Nine times, her voice echoed inside his mind. She promised him if he did her bidding, all he asked for would be his.

Her voice stroked him like a lover's hand, warm as brandy flowing through his veins. She promised him power. She promised him women. She promised him the ability to do the darkest of magic. She had one small request of him, assuring him he would find great pleasure in it as well. But he must be patient. The time would be soon. She wasn't ready for him to prove his loyalty yet. She would call upon him soon.

But until then, there would be other women for him to enjoy. After all, he needed the practice...and she craved to feed upon their fear.

CHAPTER
EIGHT

Nessa soaked up the vista of the rugged hillside as though it were her last day to walk the earth. The dusky blue crags spanning the horizon framed the rock-strewn meadow stretched out before her. The wind soughed through the nearby pines as it rushed to whisper the Highland's mysteries against her cheek. Her soul sang as she drank in the crisp, sweet air. She'd arrived home at long last. She belonged here. She'd known it from the beginning. She'd never been this contented before in her life. Peace settled to the marrow of her bones. Satisfaction hummed through her veins.

Even the nightly visits from her silent Highlander had changed since her arrival in Scotland. They were more vivid, more realistic, and more sensual than they'd ever been since he'd first made his presence known.

A smile tickled at the corner of her mouth. A shiver of lust stirred in her belly as she remembered the latest dream. His hands, his mouth, the way the man knew every delicious pleasure spot and every nerve ending set her body thrumming.

Nessa inhaled a deep breath. She mentally shook herself and

forced herself to put the dream to the back of her mind. When she opened her eyes each morning, every detail remained vivid. Her soul-shattering orgasms branded themselves in her mind. His visits were becoming almost sensual torture. There wasn't the tiniest part of her body he hadn't kissed, tasted, or caressed.

Nessa picked her way over the rocky hillside, unbuttoning her jacket to the cooling air. She had hoped the cold air of the fading day would tamp down her smoldering passion to a bearable level. Her dreams had become so increasingly vibrant it was a constant effort to put them to the back of her mind. She had found it difficult to recover once she awoke the next morning. To her frustration, she remained in a constant state of arousal; her body ached for her dream lover throughout the day.

There was just one detail about all her dreams that she hadn't quite been able to understand. Although her masterful Highlander always gifted her with mind-reeling orgasms, not once had he ever consummated the act and joined his body with hers. His hands were blissful tools of delicious pleasure; his mouth drove her insane. But not once had he claimed full possession and consummated the deal.

Was this some kind of Freudian sign? Did she think herself too plain to deserve the full attention of such a magnificent man? Had her parents' constant belittling while she was a child managed to damage her psyche so much that she couldn't even finish an erotic dream?

Nessa fanned her burning cheeks and swiped her hair out of her eyes. "I have to get my mind on something else or I'm going to spontaneously combust."

Topping the last outcropping of grass-covered stones before arriving back at the archeological site, Nessa succeeded in pushing her lusty dreams to the back of her mind.

She smiled proudly as she watched her troupe of devoted grad students brushing soil away from bits and pieces of odd-shaped shards. This was absolute heaven. She'd waited for approval on this grant for years. Studied and cataloged before, the sites weren't new digs, but Nessa knew there was more to be found. It tingled, like a sixth sense tapping at the base of her brain and her instincts were never wrong. There were several promising corded-off areas scattered across the site. The Bronze Age burial cairns and hut circles of Durness were more precious to her than a diamond mine littered with gold.

Trish met Nessa up on the hillside and handed her a mug of coffee. Nessa accepted it with a smile of thanks as she shivered in the chill of the early evening breeze. Trish took good care of her, from best friend to paperwork to the best coffee anywhere in the world. What more could a girl ask for?

Trish motioned toward two of the students and leaned close to Nessa and whispered, "James and Lyla have recommended a pub for us to try. I think they're hoping for extra credit."

Her attention turned to the two students Trish had indicated. Nessa studied them through the steam coming off her coffee as she sipped at the dark warming brew. "If they'd pay as much attention to their papers as they pay to each other, they'd both have completed their theses by now. In fact, as bright as those two are, they'd be well on their way to being published in this field as well as a couple of others."

Trish *tsk-tsked* Nessa with an arched brow as she adopted a chiding school marm tone. "There's more to life than degrees and titles, my friend. One of these days you're going to realize that Dr. Buchanan."

Grabbing Nessa by the sleeve, Trish urged her toward the large weather-stained tent serving as their central office. "Come on. It's time to call it a day. It's Friday and high time we found a little nightlife around here."

Holding her mug to keep it from sloshing, Nessa hurried along beside Trish. "So, I take it we're going to try this highly recommended pub? Did you happen to get them to write down the directions?" If Trish was going to drag her out on the town, then Nessa had to give her a little grief about always getting lost.

Trish shut down the computers and scooped loose papers into awaiting trays. "Yep, it's time for a little relaxation. Both of us are way overdue for some downtime. Several of your more devoted followers are spending the weekend at the site. So, you and I don't have a thing to worry about. We can actually enjoy a few days of civilization in real beds at the inn. And they even have running water and flush toilets!"

Grabbing her backpack, Nessa's mood lightened the more she thought about Trish's plan. The tension eased out of her shoulders as she thought about soaking in a nice hot tub. Maybe this wasn't such a bad idea. Shooting Trish a wicked look, she tossed her the keys to the jeep. "As much as I hate to agree with you, you're absolutely right. I'm in the mood for a little relaxation myself." But she couldn't resist repeating her earlier question. Nessa was determined to get a rise out of Trish. "Did you say you got them to write down the directions or are we taking the scenic route again?"

Trish jangled the car keys behind Nessa's back. "You always said you wanted to see the Highlands. I'm just helping to fulfill your dreams."

Nessa laughed as she climbed into the car. She wadded up the map spread across the seat and tossed it over her shoulder into the back full of gear. "I tell you what. You get us there as best you can and I'll just enjoy the ride."

Starting the car, Trish teased with an evil grin. "Speaking of dreams, have you had any more shrieking orgasms like the one that had you moaning on the way over on the plane?"

Nessa's cheeks as well as regions much lower flushed hot with the memory of the other passenger's knowing smiles. "Actually, my Highlander has become increasingly...umm...active since our arrival in Durness." Nessa squirmed in her seat and bit her lip. So much for tamping down her residual passions. A slow, moist burn flared between her thighs just from mentioning the man of her dreams. Trish would have to stir that up.

With a shrug, Trish glanced at Nessa before turning to scowl at a faded signpost. "Maybe that's a sign you're about to find the man in the real world that's able to make you moan. Maybe now that you're in Scotland things will turn around. It's about time your luck with the weaker sex changed and you found somebody who could ring your bell."

She pulled into the well-lit parking lot of a squat brick building and leaned over the steering wheel to peer up at the brightly painted sign. "I think this is it. See? It wasn't even a twenty-minute drive. I told you I was getting better at finding my way around the Highlands!"

Nessa sniffed a satisfied breath as they walked into the welcoming pub. Glancing about the bar with interest, she soaked up the comfortable hominess of the room like an orphan who'd just found a home. From the dark, heavy wood of the tables to the high-backed benches built into comfortable booths, the pub was everything she had thought a bar in Scotland would be. Her mouth watered at the inviting aromas wafting out of the kitchen. The yeasty temptation of warm, buttery breads mixed with the smoky roasted meats and deep-fried vegetables. Layered among the aroma of all the tempting foods was the hearty smell of ale. Nessa shivered with anticipation. It had been forever since she'd had a chance to eat like this. This was heaven. The blood in her arteries was already starting to clog. What a way to go.

They found a table beside a wall of windows. Nessa nodded toward the smiling face of the buxom waitress already ambling their way. "Maybe James and Lyla do deserve extra credit. If the food and drink are as good as the atmosphere and the smells coming from the kitchen, I'll even write them a letter of recommendation."

Trish nodded toward a dark-haired man towering behind the bar. Keeping her eyes fixed on her latest discovery, she wet her lips and tapped a finger to get Nessa's attention. "Forget about the food. Check out the barkeep. I wonder if he comes highly recommended."

The waitress giggled as she pulled her notepad from the apron tied around her slightly plump waist. "That's no' the barkeep, miss. That's the owner, Gabriel Burns."

Trish sat even taller in her seat, arching her back in her best vixen's pose. As she smoothed a finger over her lips again, she leaned closer to Nessa, nearly purring as she preened in Gabriel's direction. "The owner? Hmm, that's even better. I've got dibs on that one, my friend."

This should be good. Trish was always on the hunt. Nessa snickered as she turned in her seat. She couldn't wait to see this latest specimen of Trish's interest. Nessa's gaze locked with a pair of laughing dark eyes. The light in those eyes dared her to be the first to look away. But there was something else Nessa caught in that glance. Something dark. Something predatory and dangerous that made her recoil.

Long-legged and powerful, Gabriel crossed his arms, reclining against the wall behind the counter. Coal black hair framed his smirking face as he rubbed at the evening stubble shadowing his jaw. He nodded ever so slightly into Nessa's wide-eyed gaze.

He laughed out loud as a rush of heat burned her cheeks.

The tips of her ears scorched with fire as she whirled back around in her chair. "Why didn't you tell me he was looking this way?" she hissed as she hunkered down in her seat. Nessa cringed at the uneasiness churning in her stomach. What was wrong with her? You'd think she was some teen with a bad case of acne.

Nessa scowled at Trish and the giggling waitress as she kept her head ducked behind the high-backed bench. And here she thought she was going to be able to enjoy a night of no pressure and if she was lucky, enjoy eating enough rich foods so she'd have a grease hangover the next morning.

Trish gave Nessa a look like she'd lost her mind. "You didn't ask. Besides, I already called dibs, so what are you worried about? You have to lighten up, Nessa, and quit taking yourself so seriously. How are you ever going to meet an exciting man if you can't even look one in the eye?"

Nessa gritted her teeth and sat fuming in her chair. Damn Trish and her ability to roll with any situation. She had the self-confidence of the Queen of England. Why couldn't Nessa figure out how Trish did it? Trish must've spent a ton on shrinks and self-help lessons. That had to be the answer to such ironclad self-esteem.

With a curt nod to the snorting waitress who waited to take their order, Nessa forced herself to sit up taller and folded her hands on the table in front of her. "We will both take an order of the shepherd's pie and a pint of your darkest ale."

After one last giggle, the waitress shoved her pad into the waist of her apron and skirted her way back toward the bar.

Nessa decided Trish might as well go ahead, vault over the bar and jump on Gabriel's body the way she was ogling him and waving every five minutes. She wondered if the waitress would be willing to find her a bucket of ice water to dump on Trish's head.

"It's a long walk back to the inn," Nessa warned as she drummed her fingers on the table.

"Oh, lighten up, Nessa," Trish chided with a grin as she raised her glass to her lips. Sitting taller in her chair as though she were a cat about to pounce upon a mouse, Trish pointed across the room at a couple just arriving. "Isn't that the couple from Balnakiel who gave us directions our first day here?" Swiveling in her seat, Nessa studied their faces, then nodded in agreement. "That's them. I wonder if they've gotten their shop open for business yet. The purple globe they had was fascinating. Remember? The one that nearly vibrated off the shelf and was full of the laser lights?"

Nessa caught their eye and waved hello. There was just something about those two she had liked. The couple smiled and returned waves of their own. They put their heads together for just a moment and then scooted from their seats. They made their way over to Trish and Nessa's table, smiling as they wove their way between the surrounding chairs.

"I see ye found your way back to Durness. How have ye been enjoying your stay?" With a polite bow toward Trish and Nessa, as he spoke, Brodie unconsciously pulled Fiona closer to his side. His arm rested protectively around her waist as he shot a narrow-eyed glance in the direction of the bar.

A shiver of happiness thrilled its way up her spine. Nessa couldn't resist a heartfelt sigh. "It's so beautiful here. I feel like I've come home. If it were up to me, I'd stay in Scotland forever." She struggled to ignore the pang of jealousy at the obvious bond the married couple shared. She wished she could find the type of closeness Fiona and Brodie had found. Even though friends and co-workers surrounded her, Nessa always found herself isolated...so alone. It was hard to resign herself to the fact that she'd probably be single all her life. Nessa tried to console herself with the knowledge that at least she'd made it to the land of her dreams.

Fiona smiled and snuggled closer to her husband. "By the way, we didna introduce ourselves the other day. My name is Fiona and this is my husband, Brodie. Would ye mind if we joined ye? Sat with ye for a while?" Fiona turned and looked about the pub. "We came here tonight at the insistence of an artisan we've been seeking to join our shop. But it looks like they've stood us up again. Ye will probably think we're quite the country couple, but we love listening to the way ye speak and would love to hear more about the USA."

"Sure, pull up a chair. Trish and I decided to come here tonight with the hopes of making a few new friends." Nessa and Trish scooted to make room for the couple at their table.

Trish motioned with her glass in Gabriel's direction as he stood filling glasses at the bar. "I've found my new best friend right over there. I'm just waiting until after dinner tonight to make my introductions."

Fiona's face paled. She took a deep breath, then took a sip of her ale. "Aye, Mr. Gabriel Burns is plenty easy on the eyes. But take care, Trish. A beautiful veneer sometimes hides something rotten beneath the surface."

Brodie brought Fiona's hand to his lips and gazed into her troubled eyes. "Careful now, lass. Ye had best be remembering ye're a

MacKay now and your eyes should not be traveling anywhere but here."

Nessa worried with the corner of her napkin as she stared down at her plate. She couldn't help it.

Their closeness was really getting to her tonight. She tried staunching her growing envy at the couple's bond. She hated herself for not being happy for them and the special closeness they had found. Nessa toyed with the food left on her plate and tried to think of something to say. Wait a minute? Did they say their name was MacKay? Nessa fumbled with her silverware and barely kept it from crashing to the floor. That name kept cropping up.

"MacKay? Did you say your last name is MacKay?"

"Aye." Fiona nodded, glancing over at Brodie as she added, "Do ye know the name? Are ye familiar with any of the family's history? Or any of the clan legends of lost loves or curses, perhaps?"

Nessa frowned with a shake of her head. An unexplainable stab of uneasiness nagged at her chest. "No. The name MacKay seems to be popping up in a lot of my paperwork of late."

Brodie almost choked as he drained his glass. He fixed his wife with a warning look as he lowered his glass to the table. "Paperwork? If ye don't mind my asking, what exactly is your business here in Durness?"

With a theatrical groan, Trish shook her head as she moved her plate and pounded her fist on the table. "I'll sum it all up in a nutshell. Nessa is a professor of archeology and we're here on a grant to study the Durness sites and the history around Balnakiel. But I'm begging you, please don't get her started on Scotland's history or her career or we won't hear a word about anything but work tonight. It's the weekend. It's time to relax!"

"Excuse me." Their waitress for the night stood by the table with a gloriously sinful chocolate dessert in her hands. "Mr. Burns asked that I bring this to the lovely lady. He said she looked to be one who might enjoy a bit of a sweet indulgence."

With a victorious chortle, Trish cocked a brow at Nessa and

reached across the table toward the rich dessert. Her smile faded, when the waitress raised the plate out of her reach and mouthed the words, *Not for you.*

The waitress nodded toward Nessa and set the plate in front of her. "Not meaning to hurt anyone's feelings but Mr. Gabriel was verra clear. The dessert is for the wee blue-eyed lass. The one with the rosy cheeks that show everything she's feeling."

Her mouth dropped open in surprise as Nessa glanced around the table. One hand fluttered to her throat, as she imagined the decadence of the sweet delight. Glancing from the cake to the waitress's face, Nessa fixed her with a doubting glare. "Is this some sort of joke? Are you sure he didn't mean the dessert for my friend, Trish?"

A deep rich voice rumbled just behind her as she stared down at the plate. "Why are ye so surprised? Surely, ye don't fear a wee bit of chocolate that canna be nearly as sweet as yourself?" Gabriel had appeared out of nowhere and nudged a chair beside Nessa's seat. "My name is Gabriel. But ye already knew that since Cordelia's never kept a secret in her life."

With a giggle, Cordelia placed a fork beside the plate in front of Nessa and nudged Gabriel with her ample hip. "Ye said ye like it when I give the pretty ones your name. Don't feign the put-upon boss routine with me!" She pulled her notepad from her apron and stuffed their tab in Gabriel's shirt pocket before moving on to take the next table's order.

Gabriel clapped Brodie on the shoulder a bit hard and greeted him with a stiff nod. A flicker of malice sparked in his eyes as if the polite smile strained his face. "And you! Ye have a lot of nerve showing up in my place after stealing this fine woman out from under my verra nose."

Fiona trembled and edged closer to Brodie as she curled her hands to her chest. "I intend to be sure Nessa knows she'd best be running in the opposite direction from the likes of a cur like you!"

Gabriel's eyes narrowed just a flicker; his smile cooled a bit as he tilted his head. "Now, Fiona. I thought we agreed it would be best for all concerned if we considered the past over and done. Admit it, my lost love: we're all better off putting those days behind us."

Brodie edged forward, leveling Gabriel with a cold and deadly glare. He scooped one of Fiona's hands in his own as he leaned farther across the table. His jaw clenched, there was no missing his meaning as his lips curled into a disdainful sneer. "The past is over but it will never be forgotten. Ye would do well to bear that in mind."

Nessa watched this interplay. A great wrong had happened between these three. She didn't know what but from the malevolence hovering in the air, it must have been pretty serious. Nessa nudged Trish underneath the table. Do something, she mouthed.

Trish fixed Gabriel with a frosty look and stuck her pert nose in the air. "I thought Irishmen liked well-endowed redheads. I know you've relocated here to Scotland but aren't you veering from your ancestral DNA by chasing after little bitty brunettes?"

Gabriel laughed aloud at the tension-breaking question and stretched out a hand of welcome to Trish. He rested his arm in a subtle sign of claiming across the back of Nessa's chair. "I've been burnt by such a fire many a time before. Let's just say I feared ye would be too hot to handle and I sought to steer clear of such pain again."

"What a line of bullshit!" Trish snorted as she downed her second glass of ale.

"Ye see?" Gabriel nodded around the table. "The spitfire just proved my point!" He turned to Nessa, picked up her fork, and sliced into the decadent dessert. Rich, chewy chocolate cake surrounded a center of oozing dark chocolate swirling into the heavy cream and powdered sugar layered upon the plate.

"Taste this and tell me ye ever had better. I promise ye. Ye're going to love it and ye'll no' be able to get enough." Gabriel's tone mesmerized Nessa. She had the nagging feeling he implied a lot more than just the dessert.

Brodie coughed and scooted his chair sideways. He fiddled with his silverware on the table and cleared his throat again.

"Brodie, are you okay?" Nessa looked away from the bite of cake, grateful for the interruption. Brodie reminded her of one of her students who was in dire need of a dash to the restroom facilities.

Brodie cut his eyes across the table at Gabriel with a jerk of his head. "Careful, Nessa. Ye canna be trusting a man who'll resort to plying a woman with chocolate the first time he sees her. Ye never know what other treachery he might be planning for ye when ye least expect it."

Nessa cut her eyes back at the bite of dessert still held just within reach of her mouth. She had the distinct feeling if she took that first symbolic bite, she'd never be able to resist the rest. She stole a glance at the dark depths of Gabriel's eyes and suppressed a smile. She wondered what his definition of all night long might be.

Her decision made, she wet her lips and eased open her mouth. Leaning forward, she closed her lips around the bite of dessert, her eyes never leaving Gabriel's face.

She closed her eyes. It was pure perfection. Nessa shivered at the rich confection melting on her tongue. "Oh, my...this is absolutely wonderful. Please give my compliments to the chef!"

She had always had a weakness for chocolate. How had Gabriel known? With her past disappointing experiences with men, in her opinion, chocolate was better than sex.

"I accept your compliments," Gabriel purred, shooting a satisfied sneer in Brodie's direction. He scooped up another forkful, holding it once more in front of Nessa's mouth. His lips curled into a predatory smile as he waited for her to recover from the first delightful taste.

"You made this?" Nessa gave a delighted shudder as she swallowed the delicious morsel. The rich sweetness lingered on the back of her tongue long after the bite was gone. As she licked her lips, she hugged herself. The sumptuous cake overloaded her mouth with its wicked richness. The dessert luxuriated decadence itself, one bite was almost too much.

Trish took her own fork and stole a bite from the plate. "The man has good looks and cooks too. That's just great," she muttered as she licked the chocolate from her fork.

Nessa tried to take the fork from his hand. She swallowed hard as Gabriel shook his head.

"Nay, lass. Ye must allow me to feed ye. That way I don't miss a moment of the pleasure in your eyes as ye enjoy what I've prepared for ye."

An uncomfortable stirring rumbled in the pit of her stomach, and Nessa didn't think it was a problem digesting her meal. She didn't like the way Gabriel's words insinuated something more than the mere enjoyment of the dessert. Men didn't come on to her like this. She'd learned that lesson the hard way. She didn't know what Gabriel's problem was but there was just something about him that didn't ring true.

Nessa fended him away as she licked the chocolate syrup from her lips. "Oh, no more. It's almost too rich. I don't think I can stand another bite."

Gabriel barbed the MacKays with a smirk of victory as his self-satisfied laughter rumbled deep from within his chest. "Then tomorrow night, ye must allow me to cook ye a private dinner. I guarantee I'll fix ye something a great deal more tempting than a simple shepherd's pie." Gabriel tossed the fork upon the dessert plate and slid it to the center of the table.

"Well, I don't know," Nessa hedged, sidling a glance over at Trish for moral support. There was just something about Gabriel Burns that set off her warning bells.

Trish kicked Nessa's ankle under the table and gave her a determined best-friend look. Her eyes snapped as she mouthed the words, Are you kidding me? Go for it.

Trish pulled a notepad from her purse, jotted down an address, and tossed it across the table to Gabriel. "Forgive her, Gabriel. She's a bit off her game tonight because it's been a while since she's taken the time to forget about work for longer than two minutes at a time. Once you get to know her, you'll find out she's great. Here's the address of the inn where we're staying and that's the number to the phone in Nessa's room."

Gabriel smiled and accepted Trish's peace offering with a gracious bow of his head. Folding the paper and placing it in his pocket, his smile widened as he rose from his seat. "Until tomorrow night then, my dear, sweet Nessa. I'll pick ye up around eight. How will that be?"

"That'll be fine." Nessa kicked back at her beaming friend beneath the table. Trish had never known when to butt out when it came to fixing her up with men and apparently, tonight wasn't going to be any different.

"Please excuse me. I must tend to my business though I'd much rather stay with present company. Brodie, Fiona...'twas good to see ye again. I'll be taking care of both these tabs tonight."

Edging his way around the table, Gabriel rested his hand on Nessa's shoulder. As he spoke, his fingertips caressed the skin at the nape of her neck, and he allowed them to tarry just a little bit longer than necessary.

Trish whistled under her breath as she watched Gabriel prowl across the room. "You've hit the jackpot with that one for sure. Let's see your dream Highlander compare with that Irishman!"

"Her dream Highlander?" Brodie's expression perked as he looked between the two women.

Nessa kicked Trish under the table again. Time to go. Trish had hit her loose-lipped limit with the alcohol and was starting to spout personal stuff. "Never mind. It's just an inside joke, and Trish has had way too much ale." Rising to her feet, Nessa grabbed her friend by the sleeve and pulled her toward the door. "Come on, Trish. It's getting late. We've got to let Brodie and Fiona get home."

"Fine." Trish snorted with a roll of her eyes. "It was nice seeing you both again. We'll drop by your shop one of these days. We both really liked the purple night-light."

Fiona choked on a sip of her ale. She sputtered and coughed as Brodie pounded away on her back. "The purple night-light?" Fiona gasped and struggled for air. Her eyes filled with tears and she dabbed at them with a napkin she'd grabbed from the table.

Nessa nodded as she navigated between the extra chairs crowded around the table. "You know. The one that nearly rattled off the shelf when we shut the door? The one that looks like a crystal ball?" She paused, waiting for the MacKays to realize the object she was talking about. Nessa shifted her bag to the opposite shoulder before following Trish toward the door.

Brodie continued patting Fiona as a look of realization dawned across his face. "Oh aye...the purple night-light. We know what ye're talking about now. We've had it so long; we rarely think about the thing even being in our shop. We hardly remember to dust it." Brodie waved with one hand as he babbled away and rubbed at Fiona's back. "Be sure and stop by and visit us soon. Perhaps we'll tell ye a bit of the history behind the purple globe. I'm sure ye would find it truly amazing. Especially since ye have a penchant for the past."

CHAPTER
NINE

Latharn heard the key turn in the lock. It was about time they opened the shop. They were late this morning. They had promised him the search for Nessa would begin today. He had warned them his patience was all but gone. Where in the hell had they been?

Latharn tensed as he peered through his curved glass walls. Brodie's downcast face displeased him. He concentrated a bit harder, focusing on Brodie's aura. The hue did not bode well.

Brodie tossed his keys as he walked through the door. He grimaced as they landed with a crash on top of the counter. The metallic jangle shattered the morning silence of the shop.

Fiona entered right behind him. She went around flipping on the lights and opened the shutters to the morning sun.

Latharn studied Fiona's aura and his mood darkened. Brodie and Fiona both were troubled. What had happened between yesterday and today that had stirred their auras into such a miserable shade?

"Do ye think he's awake?" Brodie motioned toward the globe behind the counter, his voice a cautious whisper.

Latharn released his aura and rumbled it forth, reflecting the purple light of his essence off the plaster of the white-washed walls. "I am always awake and your emotions are telling me that your news does not bode well." High upon its shelf, the crystal trembled as Latharn's wariness filled the air.

"What happened with you two last night? What has both of you so troubled?"

Fiona edged closer to Brodie. She shook her head as she mouthed the words, *Don't tell him*.

"Fiona, my dear, sweet lass. It might do well for ye to bear in mind that although ye cannot see within my prison, I have no trouble whatsoever when it comes to seeing you...and I am also quite adept at reading lips."

Latharn swallowed hard against the anger rising in his chest; he clenched his fists at his sides. He struggled to control his emotions when he projected his voice outside the sphere. The light from the orb pulsated faster as his irritation fueled the beams from the witch's ball. "Now what exactly is it that Brodie is not supposed to tell me? And might I remind ye of my patience growing thin?"

"We found your Nessa," Brodie interrupted. "We had dinner with her and Trish at a pub in town last night."

"My Nessa."

At the sound of her name, Latharn's entire body relaxed. The thought of her was like a tonic to his being. When his tension eased, he reduced his aura to a contented purr. The hard shafts of lasers merged into a serene purple haze. "Ye have no idea how long I've waited to hear someone speak as though she was already mine. Someone other than myself, since in my heart, she's belonged to me since the moment I first found her."

Brodie and Fiona exhaled in obvious relief as they approached the shelf. Fiona almost whispered as she settled the orb on the counter. She stroked the glass as she spoke. "She seems verra nice. But I have to say, she doesna appear too comfortable around men. It's as if she thinks herself too plain for them to notice her. The lass is quite fetching but she acts as though she thinks herself a part of the furniture."

Latharn pounded his fists against the walls of his prison. What had Fiona said? His fury filled the orb with a surge of power that blasted throughout the room. The energy made Fiona and Brodie squint as cutting beams shot from the core of the globe.

"What man has she been around? What are ye trying to keep from me? She is mine now that she is on my land. No one will take what is mine!"

Brodie shot Fiona a reproving glare as he shielded his face and approached the globe. As he centered it in the middle of the counter, he held up his hands as he explained. "We met with Nessa and her friend in a pub in Durness. It was nice. We had a verra nice visit."

Stomping around the circumference of his cell, Latharn pounded his fists against the glass again. Did they think him daft? Six centuries imprisoned inside this damned sphere didn't mean he couldn't follow a simple conversation! The power of his fury ripped through the globe. His energy pulsated through the room. Dishes trembled and rattled on the shelves. Latharn's rage shook the building. His tone grew fiercer. Latharn repeated his words, his voice rumbling from the globe like thunder. "Ye already said that, Brodie. Do ye think me a simple fool? What are ye trying to keep from me? Your unease is drowning out your words." Thunder rumbled in the distance. Latharn paced the confines of his prison. They'd best be talking. He was ready to call up a maelstrom.

With a nervous pat on Brodie's arm, Fiona silenced him as she stepped closer to the counter. "The owner of the pub is Gabriel Burns. He seemed quite interested in getting to know Nessa better. They're supposed to be having dinner tonight. But rest assured, Latharn. Your Nessa didna seem all that enthused to be going out with the wicked man."

Latharn jostled the witch's ball in its stand as though an earthquake shook the room. He fueled blinding white light from the center of the crystal and ricocheted lasers off the walls.

Latharn roared with uncontrollable rage. His fury crackled in the air. "I will kill the bastard if he dares to touch her! No man takes what is mine. I have been waiting for centuries for her to come to me." Latharn stormed around the circumference of the sphere. This crystal hell had never seemed so small. He'd never been this close to the edge of madness before. Nessa belonged to him.

Fiona ducked her head from the energy blasts bursting through the air. She shielded her eyes as she attempted to reason with him. "Latharn, ye said ye've been watching her since she was born. Are ye saying ye have never seen her with...seen her when she was... Surely, ye canna believe she's never been with a man. Latharn, ye do realize she's quite a bit older than a newly blossomed young maid."

He allowed the blinding lights to fade from the room. The swirling glass shimmered to a weak flicker as Latharn moaned. "I know she's no' a virgin. I witnessed her seeking love and comfort at the hands of selfish, clumsy fools. I didna want to watch," Latharn choked out in a hoarse whisper. "...but I couldna bear to turn away."

A look of sadness settled across Fiona's face as she rested her palm against the dark surface of the ball. "It must have been torture for ye, Latharn, to watch Nessa lay in the arms of another. But that doesn't mean Nessa willna be able to love ye. In fact, it will make her love ye even more."

How could he make them understand? Latharn waved the globe into deeper darkness and reduced the light to a sorrowful flicker. His voice echoed with emotion as he struggled to explain his pain. "I had wished to be the one to teach her the pleasures of love. But it just wasn't to be. I understand her trying to find an end to her loneliness. I could no' very well expect her to wait until she realized I was real and could be with her upon this plane. I could never be sure that would ever happen...no matter how often I nudged her subconscious mind. But ye canna imagine the ache of watching the one ye love, search for what only you should be able to give them." Latharn crouched at the base of the globe, cradling his head in his hands.

Brodie rubbed his chin and smiled. "Apparently, ye have affected her more than ye might think. Her friend mentioned something about how Gabriel might compare to the Highlander in her dreams."

Latharn rose and increased the light of the globe, allowing the purple aura to dance about the room once more. The light waves pulsed with his voice as his presence filled the room.

"Now that Nessa is on the soil of my homeland, now that her given name has been spoken aloud upon MacKay land, she will find I'm not restricted to merely appearing in her dreams. This man had best be wary of going anywhere near my woman."

Fiona stepped forward. Chewing on her bottom lip, she wrung her hands as she spoke. "Ye must be careful, Cousin. Nessa may be accustomed to history and artifacts but I doubt verra much if she's used to the wrath of a six-hundred-year-old Highlander gifted with magic. Ye don't want to scare the lass back across the Atlantic by striking Gabriel Burns down with one of your spells."

"Brodie." Latharn's voice fell deadly quiet. He infused his simmering emotions into every word. "Didn't your wife once think herself in love with this Gabriel? Weren't they even betrothed to each other at one time?"

Brodie's lips thinned into a scowl of disgust as he frowned down into the ball. "Aye, Fiona was promised to him before I won her heart. I opened her eyes by rescuing her from the devil himself. She and Gabriel were almost as one. She thought herself in love with the beast."

"And how did ye feel...and how do ye feel now whenever ye see them in the same room together?" Latharn challenged Brodie, interrogated him with the power of his mind as the pulsing light of the orb thrummed throughout the room. Latharn ensured the fiery flashes kept pace with his prodding tone, taunting Brodie to speak what he truly felt.

As his gaze locked with that of his beautiful wife, Brodie sneered, "I want the man's neck snapped between my hands so I can close his eyes forever."

"Brodie!" Fiona gasped, her hand fluttering to her throat. "I canna believe ye would say such a thing...not even about Gabriel Burns."

Brodie ground out his words through gritted teeth. "We MacKays love with every fiber of our being. It doesna matter within what century we are born. When it comes to our mates, we revert to our most primitive emotions. When we find the one meant to be ours, we willna let her go. No one takes what is ours."

Fiona nestled her head against his chest and wrapped her arms around his waist. "Brodie, ye know I never loved the man. I couldn't when I saw him for what he really was. I've never felt for any man what I feel for you. You're the breath that feeds my soul."

"It doesna matter." Latharn projected his voice louder into the room. "Brodie's passion will never allow him to see Gabriel as anything but an enemy. This century's manners will keep him from acting on his emotions. But the hatred will always be there."

Fiona whirled upon Latharn's globe. "Hate him if ye must. But can't ye see what I'm saying? If ye cause him harm, Nessa will run back across the sea. She's no' a Scot. She wasna weaned upon the legends of myth and magic. As far as she's concerned, all ye are is a dream. She has no idea that ye truly exist. If ye mean to have the lass break the curse, ye must awaken her to the legends with care."

Latharn waved his hand across the glass with an angry swipe. Did they realize what they were asking of him? Did these two have any idea how long he'd been waiting for Nessa? Did they have any idea what he'd been through? If that bastard touched his woman... Latharn paced back and forth across the sphere, his hands itching for Gabriel's throat.

Brodie and Fiona watched the globe and waited for Latharn's response.

Latharn battled with their reasoning, warring against his emotions. Raking his hands through his hair, he threw back his head and roared. It was no use. He had no choice. This century had ruined true justice. Forcing his hands to unclench his fists, he calmed the energy and reduced the light play to a peaceful glow.

With a shuddering breath, Latharn forced his voice to echo out into the room. "I will not kill the man unless he provokes me. That's all I can promise. Dinna ask any more."

Then he shut down the aura of the globe to a flicker and it faded as he retreated into the depths of his tomb.

CHAPTER
TEN

Nessa stared into the mirror for the hundredth time. Her mouth crooked critically to one side. As she studied her reflection, she turned first one way, then the other. It didn't matter which way she turned. In her opinion, every angle sucked. This sweater made her look as flat-chested as a pre-pubescent boy. What the hell had she been thinking when she bought it?

Nessa yanked it off over her head, ripping her arms out of the sleeves. She tossed it on the growing pile of rejected outfits on the bed. Hands on her hips, she fixed a bleak stare into the closet at the number of bare hangers she'd strung along the bar.

She ought to strangle Trish for this setup with Gabriel. Her stomach churned into a knotted mass and she needed to pee again even though it had only been fifteen minutes since her last trip to the toilet. What was wrong with being alone? Being single wasn't some sort of death sentence. Being alone sure caused a lot less stress. Besides, she was sure a man like Gabriel would lose interest in her soon enough. He didn't strike her as the type of man who valued a woman for her brains.

Nessa frowned as she sorted through her last few remaining

blouses and fingered the silky cloth of one of the sleeves. She caught her lower lip between her teeth as she fingered the deep blue silk in her hand. Why in the world was he even interested in her in the first place? Whenever she and Trish were out together, his type always gravitated to the buxom redhead. Her nagging instinct to veer away from Gabriel still hammered at the back of her head. There was still something that disturbed her about that man and not a good something either. But she just couldn't quite put her finger on it.

Nessa shrugged as she spoke aloud to her reflection in the mirror. "Well, since I'm sure this is going to be not only our first date but probably our last, it really doesn't matter what I wear." She yanked the silk blouse off the hanger and slid it over her arms.

Nessa studied her reflection in the mirror, fluffing her dark curls with her fingertips until her bangs framed her anxious eyes. She smoothed a pink shade of gloss across her full lips and eyed her reflection with the usual disappointment. "At least I know I've got a beautiful brain, no matter how plain the wrapper."

She jumped at the knock on the door and almost cleared the dresser's top of its contents. She glanced at her watch and returned her reflection's wide-eyed stare. Frowning into the mirror, she once again addressed the pale-faced girl blinking back at her with apprehensive eyes. "Oh great. He would be a little early."

Nessa fluffed her curls one last time, took a deep breath, and jerked open the door. There they were again, those predatory dark eyes sizing her up as though she were a juicy, ripe tomato hanging on the vine.

She greeted him with a nervous nod of her head. "Hi, Gabriel, I see you didn't have any trouble with Trish's directions." Nessa opened the door wider and motioned him inside with a fluttering wave of her hand. "Come in while I get...er...find my jacket."

With a predatory widening of his perfect white smile, Gabriel glanced around the room. His brows rose as he spotted the clothes piled on the bed.

Clearing his throat, he turned his back to the mess and gallantly bowed his head.

"Ye look even lovelier then ye did last night."

"Thank you," Nessa mumbled, ignoring the compliment as she searched the room for her jacket. She dug through the pile of clothes like a dog in search of a bone. She didn't raise her head as she defended the chaotic mess. "I'm not usually this unorganized. It's just that I've been out in the field all week and haven't had a chance to sort things out." She wished he'd quit staring at her. Why didn't he go start the car or something?

Gabriel cocked his head to the side and clasped his hands behind his back. "In the field?" he repeated. "What is it ye do for a living that requires ye to be in some field?"

"I found it!" Nessa grunted and pulled her jacket out from under a stack of books on the chair. "I'm an archeologist. I'm in charge of a research project excavating some of the history here in Durness."

Gabriel's smile broadened. Scooping the jacket out of Nessa's arms, he held it for her with a tilt of his head. "I'm impressed. Such a beauty and obviously brilliant as well, the stars smiled upon me when they led ye to my pub last night."

Wow. Who wrote this guy's lines? An uneasy feeling crawled up the base of her spine. Didn't he realize he laid his compliments on a little too thick? Something about Gabriel just didn't ring true. Nessa stifled a shiver as she led the way out the door. He was as overly sweet as his decadent dessert. "I'm not too sure about the beauty part, but if you're interested in archeology, I might be able to explain a thing or two."

"I'm interested in anything involving you. I knew it from the moment ye walked into my pub. There's an air of mystery about ye, Nessa Buchanan. And I always have been one who loved the opportunity of solving a mystery." Gabriel rested his hand upon the small of her back as he guided her toward his car.

Nessa fought the nagging urge to outrun his hand as she walked toward his car. He was certainly much more attentive than any of the other men she'd been out with. Could he be for real? With so much charm, he must be quite the player. She still would've tagged him as the sort of man who'd be more attracted to Trish. Nessa studied Gabriel as he walked around to his side of the car. She promised herself she'd figure out his angle in choosing her instead.

"Dinner is already awaiting us in the private room at the back of my pub. Do ye happen to like poached salmon, Nessa?" he asked as he headed the car down the narrow roadway leading to the pub.

Just as she was about to reply, a gust of wind blasted the side of the car. As it swerved, Gabriel spun the wheel to keep them out of the rocky ditch running alongside the road. Tires squealing, Gabriel struggled to straighten the car in the lane. He lost the battle as one of the back tires blew out with a resounding bang.

The car landed with a disheartening thud against the steep embankment. Gabriel threw the gearshift into park and yanked the keys out of the ignition. Flipping on the interior lights, he turned to Nessa, his face filled with concern. "Are ye all right?"

She nodded, unlatched her seat belt, and let the strap slide back into the holder. Bending to the floorboard to retrieve the contents of her purse, she glanced up at him with a grin. "I'm fine. I'm glad the wild ride happened before we ate dinner or I might've ruined the inside of your car."

Gabriel chuckled as he stretched to recover her lipstick from where it had wedged itself under the gas pedal. "I'm pleased to see ye have a sense of humor. I hope ye enjoy evening walks as well."

"No spare tire?" Nessa asked, refilling her purse.

"No spare tire," Gabriel admitted. "I meant to replace it weeks ago but it just kept slipping my mind."

Nessa glanced out the window and studied their surroundings. She didn't think the pub was all that far. The stars shimmered an invitation from the clear night sky. With a shrug, she pushed open the door and smiled as she inhaled the refreshing night air.

"It looks like we've got a beautiful night for a walk. You know what they say: everything happens for a reason."

As Gabriel helped her from the car, he pulled her into his arms. His voice lowered, husky with passion as he replied, "Aye, Nessa. Everything happens for a reason." He lowered his head and brushed his lips against hers.

Nessa gave a small shriek as another mysterious blast of wind ripped him from her arms. Heart pounding, she looked up into the starry night, searching the cloudless sky. She glanced around at the tops of the motionless trees. Where had the sudden burst of wind come from? Nessa rubbed the gooseflesh from her arms as she shivered and looked around. She'd never been afraid of the dark before, but tonight's events had her spooked.

She braced her feet and reached down to Gabriel to help him climb up from the stone-filled ditch. Her breath fogged in the chill night air. She grunted as she struggled to pull him up from the rocky mire. "Are you all right? Where is that wind coming from? There's not a cloud in the sky."

Gabriel hobbled up the embankment, wiping his hands on his jeans. He brushed at the dirt and debris on his shoulders, his voice cracked with pain as he limped his way to the road. "The spirits must be bored with their usual amusements tonight. They must be tossing us about for a wee bit of fun."

Nessa noticed his pained gait and his difficulty in catching his breath. She slid under his arm and supported him as much as she could. "You're limping. Is it your ankle or your knee? And you're having trouble breathing. Did you hurt your ribs?"

Gabriel winced. His lips tightened and he clutched for Nessa as his knee buckled under his weight. "Definitely my knee. I think I may have bruised a rib or two. I must've twisted it during my dive into the ditch."

Nessa led him to the car and helped him lean against the bumper. She fished her cell phone from the bottom of her purse and steadied him with the other hand. "I'll call Trish. She can bring the car and we'll take you to the emergency room so they can check you out."

"Emergency room?" Gabriel grimaced as he lowered himself against the car. "Just take me over to the walk-in clinic. Cordelia's mother is the doctor there."

Nessa punched Trish's programmed speed dial number and waited. She frowned as she received the irritating beeps informing her that she wasn't getting a signal. She turned to face a different direction and scowled when her phone still dropped the call. "I've never had a problem getting a signal around here. Something must've rattled loose when it was thrown from my purse."

Nessa frowned at the increasing pallor of Gabriel's face and hit redial again. If she didn't get through to Trish this time, she was going to have to do something else, even if it meant she had to jog somewhere to find Gabriel some help. It was obvious poor Gabriel wasn't going to be able to move. It was apparent he was doing all he could to remain upright through the increasing pain.

"Dammit! I still can't get a call to go through." She shoved her phone back down into her purse and slung it over one shoulder. "I'm going to get you as comfortable as possible and then I'm going for help." As she brushed his hair away from his clammy forehead, Nessa's heart wrenched at his misery. "Come on, Gabriel. I'll support you as best I can. Let's get you into the backseat of the car."

Gabriel wrapped his arm around Nessa's shoulders with a half-hearted laugh. "I'm afraid I'll not be much use to you tonight in the backseat of the car."

Nessa grinned, eased him down into the seat, and patted him on the shoulder. "Great sense of humor there, Gabriel. As soon as you're well, maybe we'll try this date again."

Gabriel captured her hand and planted a kiss in her palm, then nodded with a promise in his eyes. "I guarantee the next time we're in a backseat together it'll be much more enjoyable for us both."

Nessa smiled and pulled off her jacket to cover as much of his chest as the tiny garment would warm. She feared he might go into shock before she made it back. His face had turned a decided shade of gray. "You rest. I'll be back with help before you know it."

She closed the car door to his silent nod. With a frown, she looked up and down the deserted country road. Should she go back to the inn to get the car? Or should she try to make her way to the pub? The best she could figure, they were almost halfway between the two points. As her grandmother used to say, it was six of one or half a dozen of the other.

She knew Trish had left the keys in the car and had planned on spending tonight up in her room. Nessa decided to head for the inn. Trish could help her get Gabriel into the car and for some reason, the ghostly blue light of the full moon urged her in that direction.

As Nessa settled into a mile-eating jog, she took one last glance back at the car. She stumbled as she saw the Highlander from her dreams loom over the door of the wrecked automobile. Her spine tingled. The hairs on the back of her neck prickled as though her soul had just shivered.

The Highlander raised his head to meet her startled gaze just as he reached for the handle of the door. When he noticed her, he straightened and moved away from the car. Although he took steps, he floated above the ground. Not corporeal, his form was almost transparent. The trees and bushes behind him shimmered through his body. Nessa had never seen a ghost before but she was positive that was what she saw now.

"Leave him alone. He's hurt and I'm going for help. He's got enough to deal with without seeing a ghost." Nessa spoke without fear. She knew the apparition. After all, he'd been visiting her dreams since the summer she turned eighteen.

The Highlander's eyes narrowed as he moved toward her. His pale hair fluttered in an imaginary wind. When he stood in front of her, he towered over her. She'd never met a man so tall. Nessa wasn't afraid. This was her Highlander, the gentle man of her dreams.

All that was amiss was the fiery rage flashing from his eyes. She'd never seen his face filled with such fury. All she had seen was loneliness and reassuring affection reflected in his gaze. She'd always thought that must be the reason they'd always connected. Nessa had been lonely her entire life and those who should've loved her had only caused her pain.

"What's wrong?" Nessa whispered up into the specter's grim face. "Why are you so angry...so upset?"

The Highlander's mouth tightened. His jaw rippled as he clenched his teeth. He jabbed once toward Nessa and then back toward the car then snapped his head with a negative shake.

Nessa misunderstood and waved away his worries. Her High-lander must be trying to protect her. "Look. It's just one date. I'm sure he'll lose interest and move on to Trish once he realizes I'm more the intellectual type. You know men never stay interested in me."

His nostrils flared. The apparition pointed at Nessa again, then shook his head harder as he pointed toward the car. Once more, he pointed to where Nessa's heart hammered in her chest and then pointed to his own chest, and nodded just once. Her eyes widened as his meaning became clear and Nessa grew more irritated the longer she stared into his snapping eyes. "A fat lot of good it would do for me to be in love with you! You're not even real. You're only in my head."

He shook his head, slower this time. Her phantom placed his hand upon his heart, then once again motioned toward Nessa. He reached for her as though he wished he could stroke her cheek. His face fell, his expression changing to one of suffering pain as his hand passed through her instead of resting upon her skin.

"Look. I don't know why my mind conjured you up. Maybe I shouldn't have had that second bottle of ale while I was getting dressed. But you need to take yourself back to wherever it is you go when I'm awake. I promise I'll see you later in my dreams."

Nessa turned on her heel and shook herself as she started jogging in the direction of the inn. "And I thought coming to Scotland would sort everything out in my life. What the hell could I have been thinking?"

Her face to the full moon and her determined stride headed for help at the inn, Nessa refused to look back toward the car again. She missed the loneliness aching in Latharn's eyes as he faded into the night.

CHAPTER
ELEVEN

"Strengthen blood, strengthen bone, purge spirit, cleanse soul, honored seductress hear my call...heal my body...give me all."

He lay naked on the floor with the candles burning around his body. Gabriel mumbled the ancient chant three times. The flames of the candles sputtered and danced as his breath stirred the fetid air in the room. She said she would heal him but he had to remain this way all night to prove his complete obedience and dedication to her.

It was worth it. A dislocated knee and broken ribs took too long to heal the natural way. If she healed him overnight, he could fake his injuries to his advantage. Sympathy was sometimes a woman's greatest weakness. Most women tended to be nurturers.

He drew a shaking breath and clenched his fists. The fierce throbbing worsened. Surely, her arrival would be soon. He shifted uncomfortably on the cold, damp floor. Her whisper echoed in the darkness as the chill of the room settled deeper into his swollen knee. Her icy fingertips tickled up his flesh. She searched for the broken edges of his painful ribs. His heart hammered faster as she stroked her hands up and down his sides...and then her icy touch slid lower.

The flames of the candles shot higher into the darkness even as a layer of frost crackled across the floor. His skin was seared to the frozen stone surface. As he shivered, his flesh split and tore. Now she stroked him and purred in his ear. How could anyone ever deny her? He would serve her forever and even longer. She promised him power; she promised him pleasure, and, best of all, she promised him sweet revenge.

CHAPTER

TWELVE

Nessa sat hunched in front of the glowing laptop, peering through the glasses on the end of her nose. With a groan, she yanked them off her face and threw them on the desk. Leaning back in the chair, she covered her face with her hands and massaged her gritty eyes. Last night had started out as a nervous mess and then plummeted into a catastrophe.

Gabriel had ended up hurt and now sported a wrenched knee and three broken ribs. She and Trish had gotten him tucked in at Cordelia's house in the early hours of the morning. They had discovered Cordelia was not only his waitress but more like the family he'd never had. She and her mother had more or less adopted Gabriel when he'd first settled in Durness after leaving his homeland of Ireland. Cordelia was as fiercely loyal to Gabriel as any natural-born sister would ever be.

When Nessa had gotten back to her room, she'd fallen into bed. She hadn't even moved the pile of discarded clothes, just curled her tired body around them. She'd fallen right to sleep. But her dreams had been torture, not the usual erotic bliss with her loving Highlander. With a shuddering sigh, Nessa closed her eyes, replaying the nightmare from the evening before.

Her Highlander had appeared but he'd been enraged, so angry she thought he might speak for the first time since they had met. But he'd just gestured back and forth from his heart to hers. His eyes had flashed with rage as he pounded on his chest. He'd clenched his teeth and raked his hands through his hair. He'd reminded her of a madman. Toward the end of the dream, he'd spread his hands in front of her and somehow caused an image of Gabriel to appear. Horrified, Nessa had watched as her ancient Highlander had swung his claymore and separated Gabriel's body from his head.

The Scot was an animal, panting like a primeval beast with blood and hatred in his eyes. He'd raised his bloodied weapon into the air with one hand and Gabriel's dripping head in the other. He'd thrown his head back, lips curled into an open-mouthed sneer. The corded muscles of his throat had moved as though he roared a silent battle cry.

She'd awakened with her heart in her throat, unable to breathe as though someone had held a pillow over her face. Nessa swallowed hard and sat up in bed. She shook for hours afterward. Choked with tears, Nessa hugged herself against the fury of the dream. The image had been so real. She'd clearly seen the terror in Gabriel's eyes as he'd watched the blade swing toward his neck. She'd witnessed as his body had slowly teetered forward. His warm, salty blood had sprayed over her face and arms.

How could her gentle lover be such a beast? Take such pleasure in killing an innocent man? She might not have formed any feelings for Gabriel but she'd been horrified at witnessing his heartless execution.

Nessa shook herself free of the torturous memory, rubbing her face as she slung her arm over her eyes. Maybe she should check into some sleeping pills. Some that would send her deep into a dreamless haven. If she drugged herself into a mindless state of oblivion, she'd escape any more dreams of her Highlander's rage. As a lover, he was more than welcome to visit her every night but last night Nessa had seen a side of him she never wished to see again.

She blinked hard and tried to focus on the daily reports of her students' findings. With a disheartening jolt, Nessa discovered they were running about a week behind. Enough of her dreams and enough of men, at least she still had her work. Nessa beat on the keyboard in tired irritation. Her voice cracked with fatigue. "Trish, have you uploaded the latest scans of Area Four? James and Lyla specifically mentioned a significant readout...Trish? Trish!"

Nessa drummed her fingers on the desk and turned to find Trish's chair vacant at her desk. "I wonder where she's gone to this time." Nessa grabbed her journal and rose from her chair.

Still massaging her tired eyes, she ran head-on into Gabriel as he pushed through the flap of the tent. "Oh hell! Are you all right? Did I hurt your ribs?" She steadied him on his crutches while cringing at her clumsiness.

Gabriel rubbed at his ribs and hopped on one foot as he struggled to regain his balance. "I'm fine. I just thought I'd stop in to see ye, and to thank ye for taking such good care of me on our first date. Cordelia dropped me off while she ran a few errands. I thought I'd sit with ye for a bit...if that's all right with ye and ye have a bit of time to spare?"

Nessa pulled a chair closer to him and shrugged as Gabriel eased down into the seat. "After the way you ended up, I can't believe you want to come anywhere near me. I figured you'd think I was a jinx."

"'Twas a strange night." Gabriel agreed. "But I doubt that it had anything to do with you."

Nessa fretted with the corner of her journal as she thought back over the night and everything she had seen. She remembered the strange meeting with her ghostly Highlander. She wondered if Gabriel had also noticed his presence but she was afraid to ask. If he hadn't seen the ghost, and from the way he was acting, he hadn't, he'd think her insane if she mentioned it.

"Here are the latest reports from Area Six and there's something wrong with the scans from Area Four." Trish barreled through the door, her arms piled high with papers and rolled up charts of the surrounding dig. She greeted Gabriel with a saucy wink as she dumped the load on the desk.

"How are you feeling this morning?" Before he could answer, she wagged a rolled up chart in his direction as though she meant to use it for a paddle. "I told you, you should've gone out with me instead. I've never been known to send a man away from a date with a set of crutches."

Gabriel grimaced and held his ribs as he chuckled. "I'm much better today than I was last night and somehow, I think a date with you might've left me in even worse shape."

Trish winked again and tossed a paper clip at Nessa as she fixed Gabriel with a devilish grin. "Shame on you, Nessa. Have you been telling Gabriel I like it rough?"

"I think everyone pretty much gets that impression without having to be told."

Nessa turned to Gabriel and patted him on the shoulder as she handed him an extra chair to prop his leg. "I can't believe you're already up and about. Didn't Dr. Stuart tell you to take it easy for a while?"

Gabriel grabbed her hand and brought it to his lips as he gazed into her eyes. "I had to see ye since our date didn't play out as perfect as I planned. The clerk at the inn said this was where ye would be. So, I thought I'd drop by to see if ye would go out with me again...at least out of sympathy for a poor battered man."

Nessa caught her breath and forced herself not to snatch her hand out of his. Wariness settled like a ten-pound lump of lead in the center of her chest. Gabriel Burns was trying too hard. They'd just met. What was his game? It wasn't as if she was the only female within a five-hundred-kilometer radius. But then again, maybe she was overthinking things. After all, she was exhausted.

As she remembered her nightmare of the evening before, she shook herself and shoved her misgivings to the back of her mind. As an afterthought, she made herself a mental note to stop and buy those sleeping pills. She gave his shoulder a gentle squeeze and nodded in vague agreement. "We'll see. As soon as you're better, we'll see about another date."

"Dr. Buchanan! You've got to see this!" Shouts of several students echoed into the tent from the corded off section of area one.

Nessa scooped her glasses off the desk and waved to Gabriel as she darted out the door. Grabbing her journal, she shouted back over her shoulder. "I'll be right back. It sounds like they've found something major. I've got to see what it is."

She jogged her way down the rough terrain. The old excitement roared its way through her veins. There was no emotion she could think of to describe the thrill of a new find. No way to tell someone what it was like to be the first to uncover a bit of the past. Only a fellow history hound would understand the current exhilaration coursing through her like a locomotive.

The students swarmed like a nest of ants around a tasty picnic tidbit. They parted as Nessa entered the site and waved her in to see what they'd found. She squatted down beside the student brushing away the last of the debris.

Nessa clenched a hand over her mouth. The bile rose at an alarming rate as she recognized the find. Perfectly preserved in the Scottish soil was her enraged Highlander's claymore from last night's dream. There was no mistaking the crest inset in the intricately carved handle or the still-lethal razor sharp blade.

Her stomach churned, dangerously close to overflowing. She shivered against a clammy, nauseous sweat. Gabriel's beheading replayed through her mind against all her efforts to block it. The coppery smell of the warm blood filled her mind until she tasted it on the back of her tongue. She clamped her lips tighter together. Her nostrils flared as she took deep breaths to clear her head. She had to pull herself together. She couldn't let any of them know. They'd think she'd gone mad if any of them knew the thoughts assaulting her senses.

"This is great, excellent! It's a beautiful piece. The blade and crest are still intact. You have all done yourselves proud!" Nessa lavished praise upon the students as she struggled to choke back the rising nausea. As she stood, she managed to stay steady on her feet and smile at the sea of excited faces. She couldn't let any of them know she'd been unfortunate enough to see the efficiency of this weapon in action.

Nessa eased away from the group of chattering students and made her way back to the tent. She forced herself to see the ancient claymore for the archeological find that it was. She reminded herself just how pleased the University of Glasgow and the Royal Commission for Ancient Artifacts would be with the find. This would validate her grant. Her work in Scotland was safe and her peers would give her their nod of approval.

Nessa raised her head at the sound of an approaching vehicle and gave a weak wave as Cordelia pulled up in her jeep.

"Good morning, Cordelia. Do you think you'll actually be able to make him get some rest or are you going to have to tie him down?"

Cordelia returned a dimpled smile of agreement as she joined Nessa at the pathway leading to the tent.

"He's a stubborn one that one is. Ye would do well to remember that whenever ye're dealing with Mr. Gabriel Burns."

With that opening, Nessa decided to find out just as much about Gabriel Burns as Cordelia was willing to share. If she knew the inside story of the handsome man it might answer her suspicions as to why he was so avid in his pursuit.

"Cordelia, tell me. Is he really as nice as he seems or am I dealing with just another wolf in sheep's clothing?"

As she rubbed her thumb across her plump chin, Cordelia gave Nessa a quick up and down. "Ye don't think very highly of yourself, do ye? At least not when it comes to your looks?"

Taken aback, Nessa really didn't know what to say. Cordelia's observation wasn't what she'd expected. She was looking for answers about Gabriel's ardent behavior, not an observation of her own insecurities. "I'm honest about my looks. I may not be anything special, but what's that got to do with Gabriel?"

"How can I say this without ye taking it the wrong way?" Cordelia circled Nessa's body, frowning as she gestured up and down Nessa's tiny frame. "Gabriel has always been attracted to the underdog; shall we say? A woman who's unaware of her own worth in this world is more tempting to him than a rare vintage wine."

A coldness settled over Nessa as she returned Cordelia's unwanted appraisal. "Look, I know I'm an excellent archeologist. I know I have a sharp mind. But that said, I'm also smart enough to realize that I'm nothing out of the ordinary when it comes to looks."

"Ah...but don't ye see? There's your beauty in Gabriel's eyes. Deep inside ye don't think ye deserve the attention of a man like him. In your mind, ye don't think of yourself as his equal. Ye might say ye see yourself as a bit of a lesser class." Cordelia shook her finger in Nessa's face as she nodded her head with each of her words.

How dare this woman stand there and psychoanalyze her. Nessa's growing dislike for Cordelia simmered up at least a couple of notches. "So, what are you saying, Cordelia? Are you telling me Gabriel is only attracted to me because he thinks once he's got me hooked, he'll be able to dominate me, that I'll do anything to make him mine? Are you telling me he thinks I'm so insecure that I'll bow to his every whim?" Nessa's voice shook with humiliation. It infuriated her that Cordelia had voiced what Nessa had suspected all along.

"Oh, no!" Cordelia pulled a horrified face, shaking her head as she glanced toward the opening of the tent. "What I'm telling ye is that Gabriel is attracted to women such as yourself. It...it...angers, that's the word, it angers him that society has made it so difficult for a woman to know her true worth. Society needs to learn to see...to see...to see beauty in every shape and form! It's almost as though building up your self-confidence is his...is his calling, a duty to which he feels honor bound. But if the two of ye do happen to fall in love, you'll never find a more devoted man." Cordelia stammered and sputtered her words, wringing her pudgy hands in front of her.

This conversation had gone past the point of ridiculous. Nessa smelled a rat. Why was Cordelia so nervous? Why did she keep glancing at the tent? The woman was obviously having trouble remembering her speech. If she hadn't been so irritated, Nessa would've laughed. She was positive Cordelia watched to see if she believed the words she spouted. Nessa didn't trust her. Just looking at the woman ticked her off.

Nessa hugged herself as she stood there, tapping her foot. This was just great. She would've liked to find a nice relationship but she wasn't about to become a cowering bitch on a leash. It sounded as though Gabriel Burns was looking for a woman with such low self-esteem, she'd never mind walking at least two paces behind him. And there was just something odd about the nervous emotions flashing in Cordelia's eyes. Something was wrong with Mr. Gabriel Burns, and Cordelia had just confirmed it.

Her heart fell as she realized she was going to cut this relationship off before it ever got started. Her past experiences with men had always ended in disappointment and it appeared this one wasn't going to be any different. Great. This day just kept getting better. A perfect finale for last night's fiasco.

"Well, I think it's a little early for discussions about devotion," Nessa snapped as they walked through the door. Nessa motioned Cordelia inside with a snap of the canvas flap and looked toward the corner where Gabriel sat with his foot propped in a chair.

"Devotion? What has this wee minx been telling ye about devotion?" Gabriel eased his foot down out of the seat. His lips curled into his predatory smile as he edged his way up onto his crutches.

Planting both hands on her ample hips, Cordelia adopted her fiercest stance. "Nothing about devotion, ye great hulking beast. Just a good deal about stubbornness and how strongly ye embrace that trait. Now on your way and into the car with ye or I'll be bringing

Mother over to box your ears." She urged Gabriel toward the door, casting an apologetic smile at Nessa as she passed.

Gabriel paused in front of Nessa on his way out. "I'm determined, lass, to hear a yes. So ye promise? As soon as I'm released from this tyrant, we'll retry our first date?" Gabriel leaned closer. He fixed her with his most beguiling smile and waited.

Nessa forced the irritation out of her voice and phrased her careful reply. "I promise I will think about it, Gabriel. Now listen to Cordelia and try to get some rest." She took a slight step back. Her heart sank with renewed disappointment. Even with the odd misgivings she'd felt around Gabriel, she'd hoped there was a little bit of excitement to be found. Now even the thrill of a new chase was gone. As it turned out, she'd only been wasting her time.

A puzzled look shadowed his face. Gabriel didn't miss Nessa's step away. He tilted his head and studied her. His eyes narrowed as he leaned in closer and balanced himself with his crutches and one uninjured leg. "I'll ring ye tomorrow then?"

Nessa slid another step back, shrugging as she crossed her arms over her chest. "With the new find, I'll probably be out of pocket all week. But you can always leave a message."

Gabriel's smile disappeared at Nessa's silent dismissal. "Very well then." With a curt nod, he turned and left without another word.

Leaning across her desk, Trish's face reddened as she held her tongue while Gabriel and Cordelia made their way to the car. She bit her lip until she saw they were well out of earshot and then she exploded. "Okay, Nessa. Out with it! Would you mind telling me just what the hell that little dance was all about?"

Nessa dropped into the chair behind the desk and pillowed her head in her arms. In a muffled voice filled with despair, she barely peeped above her arms as she replied, "What little dance?"

Trish rose to circle Nessa with her hands on her hips and wiggled her butt to a little jig. "You know what I'm talking about. Your obvious pink slip to Gabriel and the body language that's clearly hanging out the sign that says this chick's not for sale."

Trish perched on the corner of Nessa's desk and patted her friend's dark curly head. "I thought you said you liked him. You said last night that if not for the wreck, the evening had started out kind of okay."

Nessa propped her head and pinched the bridge of her nose, squinting her burning eyes for relief. "Things change, okay? Maybe I don't know what I like anymore. All I know is that I'm tired."

Trish pursed her lips and bent her head, scowling at Nessa with determination. "What you need is some fresh air and a change of scenery. The MacKays just called and invited us over for tea. Come on. Get your jacket." Trish swatted Nessa's shoulder with a handful of papers and hopped off the corner of her desk.

Nessa shook her head. She slumped back in her chair and folded her arms across her chest. "I am not going. I do not like tea. I'm tired. Nightmares kept me up all night. Besides, the students have made a significant find that requires my presence here."

Trish tapped one foot and motioned toward the outer flap of the tent. "You have to go. I already told them we'd be happy to come. Besides, Fiona says Brodie has several brothers that she'd be more than happy to introduce us to. Come on. Some new faces will make you feel better."

"I said I'm not going," Nessa snapped. What little control she had left crumbled away as she stood up from her chair. "I am sick and tired of your hormones dragging me around from one disappointment to the next. From now on, Trish leave me out of your sexual scavenger hunts. If I want companionship, I will get myself a dog. Heaven knows they're the only creatures on earth capable of unconditional love."

Trish stared at Nessa in open-mouthed amazement and rested a concerned hand on her shoulder. "Nessa... What is going on with you? What is wrong?"

Nessa scrubbed her face with her balled up fists and struggled to keep from bursting into tears. Her voice quivered as she fought for control and rummaged around the tent for her coat. "Nothing! Okay? I'm just tired. Just leave me alone for a while. I just need some fresh air. I'm just going for a walk. Don't look for me later because I don't know when I'll be back."

Nessa shoved her arms into her jacket and jerked the collar up around her neck. As she stomped out the door, she shielded her weary eyes from the blinding rays of the sun. Where the hell had she put her hat? As far as she was concerned, from this day forward, work was all that mattered. One way or another, Trish would just have to learn to accept it. When it came to priorities, men just hit the rock bottom of her list.

Poor Trish. She shouldn't have bitten off her head like that. A twinge of guilt banged against her exhausted mind. Nessa ducked her face even lower into her collar. Trish was her best friend, confidant, and sister she'd never had.

If she'd taken the time to tell Trish about her horrifying dream, Trish would've understood. She might not have believed it. She might think Nessa had slid over the edge but she never would've judged her. She would've just nodded her head, offered her shoulder for Nessa's tears, then suggested they go out and do something crazy to push it out of Nessa's mind.

Nessa bent to pick up a rough-edged stone and turned it over in her hand. With a cynical laugh, she rubbed her thumb across its cold, rough surface. The archeologist in her wondered what secrets it could tell.

She'd come so far. She'd reached her goal. And she'd always credited her drive to the man in her dreams. Now that same man had shattered his comforting lover's image. Now what was she supposed to do?

CHAPTER
THIRTEEN

"When will they be here?" Latharn bellowed from the sphere. He hated it when Brodie and Fiona went into the other room and left him on the shelf.

Fiona stuck her head through the door and motioned toward the clock centered on the mantel. "I told ye they should be here within the hour. Ye asked me that same question just fifteen minutes ago. Please, Cousin Latharn. I canna get the tea and cakes ready if I keep having to come in here every five minutes and tell ye what time the girls are supposed to arrive."

"If I asked ye the question fifteen minutes ago, then ye are not coming in here every five minutes to talk to me," Latharn shouted at the swinging door. It was too late. Fiona had left and gone back into the kitchen. If they would set the damned globe in the sitting room, then they wouldn't have to worry about it.

Latharn fumed as he paced the circumference of his prison. He'd been practicing more of late. Perhaps he could move the globe there himself. First, he visualized the globe sitting on the counter of the shop. He opened his eyes. With a proud smile, Latharn scanned his new surroundings. He had done it. Emrys had told him concentration and practice was the key. He rubbed his hands together and flexed his shoulders. He visualized the dark mahogany table he knew Fiona had centered in front of the window of the sitting room. It had belonged to her mother. It was her pride and joy. Opening his eyes, Latharn chuckled as he now enjoyed the view out of the parlor window. And there was Trish just getting out of her vehicle. But where was Nessa?

"Brodie! Fiona!" Latharn bellowed from his new vantage point in the center of the sitting room.

"How did ye get in here?" Brodie twisted his head from the doorway of the shop to the mahogany table in the center of the room.

"That is not important right now," Latharn hissed as he reflected the aura from the sphere off the walls. "Nessa is not with Trish. Something is wrong. Find out what it is."

Brodie turned to follow Latharn's command as Fiona walked in from the kitchen and pointed at the sphere and back at the room. He shook his head at her and waved her back toward the kitchen as a knock sounded at the door.

"That's her. Be sure and stand so I can see everything." Latharn wished he could speak to Trish. He knew he had upset Nessa the other night in her dreams. He'd lost control of his damnable temper, his uncontrollable rage...he couldn't help it. The thought of Gabriel Burns touching his Nessa made his blood boil.

Brodie opened the door to Trish's smiling face. "Trish, we're glad ye could make it. Won't ye come inside?" As he stepped aside and ushered her in, he added, "Where's Nessa? We thought she was coming too."

A suspicious look flickered across Trish's face as she stepped into the room. "Nessa had a really rough night last night. She sends her thanks and promises to make it some other time."

Latharn watched Trish's body language. This lass was a cagey one. Trish protected Nessa as she'd so often done before. Latharn chuckled as he stroked his chin. He could tell by the look on Trish's face, she'd already sized up Brodie and Fiona. He read her as easily as a book. This afternoon's tea could prove to be quite entertaining. Brodie and Fiona could end up having their hands full. Latharn leaned against the glass and prepared to enjoy the show.

Fiona led Trish to a comfortable chair right beside the mahogany table. An innocent look plastered across her face, Fiona's hand fluttered to her chest. "A rough night? Is she okay? I thought last night was her private dinner with Gabriel Burns."

Careful, Fiona. Dinna overplay your hand. This one is not a fool. Latharn shifted closer for a better view as he waited for Trish's reaction.

Trish settled into the cushions and smiled. She hesitated before she answered. "Dinner didn't go quite as planned. There was an accident and they had to cut the date short."

"An accident?" Brodie shared a fierce look with his wife as he set the platter of sliced cakes upon the table in front of the chairs.

Latharn rubbed his jaw and grinned. Aye. An accident, all right. Unfortunately, the bastard had survived it. Latharn had been gentle and sent just the barest puff of wind. This should be good. Trish was toying with Brodie and Fiona. She waited for them to drag the information from her. The minx. She must've been a cat in a previous life, playing with her prey before the kill. What else would she tell them?

Trish stirred her tea as she perched on the edge of her chair, then leaned forward and selected a cake. "Nessa said Gabriel lost control of the car when it was sideswiped by a blast of wind. They ran off the road and then Gabriel was blown into the ditch while trying to help Nessa out of the car." She sipped her tea. Her eyes narrowed into speculative slits as she watched the couple's reaction over the rim of her cup.

"A blast of wind, ye say? How frightening that must have been for them. Was either of them hurt?" Brodie's hands curled into fists and he moved to the edge of his seat.

Trish shrugged and swirled the amber liquid in her cup with the delicate silver spoon. "Nessa's fine. Gabriel didn't fare as well. He ended up with a wrenched knee and three broken ribs." Trish set her cup of tea on the table, then folded her hands in her lap as she relaxed back in her chair. "Of course, Nessa had to jog all the way back to the inn for help and then mentioned something about having nightmares the rest of the night."

Fiona and Brodie fidgeted in their seats, stealing glances at Latharn's sphere. Fiona cleared her throat as she rose to refill Trish's cup, her hand trembling as she clenched the handle of the delicate teapot.

"We're verra sorry to hear Gabriel was hurt. These narrow country lanes can be quite treacherous at times. He's lucky Nessa was able to go for help since we just learned the local ambulance is back in the shop."

Trish set her cup on the table and folded her hands in her lap. "Why don't you two make it easier for all of us and just tell me what's going on?"

Tightening her lips into an irritated line, Fiona spun on her heel to face her squirming husband. "Ye see, Brodie? I told ye this was a bad idea. Neither one of us has ever been any good at playing these games."

Brodie groaned, set his untouched tea upon the table, and rested his head in his hands. "This isna going verra well at all. It just proves I shouldha' never been chosen."

"Never been chosen for what?" Trish leaned forward, glancing back and forth between each of the MacKays.

Fiona rose to pace about the room. She wrung her pale hands in front of her aproned waist as she fretted. "Trish, are ye an archeologist as well? Do ye know anything about the history of this area? Are ye familiar with any of the legends surrounding the clans?"

Trish frowned as she sat back in her chair and folded her hands across one knee. "I don't have my doctorate but I do have my master's degree in ancient history. Nessa hired me as her assistant when we met on campus years ago. I know it usually comes as a shock to everyone but I'm not just a pair of boobs with legs. If I do say so myself, I have a pretty sharp set of brains rattling around inside this gorgeous red head. What has the history of this area and the legends of the clans have to do with Nessa and Gabriel's accident?"

Latharn chuckled as he relaxed against the wall. His brothers would've loved Trish.

With a curt shake of his head at his wife, Brodie took over the conversation. "I am sworn to secrecy regarding the duty with which I've been charged. I can only advise ye that it would be in the best interest for the safety of all concerned if ye looked up the history of Clan MacKay."

"The best interest for the safety of all concerned," Trish repeated, a look of confusion wrinkling her brow. "What in the hell are you talking about? Is it some curse about the dig? This isn't some newly found mummy's tomb we're defiling. This site has been under research for years and there have been no cases of anyone ever dying of any strange curses surrounding the digs."

Brodie ground his teeth as he yanked his hands through his hair. "It has nothing to do with the Durness research sites or any of the burial cairns. The legends of clan MacKay will answer a lot of Nessa's questions. Not only about last night, but about herself as well."

"Why can't you tell me?" Trish rose from her seat and crossed the room, to poke her finger against Brodie's chest. "If you're insinuating that Nessa's in some sort of danger, you'd best be letting me know!"

His teeth clenched; Brodie glared down his nose at the angry redhead fuming in his face. "I'm sworn to secrecy. I've taken a vow. I canna tell ye anymore."

"Oh Brodie, enough! I've taken no oath. I'll tell her what she needs to know." Fiona edged her way over to the sphere and slid it across the table to Trish. "Trish Sullivan, I'd like ye to meet Latharn MacKay, the man who is in love with Nessa Buchanan and destined to be her husband." As she turned the pulsating crystal toward the center of the room, Fiona acknowledged Latharn's globe with a flourish.

Latharn straightened, every sense alert, watching Trish for any sign of panic. He bided his time, waiting to see her reaction before he made his presence known. Over the centuries, he'd learned the value of timing. It made all the difference in the world.

Trish looked at them with an expression that said she thought they'd all lost their minds. Stroking her chin, she circled the table, studying the ancient stand and the mystical carvings decorating every side of the stand supporting the globe. With a nod toward the crystal, she took a deep breath as she looked into the MacKays' worried eyes. "Okay. I'll bite. What's the legend say about this thing? What exactly is it I need to know?"

His arms folded across his chest. Brodie gave her his back. He turned his face to the drawing room window and refused to speak a word.

As if on cue, Fiona stepped forward. "Six hundred years ago there existed a powerful young mystic by the name of Latharn MacKay." Fiona traced her finger around the glowing crystal, her fingers shadowed in the violet light. "He was quite handsome and...shall we say, very skilled in pleasuring the lasses. All the maids fought to be the one to warm his bed each night."

"Sounds like Latharn MacKay was my kind of man," Trish interrupted with a grin.

Her eyes wide, Fiona shuddered as she continued. "He made the fatal mistake of bedding a powerful, dark sorceress. One who was determined to win his heart. When she found Latharn unable to share his love, she imprisoned him within this crystal instead."

Trish planted her hands on either side of the globe and peered deeper into the crystal. Reaching out, she turned the orb in its stand, obviously studying the swirls of energy at its core. "So, if she couldn't have him, then she made sure nobody else could. Why didn't she just kill him?"

Brodie exploded as he whirled from where he stood at the window. "Do ye no' have a vindictive bone in your body? Wouldn't ye rather torture someone who's done ye wrong instead of giving them a quick and easy death?"

Trish clasped her hands behind her back and remained bent over the crystal ball. With a shrug of one shoulder, she leaned even closer as if mesmerized by the energy whorls.

"I guess I never quite thought of it that way. But I must admit, what you say does have some merit." She straightened and circled around the table, with a nod for Fiona to continue the tale.

With a shaking breath, Fiona drew closer to the table. "Before taking her own life, Latharn's mother found the secret to the curse. Rachel was a powerful white *bana-buidhseach* herself. But she only used her powers for good. She discovered that for Latharn to walk among his clan once again, he must be called forth by the one woman capable of winning his love."

Trish frowned, looking up from the globe where her eyes met Fiona and Brodie's watchful gaze. "Nessa?"

They nodded.

"Okay. There are just a few things I'd like for you to clear up." Trish picked up the globe, turning it about in her hands as she squinted deeper into the swirling depths. "First, how do you know Nessa's the one? Second, if she doesn't know about him, how's she going to call out to him in a loving way to somehow break this spell?"

"I'm no' a child's bauble to be shaken about. Set me down, and I'll explain it to ye as best as I can." Latharn stumbled against the glass as he released his voice to echo into the room.

"Holy hell! It talks." Trish settled the globe on the table as though it were a ticking bomb.

"I am no' an it. I am Latharn MacKay and I would appreciate it if ye would take a bit more care with the wee crystal tomb." Latharn increased the violet aura as his energy pulsated throughout the room.

Trish backed away from the flashing orb and wiped her hands on the seat of her pants. Raising her hand to her chest, her mouth opened and closed without making any sounds.

Latharn had seen this reaction before. As long as Trish didn't bolt, he'd have time to explain. He kept his voice to a soothing echo, accented with the pulsating lights. "I have known my Nessa since before she took her current physical form. I've waited for over six hundred years for her soul to choose a body and decide to join us on this plane of existence. I've been walking her dream plane since the summer her parents broke her spirit."

Latharn paced the globe and allowed his energy to swirl about the room. His voice strengthened and the light pulsed as he explained the mystery to Trish as best he could.

"Nessa doesn't realize I truly exist for the curse has prevented me from ever speaking to her while I walk in her dreams. She thinks I'm but a creation of her imagination, brought on by years of loneliness and pain."

Trish finally found her voice. "Then we'll just tell her. We'll tell her what she needs to say and then you two can live happily ever after."

With a sorrowful shake of her head, Fiona linked her arm through Brodie's as they both gathered around the table.

"Trish, we canna tell her about Latharn and neither can you. The dark witch was quite shrewd when she cast her spell. Nessa must whisper her love to Latharn and call him forth without any prompting from anyone else. If anyone reveals the details of the curse to Nessa, the globe will shatter and send Latharn's soul into the eternal abyss."

A frustrated scowl crossed Trish's face as she paced around the room. "You've got to be kidding me. How in the world are we going to get her to whisper him out of that thing without telling her how to do it? I can't even get her to follow explicit instructions on how to power down her laptop when I give them to her word for word!"

With a deep sigh, Brodie kissed the top of Fiona's head and pulled her close. "We can only hope the goddess will finally smile upon our family as she did when our clan followed the Old Ways."

Circling the table, Trish studied the globe as though plotting how to kill it. "Wouldn't she be more likely to whisper to this thing, if we kept it constantly in her presence?"

Scooping up the witch's ball, Brodie held it protected against his chest. "A MacKay must always be the caretaker of the crystal orb. It must always reside in a clan member's home."

"Why?" Trish huffed, scowling at Brodie as though she were about to snatch the orb out of his grasp.

"The curse," Fiona retorted. "The black witch was no' the fool. She knew no one could tell the intended woman how to break the curse but she also wanted to ensure the globe would never accidently become the woman's possession...the less likely for it to hear her muse."

"Set me down, Brodie. I tire of being tossed about," Latharn roared from the depths of his tomb. Brodie immediately settled Latharn back to the center of the table, his face flaming at Latharn's scolding.

"Well, dammit!" Trish paced around the table centered in the modest sitting room. With a look of determination, she spread her hands on either side of the globe and peered into the pulsating ball. Latharn spread his hands on the frigid walls of his prison and eyed her back. "Well then, that leaves us no other choice. Either the two of you must move in with us, or we have to move in with you. Either way, Nessa will be around that thing enough to start talking to it and will accidentally say what the curse needs to hear."

"Would ye kindly stop referring to me as that thing?" Latharn calmed the lights emitting from the sphere, lowering them to a serene flicker about the room. Trish's reasoning pleased him. Her unwillingness to let the puzzle go meant he had another ally outside of his prison walls.

Trish shrugged a shoulder with a sheepish grin. "Sorry. No offense. But it's hard for me to relate to something that looks like a yard ornament from my grandmother's garden."

At Trish's retort, Latharn's laughter rumbled like thunder rippling through the room. He intensified the aura to a blinding cloud as his energy centralized in the air just above the sparkling globe. For the first time in several hundred years, he projected the image of his face within the aura. He allowed them to see his amused eyes echoing his flashing smile.

"Thank ye, Trish, for being the first one to give me a hearty laugh in well over five hundred years."

"Wow." Breathless, Trish stared at Latharn's visage, suspended in the air above the globe. "I wish I could whisper you out of that thing. No wonder she trapped you in there."

FOURTEEN

"Trish, are you sure they've decreased our housing stipend? I just saw a letter stating they were increasing our grant money since the documentation of the fifteenth-century claymore."

Nessa sat at the desk with her chin propped in her hand, trying not to fall out of her seat. Her eyes were so gritty they felt like they'd dropped in a child's sandbox and been shoved back in her head. Exhaustion pounded at the back of her skull and ached through all her muscles.

Trish nodded, reaching across the desk to slide all the mail out of Nessa's reach. "I got the call this morning. We're going to have to move out of the inn. The sooner we're out the better."

Nessa rubbed her face. Trish's words didn't make any sense but maybe it was because she was so tired. "I guess we'll just have to stay here at the site full time then. We can sleep on the cots in the back. We've been sleeping here off and on anyway. We'll just have to make it permanent."

"There's another option we might consider." Trish nervously shuffled papers from one desk to the other. "The other day when I was having tea with the MacKays, they asked me if I knew of any of our students who might be looking to rent a room."

Nessa pinched the bridge of her nose and closed her stinging eyes. They burned like two orbs of glowing hot embers. She hadn't had a decent night's sleep since she couldn't remember when. The one night she'd taken the sleeping pills, she'd spent it trying to flee from the Highlander in her dreams.

Her feet had been like two blocks of solid concrete plowing through a swamp. She'd managed to keep just out of his reach, but she'd been terrified she'd fall into his hands. His weapon was gone, but fury flashed in his eyes, a storm threatening to unleash at any moment.

For some odd reason, she'd gotten the distinct impression that she'd angered him by trying to escape his visits with a drug-induced sleep. Somehow, he'd overpowered the drugs and pulled her from the dark, fuzzy depths. She'd struggled against him. She'd pounded on his chest until she'd finally wrenched free of his grasp. She'd struggled and pushed her weighted feet into an endless run. She'd awakened gasping when she'd barely escaped him.

Since that nightmare, she'd forced herself to spend the night's upright in a chair. She'd struggle through the hours, dozing just enough to function the following day. She didn't know how much longer she'd be able to keep this up; all she knew was she dare not fall asleep. Who knew what might happen the next time he showed up in her dreams?

"Nessa!" Trish tapped a chisel on the desk, pulling Nessa from her daze. "How long has it been since you've slept? Really slept...in a bed...lying down?"

"I've lost track," Nessa mumbled, rising from the desk to refill her already full coffee cup. She rubbed her forehead and tried to concentrate on what Trish had said about the rent. "I'll be fine. Now what were you saying about the MacKays? They've got a room to rent?"

Trish bit her lip and nodded. "Yep. It's roomy enough for the both of us and just a quarter of what we're paying at the inn."

Nessa shrugged into her jacket and waved a weak hand. Maybe she'd been wrong about that letter. She was so tired. She didn't know if she was coming or going. "Fine. Do whatever. Just point me in the right direction when it's time to leave the site." Donning a scarf against the chill of the dying sun, Nessa slipped on her sunglasses to hide what she knew were her bloodshot eyes. "I'm going for a walk around the sites. When I get back, we can call it a day."

"No problem," Trish replied with a smile. She picked up her cell phone as Nessa stumbled toward the door. "We're all set. If you can swing by and pick up our bags today then we'll be your new tenants tonight."

Ignoring as Trish murmured to someone about bags, Nessa paused just outside the door. She filled her lungs with a deep breath of the sharp, clean air. She hoped to find a miraculous revitalizer somewhere in the stiff Highland breeze. The day was clear and unusually cool for so early in the afternoon. Nessa welcomed the chill. It would keep her awake and help her concentrate in her current state of exhaustion.

Nessa scanned around the dig at the various cordoned-off sites. She sighed as she watched the students milling about. From where Nessa stood, not one of them looked like they had a care in the world other than striving to be the first one to come up with the next big find.

Nessa decided against wandering among the students. She was in no mood or condition for small talk of any kind. She did good just to stay on her feet. Turning toward the open field, Nessa pulled her collar closer about her face. She scanned the horizon and found herself drawn to a peaceful-looking grove of pines.

Nessa picked her way into the heart of the inviting thicket. A gurgling spring broke free from the earth and tumbled down into a deep, tranquil pool. The clear water bubbled forth from the depths of a massive limestone fissure, the opening hollowed by years of the running water. Ancient Picts had fashioned out an altar from the great stone shelf where it protruded from the bank. Nessa recognized the triple spirals and the serene face of the woman peering out at her from the center of the ancient stone. This was a shrine to honor the blessed mother goddess. The people would have worshipped the well for its healing powers.

Nessa knelt upon the mossy embankment. She took a deep breath and splashed the icy, sweet water upon her face. The sting of weariness disappeared from her grainy eyes. Her exhaustion evaporated. She felt more rested than she had in days.

"Thank you. I needed to find this place," she murmured to the peaceful image. As she looked into the serene gaze of the goddess's face upon the stone, Nessa sighed and bowed her head. She'd sought this tranquility for days. No Gabriel. No Highlander. No students buzzed around her with a thousand mind-numbing questions that she was in no condition to field. She toyed with the thought of returning to the encampment to get her sleeping bag and bring it here to spend the night at the side of the pool.

The snap of twigs and the rustling of dried pine boughs tore her attention away from the pool. The sounds came from the bushes on the other side of the pool. Nessa wondered if it were some sort of animal looking to quench its thirst in the cold waters of the crystal spring.

A woman eased her way out of the trees. She hesitated, her deep, violet eyes scanning the clearing as though searching for an item she'd lost. Nessa wondered who she could be and why she was so oddly dressed. Her flowing hair glinted silver, hanging in heavy tresses to her waist. She wore a thick velvet cloak clenched at her throat with a pale, delicate hand. Her cloak covered her entire body. The hood fell back upon her shoulders. The garment was so long that even her feet disappeared from view.

Her wandering gaze settled upon Nessa. She smiled in recognition. Her eyes sparkled, crinkling at the corners. She nodded her head in greeting as she made her way around the pool.

"I was wondering how long it was going to take you to find Brid's special place."

Confused, Nessa rose to her feet as she peered closer into the woman's face. "Have we met?"

The woman had a nagging sense of familiarity about her but Nessa was certain she'd never seen her before.

"Not exactly," the woman replied with the slightest shake of her head. She smiled as she circled Nessa as though she were a newly acquired possession. "Let's just say, I'm familiar with the history of this area and I thought I could be of some help to you in your quest."

She thought she understood. Nessa smiled her polite visiting-archeologist smile. This woman was obviously an eccentric local who'd heard about the research of the Durness sites.

"Ah, I see. Thank you. But currently, we're cataloging items from the Bronze Age. I appreciate your searching me out but I'm afraid I'm more interested in a bit further back along the timeline then you might realize. My specialty isn't this area's more recent history."

A knowing smile curled the side of the lady's mouth as she gazed out across the pond. "The Highlander from your dreams is not from the Bronze Age. He's from the Scotland of 1410."

Nessa almost choked as her throat constricted. She clapped her hand to her chest. How could this woman know about her dreams? She'd never seen her before. She'd never told anyone except Trish about the nightly visits from her Highlander.

"Who are you?" Her voice trembling, Nessa struggled against the swell of uneasiness in her chest. She edged her way closer to the mysterious woman who now stood at the mouth of the well.

"A friend," the woman replied, with a mysterious smile reflected in the water. Her shoulders shrugged inward as she tightened her cloak. With a lingering sigh, she continued as she turned toward Nessa. "Your Highlander's name is Latharn MacKay, and you must know he would never harm you. He cannot speak while in your dreams. But if you take the time to look into his heart, you will know everything he needs to say."

Nessa's body was chilled to the bone by the eeriness of the woman's words. Was this woman a ghost? A seer? A psychic? She peered closer at her. Relief flooded through Nessa's mind when the woman appeared as solid and as much of this world as Nessa herself.

Nessa took a deep breath and swallowed hard against her pounding heart. "Since you seem to know so much about this… Latharn MacKay, why is he forbidden to speak?"

The woman's eyes filled with sadness as she turned away. Her voice quivered with emotion as she pulled her hood back over her head. She didn't look back as she continued moving deeper into the pines. "Everything you need to know about Latharn can be found in your dreams. If you will trust him, everything will become clear to you in your heart in its own good time."

"Wait!" Nessa grew alarmed as she realized the woman was leaving the well. "What else do you know about him? Is there anything more you can tell me? Surely, you're not going to leave me here without saying anything more."

The woman stopped. She didn't face Nessa; instead, her hooded form turned away. She kept her head bowed as she instructed in a firm commanding voice, "Trust him, my child. That is all I can tell you. Trust him and trust your heart."

With the mysterious woman's final words, a brisk whirlwind swirled through the trees. Dust, sticks, and bits of leaves flew wildly into the air. Blinded by debris filling the wind, Nessa choked against the dust cloud covering her face. When the wind died down and she'd rubbed her eyes free of the dust, the cloaked woman by the pond had vanished.

CHAPTER
FIFTEEN

"Counterclockwise, fool!" Deardha roared against the crystal, her breath fogging the glass.

Damn, the fool was weak and did not follow instructions well at all. The idiot couldn't even read a basic grimoire. She tapped the crystal with a blackened nail as Gabriel stumbled in circles about the room.

What a pathetic failure. Deardha propped her chin in her hands and leaned her elbows against the pedestal. She was going to have to possess the imbecile's body after all. Possession was always so unpleasant. She hadn't possessed anyone since the thirteenth century and at least that had been a dear little child. Men were such filthy, piteous beasts when she took them over. Always obsessed with grabbing their cocks to make sure it still hung between their legs.

Deardha blew out an irritated sigh. It was the only way. Latharn appeared to be growing stronger now that his little bitch was on the soil of his homeland. Apparently, she should've taken into account his mystical abilities when she conjured his crystal cell. If only she'd foreseen his ability to travel the cosmos with his mind. No matter. She still would have him.

No man dare cast her aside, least of all Latharn MacKay. He would beg to return to her bed. She would force a pledge of his heart to her. And then he would die a delightful death of her choosing, one that involved something wondrously painful and excruciatingly slow.

CHAPTER

SIXTEEN

Her cell phone jarred her out of her head-jerking doze. Nessa scowled at the contraption as she pulled it from her pocket. With a bleary-eyed squint, she focused on the display, unable to identify the number demanding her immediate attention.

"Hello," she snapped. Nessa rubbed her eyes as she held the phone to her ear. She shot Trish an angry glare as her head whacked against the window for at least the third time since they'd left the dig. If there were a single pothole anywhere in the road, Trish would always manage to plow right through the middle of it.

"Nessa?" Gabriel's voice buzzed in her ear. He sounded uncertain he'd dialed the correct number.

"Oh, Gabriel. Sorry. I didn't mean to sound so harsh. It's just that I'm in the process of having my teeth rattled out of my head as Trish explores every pothole in Scotland."

Nessa thumped Trish's shoulder and covered the mouthpiece of her phone. "Slow this damn thing down," she hissed.

His rich laughter rumbled in her ear as Gabriel snorted his reply,

"I'm not even going to ask ye what that means. I'm just relieved your anger isn't directed at me."

Nessa yawned and sat up straighter in the seat. Wiping the mist from her side of the windshield, she focused on the road ahead. If she remembered her landmarks, once they passed that last weathered cairn on the right it wasn't much farther to the MacKays' house. As she tried to rub the bleariness out of her eyes, Nessa gave up and decided to take the polite route for this conversation. "So, how are you feeling?"

His voice a bit strained, Gabriel was quick to reply, "I'm quite a bit better. I've been able to graduate from the crutches to a cane and my ribs are not paining me nearly as much. Ye would know that if ye would listen to your messages that I've been leaving every time I call." A reproachful tone crept even deeper into his voice as Gabriel hurried to scold her even more. "And I canna believe ye have not stopped by the pub. 'Tis been almost three weeks since I've seen your lovely face."

Nessa closed her eyes, clenching the phone tighter. She should not have answered it, especially when she didn't recognize the number. She squelched the tendril of self-imposed guilt by rerunning Cordelia's words through her head. She'd be damned if she'd become any man's lapdog, even one as handsome as Gabriel Burns. She might be plain, but she had a lot going for her and she wasn't afraid of being alone. If true love really existed, that would be great. But she wasn't about to go fawning after any man, no matter how great he looked in a pair of tight-fitting jeans.

"Nessa? Are ye there?"

Gabriel's voice interrupted her fuming and pulled her back into the conversation. "I'm here. Sorry. I guess we must have a bad signal here." Nessa shrugged her shoulders at Trish as she scratched her nails on the phone in her own simulation of cellular interference.

"Promise me ye will be good enough to stop by the pub tomorrow and allow me to fix ye a bit of lunch." His voice smooth and cajoling, Gabriel purred into her ear.

Too tired to argue, Nessa latched onto the next best thing she could think of; she decided to play the clueless female. "That'll be great. Trish and I have to come into town to file some papers. We'll stop by the pub on the way out and you can treat us both."

Nessa grinned when Gabriel went silent. She knew he had intended for her to come alone. She closed her eyes, leaned back against the headrest, and waited for his reply.

"That'll be grand. I'll see the two of ye tomorrow and I'll fix ye a fine repast."

Nessa stifled a giggle. She was almost disappointed. Gabriel had recovered well. His voice held only the slightest tinge of frustration over a strong layer of determination.

"We'll see you then." Nessa clicked the phone shut and stuffed it back into her pocket. She reveled in an eye-watering yawn and then turned to face Trish's expectant you-better-tell-me face. "What?"

"Okay. First, you're so insecure you're afraid to go out with this guy. Then you attempt a date with him and decide he's okay but you're not really interested. But you're still kind of wishy-washy and could go either way. Now, although he doesn't realize it yet, you're cutting your ties to him by dragging along the old best friend. What gives with this guy?" Trish waited, one brow arched as she darted glances between the road and Nessa's face.

Nessa rubbed her face with her hands, yawned again, and scrubbed her fingers through her hair until it stood on end. "Let's just say I don't think Gabriel is quite what he seems. I've rethought my first impression of the man and I think holding him at arm's length isn't such a bad idea right now."

Trish shook her head. "Pass him on to me. I'll hang onto him for you. I think he's hot."

Trish pulled the car into the gravel driveway around to the back of the building. "They said we could park here in the back. There's a separate entrance to the room we're going to rent."

At the sight of the quaint structure with the weather-stained boards, Nessa attempted to stifle another jaw-cracking yawn.

Pawing for the handle to open the car door, she noticed the starched white curtains freshly hung in the spotless windows. "I can't believe Brodie came by and picked up all our stuff from the inn. They must've really been anxious to find someone for the room." Sliding out of the car, Nessa stretched and rubbed her aching neck. She didn't know how she would manage to stay awake tonight.

Trish turned the key in the lock and edged the door open with her shoulder. Swinging the door wide, she stood aside, motioning Nessa into the oversized room.

Two comfortable-looking twin beds stood in opposite corners, each paired with its own nightstand and cozy reading lamp. A slightly used but clean kitchen table and chairs inhabited the other side of the room. A door led to an adjoining bathroom lit by the welcoming glow of a hostess light. A dormitory-sized refrigerator hummed, stuffed with sodas and snacks. It squatted between two dressers with several tins of biscuits and sweets in a welcoming basket on top.

Brodie had placed their bags just inside the closet door that he'd left open for them to find. As Nessa looked around, she realized with pleasant surprise that they were going to have quite a bit more space here than they'd each had in their separate rooms at the inn.

"Are you hungry, Nessa? Looks like they've stocked the refrigerator and there's a hot plate on the kitchen table." Sorting through the contents, Trish emerged with a can of soda and popped the tab as she walked about the room.

Nessa shook her head and bent to unlace her boots as she settled on the edge of the farthest bed. "I think I'm just going to prop up here for a while and read through a few of these papers. I didn't have a chance to go over them today and the students have been bugging me for my opinion."

As she headed for the doorway, Trish tossed a separate key on the table and wrinkled her nose in Nessa's direction. "Suit yourself, chick. I'm going to walk around to the shop and let them know we're here and that the room's going to be great. Why don't you try to turn in early tonight? You're really starting to look pretty rough."

Nessa pinched the bridge of her nose, shut her gritty eyes, and forced a tired smile onto her face. "Thanks a lot for your honest observation. I'm fine. I have to get through these papers tonight so we can include them in the overnight packet to the university tomorrow. Tell the MacKays I said hi and thank them for the room. This'll be great while we're here for the rest of the dig."

Nessa pulled her backpack up on the bed beside her. She wadded up the pillow and stuffed it behind her back. As she sorted out papers, she was careful not to look up. She knew Trish would notice she feared falling asleep. She knew it had to be a flashing red light strobing on top of her head. She heard Trish clicking her nails on the door facing while she waited. Not good. Trish always fidgeted when she worried.

Trish finally relinquished with a grudging sigh. "Whatever you say. I may be out for a bit. I'll try not to wake you when I come in." Without another word, Trish slipped out the door and eased it shut behind her.

Nessa plunked her head against the wall. She took a deep breath as she glanced around the room. This place was going to be too comfortable. She'd never manage to catnap in this cozy atmosphere.

Her eyelids grew heavier, as though weighted. They risked slamming shut. Her head noodle-necked off her chest. Nessa fought against the relentless fatigue. Maybe if she just closed her eyes for a couple of minutes, she'd doze just enough to stay conscious enough to control her dreams.

He stood a bit away from her. He kept his hands clasped behind his back; his head slightly bowed. It was almost as though he waited for judgment—waited for his sentence to be read. Her heart quickened as she realized she was well within his reach. Nessa's hand fluttered to her throat. Her breath came quickly through her parted lips. Her heart pounded in her ears. She debated whether she should run.

If she turned now, she knew she could escape. He couldn't reach her yet.

But he just stood there. Sorrow and pain filled his eyes. His usual heart-quickening smile narrowed into a soul-wrenching line. Nessa waited. His anger had disappeared; he seemed so defeated. She swallowed hard and caught her lip between her teeth as she moved just a bit closer. Her fear of him lessened. The torment in his face tugged at her heart; the suffering in his eyes cried out to her louder than words. She recalled what the mysterious woman of the woods had said.

Nessa had to let him know what he'd done. "You frightened me. What you showed me you were capable of doing to Gabriel...your rage...your anger... It frightened me."

For the first time since he'd introduced himself into her mind, she spoke to him while he was in her dream. She reasoned with him about what she felt. She had to make him understand.

She frowned and reached out to him as she tried to explain. "I don't know what you want from me. You've been in my dreams since I was so young...but you've never been this way before. You've never been this difficult to understand."

Latharn took a deep breath. He nodded his head just once, then lowered himself to his knees. He bowed his head and held out his hands to her, pleading for forgiveness of his sins.

Nessa's eyes stung with unshed tears and she pressed her hands to her cheeks. A mountain of a man kneeling at her feet was more than she could bear.

She placed her hands in his. Her tiny fingers disappeared inside his muscular fists. She moved closer. As she bent, she pressed her cheek to his. Her breath caught in her throat as she touched the moisture of his tears. That's all it took. Her fear was gone. This man was brave enough to show her his heart. He had bared his emotions.

"I wish you could tell me why you keep appearing in my dreams. It seems like you've been with me forever." Nessa dropped to her knees, looking up into his eyes. She held his face between her hands, drowning in his gaze.

A sad smile played across his lips. Latharn shook his head as he turned to kiss the palm of each hand. He buried his face in her neck and crushed her against his chest. He covered her throat with desperate kisses, nuzzling a trail to her mouth. He closed his hungry lips over hers. He devoured her as though he were a man possessed. He claimed her with his kisses, deep and ardent. He branded his possession of her soul.

She clung to him as though he was a life preserver keeping her afloat on the sea of her emotions. She would open to whatever he asked. However, tonight Latharn was different. He didn't go any further than the hungry possession of her mouth or the desperate, crushing embrace. Nessa sensed he needed this night to be different. His body tensed beneath her touch; he restrained his caress as if he wanted her to reason rather than just shatter into mindless bliss.

He raised his head and gazed into her eyes. Nessa flinched at the depths of pain and frustration etched in his face. He struggled, trying to communicate, to connect with her deepest emotions without the use of words. He took his palm, flattened it against his heart then placed it upon her chest. His brows drawn together in a questioning frown, he tilted his head and waited for a sign that she understood.

Her lower lip quivered at the very obvious gesture. Nessa whispered and covered his hand with hers. "Are you telling me you love me?" Her whisper caught in her throat.

One corner of his mouth pulled up into a relieved smile as Latharn nodded and brushed his lips across hers. He took a deep breath as though steeling himself against his own deepest fears. He took her hand and repeated the heart-touching gesture from her chest to his. Then he raised a brow and awaited her answer, anxiety filling his eyes.

A lone tear escaped down her cheek as Nessa stared at her hand splayed upon his broad chest. "You know I love you," she murmured with a soft moan. "I just wish you were real."

He squeezed his eyes shut, pulling her into his arms to cradle her against his chest. Holding her close, he stroked her hair as she gave way to tears. His arms tightened around her and he gently swayed as she softly wept in his arms.

"Nessa. Are you all right? Nessa. Wake up! Was it another nightmare?" Trish shook Nessa by the shoulders to pull her from the dream. As she pulled her closer, Trish raised Nessa's head from her tear-stained pillows.

"I'm fine," Nessa hiccupped through her tears as she accepted a handful of tissues to wipe her face.

"Do you want to talk about it?" Trish asked, sitting cross-legged on the side of the bed.

As she drew a deep breath, Nessa shook her head. "Not tonight. It's still too fresh in my mind. It's late. You go back to bed. I'm going to try to go back to sleep. Somehow…I don't think he'll be back tonight." Flipping her pillow over, dry side up, she curled over onto her side.

Trish pulled the covers around Nessa's shoulders. She tucked Nessa in as though she were her child. "Well, okay. You try to get some rest. You can fill me in tomorrow."

"Tomorrow." Nessa closed her eyes, sighing as she slipped back into the lonely darkness.

CHAPTER
SEVENTEEN

Nessa slung her backpack over her shoulder as she entered the front of the shop. She smiled her good mornings at Brodie and Fiona where they stood chatting behind the counter. "Have either of you seen Trish this morning? The minx got up early to beat me to all the hot water and now I can't seem to find her. We've got to get some data sent out so that it gets to the university by Monday."

Rummaging through the cluttered shelves behind the counter, Fiona found the note from Trish. "She's already gone to overnight the papers. She said she didn't have the heart to wake ye this morning since ye've been so exhausted of late. She said there was no need for ye to come along. She said something about having everything covered."

Unfolding the piece of paper, Nessa groaned and dropped her bag to the floor. Trish and her meddling. How many times had she told that chick to butt out? "She knows I promised Gabriel we'd stop by the pub for lunch. I really hoped our visit to him today would get him to take the hint he's wasting his time. Did she say she was going to be coming back in time to pick me up? Her note is kind of vague."

Brodie lowered Latharn's globe from the shelf above the counter and placed it in front of Nessa. "She mentioned something about going to the pub without ye and relaying your regrets to Gabriel. She said ye told her yesterday ye were trying to find a way to back off a bit from that evil bastard."

"Brodie!" Fiona scolded. "Gabriel is no' an evil bastard, Nessa. But Trish did mention ye weren't quite as taken with him as ye had first thought when the two of ye met."

Since when did everyone have full rights to her love life? Nessa fumed, her aggravation tightening in her chest. "That still doesn't give her license to interfere. I've talked to her about his before." She slid her over-stuffed backpack across the floor and propped it against the counter. When she did, the hypnotic pulse of the glowing witch's ball captured her eye.

Mesmerized, Nessa's irritation with Trish disappeared as she gazed into the swirling purple vortex. She cupped the globe between her hands and sank into its endless depths. Nothing else in the room existed. The whirling energy captivated her within its dancing lights.

Fiona elbowed Brodie and nodded toward Nessa. "Look at the aura. The light surrounds her. It's as though the globe cradles her in its energy."

With a nervous cough as though to clear his throat, Brodie tapped the counter beside the globe. "What do ye think of our wee bauble here? It's been in the MacKay family for years."

Nessa tore her attention from the vibrating energy. She found it difficult to look up from the crystal orb. "Oh it's...it's lovely. I don't know why but it seems to draw me into it. It's as though the lights are dancing to some silent song." She trailed her fingertips across the surface. Nessa smiled as the energy patterns changed with her touch. "Look! The lights are following wherever I touch. It's almost as if it's following my fingertips. How does it do that?" The glass felt warm. She swore it pulsed as though it had a heartbeat.

Brodie's lips twitched. Then he shrugged his shoulders. "I've never seen the globe react that way before. Not in all the years I've had it in my possession."

Her eyes widened in surprise. Nessa touched the ball again. The light sprang from within its core in response to her touch. "Really? I wonder why it responds to me. You said it's been in your family for years. What's its story? Where did it originate?"

Fiona edged her way between Brodie and the counter. "They say it was given to Laird MacKay and his wife, Rachel, in the early 1400s. They were the laird and lady of Clan MacKay at that time. The globe has been protected and passed down through the family since that era until it came to be Brodie's and mine."

The dancing lights entranced her senses. Nessa had to drag herself away from the counter. The globe drew her in. It mesmerized her and made her feel as if she floated on a cloud of purple down.

"It's addictive. I could gaze into that thing forever. It's so hypnotic. It's almost as though it's alive. Who gave it to Laird MacKay and his wife? Some sort of wizard maybe?"

Her fingers trembling, Fiona smoothed her hands across the top of the counter and dusted around the globe. "No one knows the true identity of the giver. That information seems to have been lost." Brodie coughed and shuffled his feet, backing away from the edge of the counter.

Nessa couldn't resist a mischievous grin at Fiona as she bent to retrieve her bag. "Wouldn't it be great if it was like a genie's lamp? We could just tell it our deepest desires and poof...our wildest dreams would come true."

Brodie's eyes bulged; he coughed and wheezed until tears streamed down his face.

"Brodie! Are you okay?" Nessa dropped her bag and rushed around the counter. Brodie's face flamed a bright cherry red.

Thumping him on the back, Fiona waved her away. "Oh, he's fine. He just gets choked verra easily sometimes." With a smile, she nodded in the direction of the globe. "Now wouldn't that be grand if that crystal ball was just like you said! Our verra own wishing ball.

Perhaps that's what it was meant to be all along and it was just forgotten down through the passage of time."

Fiona pulled a box of tissues from under the counter and shoved them into Brodie'schest. Turning back to Nessa, her eyes sparkled and her voice dropped to a conspiratorial whisper. "And if it were such a magical thing? What would be one of your dearest wishes? What would ye ask of the ball?"

Nessa paused before hefting her bag up on her shoulder, half-tempted to play along. Wouldn't it be great if she could wish her nocturnal Highlander into reality and fall right into his arms? Wouldn't that be her lifelong dream come true? Who was she kidding? That's the stuff fairy tales were made of. Her old self-preservation habits kicked in at the last minute and she recoiled back inside her carefully constructed shell. Settling her backpack on her shoulder, Nessa shuttered her emotions as well. "Oh, I don't know. I've pretty much got everything I need."

Fiona's face fell at Nessa's reply. "Ah well...then ye truly are blessed. Ye not only have everything ye need but ye are wise enough to know it."

Sure, she did. Nessa turned toward the door. She wasn't about to share her deepest desires with the MacKays. They were a kind and generous couple who she felt certain would become friends. However, she just wasn't ready to open up and bare her soul.

She'd learned at a young age that when you shared your innermost thoughts and feelings it only exposed you to painful barbs. In her experience, Trish was the only person who'd never hurt her and she just wasn't brave enough right now to enlarge that elite circle of trust.

Remembering the words of the mysterious woman at the goddess well, Nessa paused and turned back into the room. "By the way, do either of you happen to remember any stories about an ancestor of yours by the name of Latharn MacKay?"

A new fit of coughing seized Brodie, his hands flying to his chest as panic registered in his eyes. Fiona renewed her pounding on her husband's back, her eyes wide as she replied, "Latharn MacKay? Why do ye ask? What have ye heard about the name?"

The lights in the sphere danced into hyper-drive. The agitated energy of the orb bounced off the walls, reflecting off every item lining the shelves. Nessa dropped her bag back to the floor and stared at the vibrating globe. She edged her way toward the counter. Uneasiness stirred in the pit of her stomach. Her skin tingled at the reaction of the lights.

"Latharn MacKay," she whispered, leaning closer. She waited for the globe's response. Violent purple energy shot from the globe. It crackled and filled the entire room.

"Look at that. It's like the light responds to his name," Nessa whispered and spun on her heel. Watching the frustrated energy spark about the room, she grew breathless with anticipation. It bounced from the windows to the ceiling, to the floor, and on every reflective surface in between. Her skin tingled with excitement; every hair stood on end as Nessa called out to the traveling light. "Latharn MacKay, are you in this room?"

The energy responded and concentrated into one spot. It caressed and swirled around her body. A familiar stroke brushed her cheek. Nessa recognized the warmth of this touch. This comforting embrace had pleasured her many times from her Highlander in her dreams.

"You're real," Nessa whispered, a shiver of recognition rippling across her skin. "You're not just in my dreams."

The aura surrounded her, swirling, touching. The essence warmed gentle feather strokes against her skin, swaddling her in a cloud of vibrating color. The cursed globe sat poised, squatted on its pedestal, the colors flowing freely from its center.

Her heart hammering so hard she couldn't breathe, Nessa fought against rising hysteria. Backing away from the ball, apprehension churned inside her like a mounting storm. In all her years, in all her finds, she'd never come across any artifact as powerful as this crystal appeared.

"What is this thing?" She nudged her chin in the direction of the globe as she stole a glance at Brodie and Fiona.

Shaking their heads, they remained silent. They just stood there, mouths clamped shut, watching Nessa and the globe.

Nessa gritted her teeth, trying to remember to breathe as she edged her way toward the door. Whatever was happening with the wildly glowing crystal, it was eerie and she wanted it to stop.

Fiona recognized that Nessa was about to bolt. She rushed from around the counter to pat her on the arm. "It's all right, Nessa. Dinna fear. It's just a wee energy ball that reacts to the static in the room. If ye look out the door, ye will see it's about to storm. We figured that out a few years back when we first brought it into our home."

Glancing out the window, Nessa almost wilted at the sight of the darkening clouds. Fiona was right. Nessa blew out a breath of relief as lightning splintered through the blackened banks of thunderheads. She spun on her heel and shot Brodie a withering glare as she poked a finger in his chest with every word. "Then why did you say you had never seen it respond to anyone's touch like it did mine? Out with it, Brodie!"

Brodie backed away and struggled to apologize. "I was merely teasing ye. 'Twas just a wee bit of Scottish superstition meant to lighten your day. Forgive me, Nessa, I meant ye no harm."

Nessa scooped her bag up and slung it over her shoulder. "Oh, ha ha. Let's make a sucker out of the silly American. Very funny." With a yank on the door, she laughed at herself and the tension eased out of her chest. "If Trish shows back up any time soon, tell her I've decided to take a cab to the dig. She can pick me up there and then we'll go over to the pub and finish off Mr. Gabriel Burns."

As Nessa stepped out into the street, she cringed as lightning pealed down through the clouds. It struck so close the air reeked of sulfur. Leaning against the doorway, Nessa covered her ears against the deafening thunderclap that shook the ground. A tree split in front of her, bursting into flames as each half crashed to the ground.

Pinned back against the building, she wiggled her way back to the door and slipped her way inside.

"Are ye all right?" Fiona rushed to her side, grabbing her shoulders as she searched Nessa's pale face.

Nessa nodded as she brushed the singed leaves from her hair and blew a burnt leaf off the end of her nose. "Whew! I've always loved thunderstorms but that one was a little close for comfort. Looks like I'll be waiting for Trish here in the shop."

Just at that moment, Trish pulled up in the jeep and parked it a good distance from the burning tree. She fanned the smoke out of her face as she slipped into the shop. Motioning toward the blaze, she brushed the ash from her clothes. "Have you guys called the fire department yet?"

Brodie shook his head as he looked out the window. "No need. The rain is dousing the flames. 'Tis coming down in sheets."

With the downpour and the water rising in the storm drains, Nessa tossed her bag onto the floor with a sigh. They weren't going anywhere in this weather. The trip to the pub was out. She turned to the MacKays and Trish with a shrug of her shoulders. "Anybody want to play cards?"

CHAPTER
EIGHTEEN

"Y ou had her that close and you couldn't trick her into saying it? You couldn't get her to call him out of that ball?" Trish paced back and forth in front of Brodie and Fiona, then turned and tapped on the top of Latharn's sphere. "And you! They said you frightened her. Maybe if you had toned down the light show a little bit she wouldn't have headed for the door. Did you ever think of that?"

Latharn bellowed from his crystal cell, sending the lasers cutting across the walls. "I will not be spoken to in such a manner." He rumbled the globe across the table, disappeared, and reappeared on a shelf across the room. He didn't care if Trish was Nessa's best friend or not. The woman would not scold him as though he were a child. Latharn glared at them from across the room. He would watch them from the mantel above the fireplace.

Brodie pounded his fist on the table and made his own defense to Trish. "We dared not speak any more than we did for fear of sending Latharn's soul into the abyss." Raking his hands through his red hair, he jumped to stalk about the room.

Latharn sympathized with his descendant. Trish obviously

understood very little about Scottish curses. One wrong word, one wrong move and your arse sizzled in eternal hell.

Trish resumed her pacing, while massaging her temples. "Is this curse written down in some ancient text somewhere? Maybe recorded in a family journal? Or were all the details just passed down word of mouth from one generation to the next?"

Latharn spun the globe to improve his view and leaned against the glass. What was Trish looking for? They already knew how to break the curse. Nessa had to whisper his release. "Why do ye want the texts, Trish? What good will reading the grimoire do?"

Brodie jerked his chin toward the globe. "I agree with Cousin Latharn. I see no point in reviewing the curse, but we do have it recorded here. There's an ancient journal written in Rachel MacKay's own hand listing everything she discovered about the curse. But I don't see what good it will do to go over it again. 'Tis just a waste of time."

Trish's eyes narrowed into plotting slits as she leaned back into her chair. "The way I figure it, a curse is like a contract. All we have to do is find the loophole. I handle all the contracts for our digs. The contract lawyers hate me. I have a knack for seeing loopholes." She offered a saucy smirk.

"This is no contract, Trish. It's a complicated curse spelled by a powerful dark *bana-buidhseach*." Fiona handed each of them a cup of tea from the tray she balanced on one hip.

Tea. Latharn cringed. They should drink ale or at the very least mulled wine when they plotted a battle. Now, what had Trish said about contracts and curses?

"You've obviously never been around many contract lawyers," Trish retorted with a grin. "So, have you got this journal here or what? Is there any way I could get a look at it or is it locked away in someone's library?"

With a shrug of agreement from Fiona, Brodie ceased his restless pacing and headed to the built-in bookshelves lining the opposite wall of the room. He pushed aside several trinkets and baubles to reveal the combination lock of a safe. Brodie unlocked the safe and swung the door aside. He lifted a leather-bound book from the box.

Latharn stared at the journal from across the room and drew a ragged breath. The sight of the book nearly knocked the wind from his chest. It had been one of his mother's last grimoires. They had spoken every day until the morning before she'd leapt to her death. He'd pleaded with her not to take her life. Latharn choked against the painful memory of her final words. She had told him she couldn't bear life without Caelan. Latharn had never understood the depths of her pain until he'd found his Nessa.

Brodie set the book on the table in front of Trish. "This is the last journal of Rachel MacKay. The faded purple ribbon marks the passage about Latharn's curse."

Trish held her hands over the well-worn book. As she opened the journal to the designated spot, Latharn watched her mouth drop open in surprise. "This is in English. Modern English. Is this supposed to be some kind of hoax? I thought you said this came from the 1400s."

Brodie MacKay hissed as he turned from the window. "Rachel MacKay was not from the past. She was a time traveler from the year 2008."

Trish's hands dropped into her lap as she leaned back in her chair. "What you're saying can't possibly be true. This MacKay history just keeps getting wilder. How could a woman from the year 2008 be the mother of a man from 1410? You cannot be serious."

"I can and I am," Brodie challenged, his chin jutting into the air.

"He speaks the truth," Latharn added from his globe shimmering on the shelf.

Fiona stepped between them shaking her head, holding up her hands for silence. "It's a long story, Trish, that of Rachel and Caelan and how they came to be joined. Suffice it to say, they were meant to be together and nothing, not even time or space, could ever keep them apart."

"Trish," Latharn said. "Sometimes knowing in your heart is all that matters. There are many things in this world and beyond that are yet to be explained."

Her eyes widened in amazement. Trish looked up from the journal, disbelief written on her face. "This story just keeps getting better. Time travelers, witches, and cursed Highlanders in a ball. Is there anything else I need to know?"

Fiona pointed at the faded words upon the page. "That should just about cover it. Now can ye read Rachel's inscriptions? The dark outline, there. That surrounds the part about the curse."

Trish leaned closer to study the faded pages. She ran her finger back and forth just above the words, keeping space between herself and the yellowed page. "Okay. Here's the part about Latharn not being allowed to speak to Nessa so that he can't tell her how to break the curse."

Latharn watched impatiently as her lips moved while she read.

"And here's the part about no one of MacKay descent being allowed to tell her how to break the curse." Her mouth fell open. Trish lifted her head. "I can tell her."

"No." Brodie's hands clenched into fists. "Ye will shatter the crystal and Latharn will be lost. Ye must not break the terms."

For the first time in centuries, hope surged through Latharn's body at the excitement in Trish's voice.

"Don't you see, Brodie? I am not of MacKay descent. Therefore, it doesn't apply to me." Trish eased the book closed as she hastened to explain, "Only those of the MacKay line are forbidden to reveal the way to Nessa's true love. I'm a mutt. I traced my family tree once and trust me, there's not a drop of Scottish blood flowing in these veins."

"It canna be that simple." Fiona dropped into a chair. "Then we wasted our chance. I could've told the lass yesterday when she was so close to calling him out."

Trish shook her head, in disagreement. "No. You did the right thing by keeping the pact and holding your tongue. When you married Brodie, technically, you became a MacKay. If you had said any more to Nessa then what I understood you to say, the crystal would've disintegrated along with his soul."

Latharn shouted, "Then go get her! What the hell are ye waiting for?" He beat on the glass, rattling the globe across the length of the mantel. Could it be this simple? Could Nessa's friend tell her what she needed to do?

Brodie grabbed Trish by the arm, pulling her out of the chair. "Do as he says. Go to her then. Tell the woman. Let this damnable curse be at an end."

Trish shook her head and remained in her seat. She picked up her tea and took a sip as she studied the sphere upon the shelf. She set the delicate china cup back in its saucer and ran one finger around the rim of the cup. "No. We still have to play this out just right. If we spook Nessa, she'll never break the curse. She'll be especially leery after Latharn's visitation at the car wreck and the nightmares she had afterward. She's just now beginning to calm down again. He must've smoothed things over in another dream. He's been trapped in there for almost six hundred years; a few more days will just have to do."

"Are ye insane? Have ye any idea how long six hundred years can be?" Latharn roared and pelted the room with energy blasts until they dove beneath the table. "Just explain it to her and she will be fine. Just tell her. Once I'm out, I will soothe things over."

"Don't you remember how spooked she was after

the car wreck and the nightmare she had that night? Remember how nervous she got when she thought the orb was you...she almost ran out of the shop yesterday just from the light show you put on. We have to take this slow," Trish shouted at him from underneath her chair. "Nessa has trouble accepting the supernatural. Think about it, Latharn."

The room fell silent. Latharn scowled from his prison and glared at Trish as she opened one eye.

"Is it safe to come out?"

"Aye. Ye can come out. I will not blast ye," Latharn grumbled. "Perhaps I can bear this hell a few more days."

Crawling out from under the furniture, Trish dusted off her knees. "By the way, I haven't seen Nessa this morning. But I noticed the jeep is gone. Did she say where she was going? It's Sunday. I figured we'd just laze around here today."

Fiona straightened her skirts as she crawled out from under the table, retying the strings of her apron. "She didna say. She was just out the door with a smile and a wave. But come to think of it, she was dressed as though she was going someplace nice."

Brodie nodded in agreement as he dusted off his trousers. "Perhaps she was going to church?"

Trish shook her head as she closed the journal and pushed her chair under the table. "I doubt that. Nessa views religion as a cultural enigma. I really don't think she follows any specific faith herself."

"Someone needs to find where she went. I'm trusting ye all to take care of my Nessa." Latharn bounced warning lights around the room. They needn't stand around gaggling like a bunch of geese.

Trish paused, tapping her fingers on the back of the chair, ignoring Latharn's display as she mused aloud. "Gabriel seemed unusually disappointed yesterday and very determined to meet with Nessa sometime soon. It's strange. I'm not saying he shouldn't be interested in her but he's just a hair shy of being completely obsessed."

Brodie straightened the chairs around the table. "It would be unwise for the fool to try to get too close to Nessa. Latharn may not be able to speak to his love but there's not a power on earth that will keep him from protecting her."

"I will kill the bastard if he so much as stirs the air in which my Nessa breathes," Latharn stated.

With a look on her face that said she was clearly fed up, Trish squared off between Fiona and Brodie. "Okay. Out with it. What's the story on Gabriel Burns? I have the distinct impression here that there's something I need to know. If he's a serial killer, I think I have the right to know. After all, Latharn has officially inducted me into the MacKay Mystery Club."

Latharn couldn't resist a chuckle at Trish's comment but he dreaded hearing the story that was about to ensue. If he hadn't been trapped in this accursed globe, he would've rendered justice himself.

Fiona bit at her lower lip and rubbed at an invisible spot on the table. "Before I became Brodie's wife, Gabriel and I were engaged to be married." With a trembling voice, Fiona swallowed hard before she continued, "Gabriel seems kind and wonderful at first until he's positive that he has ye in his snare. Then he becomes quite controlling...even cruel, some might say."

Latharn itched to clench his hands around Gabriel's throat as Fiona's hands trembled at her side.

"Are you saying he's physically abusive?" Trish leaned closer, her hands tightening around the back of the chair.

Latharn's heart went out to Fiona. That was another reason he'd chosen her for Brodie. The lass had suffered so.

That was also why the bastard deserved to die. Latharn still didn't understand this twenty-first-century justice.

Fiona nodded. "I think, given enough time, he might even become truly dangerous. Thankfully, Brodie came along before I found out just how much damage he was willing to do." She wrapped her arms around her husband's waist and buried her face in his chest.

As he clutched Fiona to him, Brodie sneered, "She's saying that the night I found him in the alley, he had his hands around her throat. I almost beat the bastard to death until she begged me to stop. To keep him from pressing charges against me, Fiona promised not to tell anyone of his abusing her over something as minor as running thirty minutes late. His pub wouldna do too well in Durness if people found out he enjoyed beating women."

"Thirty minutes late?" Trish repeated, "Just being thirty minutes late was enough to throw him into a rage where he thought it was okay to strangle you?"

Fiona sniffed and pulled a tissue from her sleeve to dab at the corner of her eyes. "Aye, my car had a flat tire. I was thirty minutes late to our wedding rehearsal. He felt as though I had shamed him in front of all our friends. Gabriel Burns is verra concerned about the perceptions of others. He not only demands to be respected, but he also prefers to be revered."

Trish stormed about the room. "The man seems so nice. Everyone seems to like him. He can't go around abusing women! Why in the hell isn't he in jail? Latharn, did you know about this?"

Latharn remained silent. His fury raged too strong right now. The energy blast would destroy the entire building.

He would have killed the bastard a long time ago if they had consulted him. He missed the days when the laird settled such things.

Justice had gone to hell.

Brodie pulled his wife back against his side and dropped a tender kiss to the top of her head. "The man is careful, and that was over six years ago. He pretty much keeps to himself. Cordelia says he's been seeing a professional counselor. Perhaps he's been able to change."

Trish whirled and shook her hand in his face as she yanked up her shirt to reveal a jagged scar running up her side. "Bullshit! Men like that never change. The only cure for their disease is a slow and painful death."

Both Brodie and Fiona averted their gaze. Latharn bathed the room with a calming glow. He would cleanse the room of Gabriel's poison. "I will keep my Nessa safe. I have surrounded her with protection spells. But I would still like for ye to watch over her as well."

A knowing grin spread across her face as Trish smoothed her shirt back down over her scarred body. "No one had better make the mistake of underestimating Nessa. She might be small but she packs a punch."

Brodie put his hands on his hips as Fiona eased out of his hug to clear the table. He tucked his chin to his chest in disbelief. "That wee lass?"

With a nod, Trish handed Fiona the extra dishes and napkins from her side of the table. "That 'wee lass' has been practicing kick-boxing for years and is single-handedly responsible for saving my life." A faraway look crossed Trish's face. "I won't bore you with the gory details. But let's just say our little Nessa can take care of herself."

As he folded his arms across his chest, Brodie smiled. "That almost makes me wish the bastard Gabriel would test the waters. If wee Nessa doesn't snap his neck, ye can rest assured Latharn will."

CHAPTER
NINETEEN

Nessa sipped her coffee and searched for another Web site referencing any mention of clan MacKay. Her gaze scanned back and forth across the screen. She frowned as she continued her research. She'd sat at the Wi-Fi Café for hours. She'd first logged onto the university's library, then expanded her search to encompass the World Wide Web.

She'd stumbled across several Web sites with vague stories and legends, a few of them had referenced some sort of family curse. The only place she'd found Latharn MacKay's name specifically mentioned was one site listing the children of Caelan and Rachel MacKay. While that particular website went on to list what had become of each of the children, it had omitted any details about how Latharn's life had played out.

The MacKay history read like a compilation of fantasy legends. Nessa took a deep breath as she scrolled down the page. The laird of the clan always destined to dream of his intended wife, he never found peace until he found her and made her his own.

Time-traveling wives, witches, powerful druids...consorting with the goddess for the promise of destinies fulfilled. She knew the Scots

BEYOND A HIGHLAND WHISPER

loved their legends but this was getting ridiculous. Where was she going to have to go to find out the truth about the MacKay line?

Latharn's sister, Aveline, was reported to have been immortal. Nessa peered closer at the screen and selected another link. Several accounts listed her joining to a god and then her disappearance into the sky on her brother Ronan's wedding day.

Nessa propped her chin in her hand and wrinkled her nose to shift her reading glasses higher as she clicked and continued her search. If there was anything the science of archeology had taught her, it was persistence and patience.

She found Caelan and Rachel's romantic legend. Her heart swelled as she read of their love that had reached across the barrier of time. Nessa scanned the passage where Rachel jumped to her death after her husband Caelan arrived home, shield on his chest, a fatal wound beneath it. Swallowing hard against the emotions knotting in her throat, Nessa blinked back the tears and continued her search.

She smiled as she read of Ronan and his wife Harley's life upon the sea and the legacy of seafaring children they'd brought into the world. Her brows arched in surprise as she found several mentions of the sister Aveline. She'd reappeared at different moments through the annals of time to assist several descendants of the ancient clan.

"I wish she'd appear to me and give me a little guidance," Nessa mumbled aloud as she widened her Google search to include any mention of witches and druids in the clan. While she massaged the tension from the back of her neck, she read of Faolan's powerful leadership of the family and his children's unbelievable gifts in the mystical ways.

With a heavy sigh, Nessa tucked her glasses into the vee of her sweater and massaged the corners of her eyes. She glanced up from her corner and stifled a groan as she noticed Gabriel walking in her direction.

"Good day to ye, Nessa. Are ye feeling better? Trish said ye had been unwell." Gabriel pulled out a chair and slid into the seat with the grace of a stalking panther.

Nessa closed her laptop and rubbed the top of the machine as though it were a wishing stone. She forced a polite smile across her face and nodded in reply. "I'm feeling much better, thank you. I was finally able to get a good night's sleep in our new room. There must've been some bad chi or something at the inn."

A look of confusion registered on Gabriel's face. He pursed his lips as he motioned for the waitress to bring another cup of coffee to Nessa and one for himself. "So, that's why my calls to the inn have gone unanswered. Where are ye staying now?"

Nessa damned herself for accidentally confessing her new location and smiled over gritted teeth as the waitress refilled her cup. "Didn't Trish tell you? We've rented a room from the MacKays'. It's really nice and a lot more spacious than we had at the inn."

"The MacKays." Gabriel spat the words, his nostrils flaring as he sipped at his steaming cup. "I would have thought a well-educated woman such as yourself would have had nothing in common with those two."

Nessa studied Gabriel over the rim of her mug, her hands tensing at the venom she heard in his voice. So, there truly was bad blood between Gabriel and the MacKays. Nessa wondered why she hadn't picked up more on this bit of tension the first night they'd all gathered at the pub. "I like Brodie and Fiona. They're warm and friendly. Since I'm a stranger in this country, I'm grateful for the way they've taken us in."

Nessa reopened her laptop and powered it down. It was obvious Gabriel wasn't going away.

His face darkened into an even uglier scowl. Gabriel sneered in disgust as he waved his hands in the air. "They're backward. The two of them live in the past. Apparently, they've not even got the Internet or else ye wouldn't be stuck here in this café." He folded his arms with an air of superiority and sat back in his seat.

Nessa clenched her teeth. She drummed her fingers on the table and returned his haughty glare. Gabriel was really getting on her nerves. She'd had about enough of Mr. Burns.

With an arched brow, she sat a bit taller in her seat and adopted her own superior air. "Perhaps you've forgotten. I'm an archeologist. The past is what interests me the most."

Gabriel leaned forward in his seat, his hands tightening into fists. Nessa pressed her lips tightly shut to keep from snickering in his face. Gabriel had heard the cynicism in her voice and he wasn't taking it well.

"Ye know very well that's not what I meant, Nessa. Apparently, ye're still not feeling yourself. Ye seem a bit on edge today."

She slid her laptop into her bag and zipped it shut with a bitter chuckle. From what she could see, Gabriel was only Prince Charming when everything went his way. She was relieved she'd found out he was an absolute toad before they'd developed any type of relationship.

She forced a smile as she smoothed the strap of the bag between her hands. It was definitely time for a parting of ways. "I have to go now. It was nice seeing you, Gabriel. I'm sure we'll drop into the pub sometime soon." She swung her bag up to her shoulder and gestured to the waitress to bring her the bill.

Gabriel snatched the tab from the waitress's hands and gifted Nessa with his most irresistible smile. "That'll be mine. No woman sits at the table with Gabriel Burns and ends up paying her own way."

Nessa strained to keep the polite smile on her face with a gracious nod of her head. "Thank you." Now all she had to do was make her escape and be done with this guy.

Gabriel leaned close and laid a restraining hand on her arm. "Would ye mind giving me a lift back to the pub? My knee's grown a bit stiff for the return walk home. I must've overused it on my stroll across the square." As he rose from the table, Gabriel winced, obviously feigning a slight limp as he edged closer to Nessa's side.

Her lips tightened with a stifled sigh. Nessa never had this problem with a man before. She pretty much disappeared into the woodwork and let the cute girls take over the room. What the hell was Gabriel's problem? Couldn't he take a hint? He must be one of those men whose pride never let the woman be the one to sever the ties.

Something about Gabriel nagged at her heart. Not a good nag, but a sense of dread. Whenever she looked at the man, she sensed a slow-growing cancerous rot. An aura of negativity surrounded the man and she wasn't the least bit interested in finding out why.

Nessa drew a deep breath. Her face ached from the polite smile stretched across it. Nessa answered with a sharp jerk of her head. "Sure. I think I know the way to the MacKays' from the pub. I can take the shortcut and drop you off." Nessa knew her answer border-lined sheer rudeness but she didn't care. She shot Gabriel a challenging glare and hoped he'd change his mind.

His eyes narrowed as he cocked his head to one side. Gabriel held out his hand and he bowed his head. "That'll be grand. I appreciate the lift. Here, let me carry your bag."

Nessa hitched her bag closer to her body. She wasn't about to hand over her precious laptop resting snugly in its bag. How stupid did he think she was? With that anger flashing in his eyes, the jerk would probably smash it to the ground. She sidled away from him and headed toward the door, tossing a smile back at him over her shoulder. "That's okay. I've got it covered."

Making her way out the door, she tucked her chin to hide the mischievous grin she couldn't quite resist. She hadn't missed the ripple of Gabriel's jaw when he'd clenched his teeth at her refusal.

The rising wind tugged at her hair as she stepped out into the street. With a glance to the sky, Nessa sniffed the strong breeze. The scent of rain rode upon the air. That was another thing about Gabriel. Whenever he was around, the weather always took a turn for the worse.

The storm clouds gathered, banking and roiling like a cook pot set to a boil. Nessa pulled her jacket tighter about her chest. The day plunged into an uneasy darkness. The clouds erased the sun from the sky.

Nessa didn't wait for Gabriel to open her door and laughed out loud at the look of irritation on his face. "Get in!" she shouted over the rumbling thunder. "We don't have time for chivalry. It's getting ready to open up and pour."

Gabriel scowled and stomped around to the other side of the car. He slid into the seat and slammed the door shut with a muttered curse. Crossing his arms over his chest, he stared out the windshield with a face as dark as the thunderous sky.

Just as Nessa slid the keys into the ignition, he covered her hand with his. He squeezed her fingers and held her hand captive as he forced her to turn and look into his eyes. "Why are ye no' interested in seeing me again, Nessa? Have the MacKays filled your head with lies?"

"First of all"—Nessa lowered her voice and turned to Gabriel with deadly intent— "you're hurting my hand. Now I suggest you let me go or I promise, you will regret it."

A look of surprise flitted across his face. Gabriel released her fingers. His hands curled into shaking fists as he pulled them away. "I'm sorry, Nessa. I didna mean to hurt ye. I just thought there was a spark between us worth pursuing. I don't understand what went wrong."

Nessa clenched the steering wheel. She swallowed hard against the bile rising in the back of her throat. They hadn't known each other long enough for him to act this way. All of her alarm bells blared at top volume. Gabriel just wasn't right. She'd better be careful. She had to get him back to the pub and out of her life, the sooner the better.

"I'm sorry, Gabriel. You're a great guy. But I'm afraid my work has picked up so much right now that I just don't have enough time to give you the attention you deserve." Nessa forced the most helpless female look she could muster on her face. She blinked at him in feigned wide-eyed innocence.

It was as if she had pushed a button. Gabriel relaxed. His easy smile replaced his scowl. "I thought perhaps I'd done something wrong. I would never do anything to offend ye."

Nessa exhaled and reached to start the car, relieved when he didn't attempt to stop her again. He'd taken the bait, now to get him home and out of her life. As she steered out of the parking lot, she turned on her windshield wipers. The skies had opened the floodgates.

She raised her voice to be heard over the rain as it pounded against the windshield. "You've been nothing but kind. That's why I think it's best if I'm honest with you now. I've been trying to get into this research project for years. It's my first priority right now."

The lights of the pub flickered in the distance. Only a little farther and she'd have it made. She just needed to keep playing to his inflated male ego and then she'd have him out the door before he knew what had happened.

Gabriel reached over and stroked her cheek, his voice dropping to a coaxing purr. "'Tis a very lonely life ye have chosen for yourself, Nessa Buchanan. I know I could make ye happy."

Nessa tried not to gag. Her skin crawled beneath his touch. As she pulled into the lot in front of the pub, she forced herself not to jerk away from his hand. The longer she was around him, the more nauseous she became. Something malicious brewed just below the surface of this man's shell. If she believed in demons, she'd think he was possessed.

Nessa smiled into his eyes and feigned a nod of agreement. "I'm used to making sacrifices for my work. I'm sure someday I'll look back on this with regret. You're a good man, Gabriel Burns, and I wish you all the best."

Gabriel slid his hand to the back of her neck and pulled her into his arms. He bent her head back, covered her mouth with his, and ravaged her with his tongue.

Nessa held her breath to keep from retching. One thought ran through her mind: He's going to get out of this car and then I'll be done with him forever. Gabriel slid from her mouth and grazed at her ear, his voice husky with desire. "We could have one night, Nessa Buchanan. It might help ye change your mind."

No way in hell. She gasped a different reply out loud. "I wish I could, but it's really the wrong time of the month...if you know what I mean."

With a disappointed sigh, Gabriel smiled as he opened the door. "Once again I am bested by the phases of the moon and their pull upon a woman's fate."

Nessa gave a weak wave goodbye and stifled a shudder as she watched him slide out of the car. Thank goodness, he was one of those men who wouldn't go near a woman if he thought it was her time of the month. "Good-bye, Gabriel. Take care of yourself."

Gabriel bent to look back inside the car and blew her an airy kiss. "Goodbye, sweet Nessa. I guess we'll never know what we could have been." He closed the door and trotted through the rain to the pub, his stiff knee miraculously healed.

Nessa shuddered, wiped her mouth on her sleeve, and hurried to click the locks on the doors before she pulled the car out on the road. "Yuck!" she sputtered and spit into the air, the taste of him turning her stomach. "What a jerk! Thank goodness I didn't fall into that trap." As soon as she'd said the words aloud, the flickering image of a young woman appeared in the passenger seat of the car.

"Ye just don't realize how right ye are, lass. His punishment will be great for his crimes against women. The goddess is no' pleased with that scoundrel at all." Patting her reddish blonde curls behind her ears, the young girl turned and smiled into Nessa's shocked face. "Ye said ye wished I'd come and give ye a visit and guide ye upon your way."

"Aveline?" Nessa jerked the steering wheel to keep the car from landing in the ditch. She headed for a graveled parking area farther down the road so she could stop the car.

"Aye." Aveline smiled in agreement. She toyed with one long curl of hair, winding it about one finger as she coyly tilted her head. "I've been noticing ye seem to be having a bit of trouble accepting the legends of the MacKay clan."

"Are you a ghost?" Nessa pressed her clammy hands to her throat. She hadn't eaten very much today. Could low blood sugar cause hallucinations? She swallowed hard and took a deep breath to try and clear her head. Was she losing her mind? This day just kept getting worse.

"Oh, nay." Aveline shook her head, frowning as she toyed with the dials on the dashboard of the car. "When mother appeared to ye...she is a ghost. But I am an immortal. I canna die."

Nessa's blood pounded in her ears. She had hit sensory overload. She covered her face and thought back to the woman at the goddess Brid's well. "Now wait a minute. The woman in the woods...that was your mother, Rachel?"

Aveline smiled again in agreement and folded her hands in her lap as she settled against the seat of the car. "Aye, Mother wanted to meet ye. She also pops in from time to time to help people along their way."

Her hand to her chest to settle her pounding heart, Nessa struggled to catch her breath. This wasn't good. She couldn't breathe. She really needed to calm down. Aveline meant her no harm. Perhaps she could tell her a thing or two. If Nessa passed out from not breathing, she couldn't ask any questions. She had to breathe. Being an immortal, maybe Aveline could provide some insight as to how Nessa could bring some order into her life. Nessa inhaled a slow, deep breath. Much better. *Why not?* she decided, and turned to speak with her shimmering guest. "What can you tell me about Latharn MacKay? Any ideas as to why he keeps showing up in my dreams?"

Aveline's smile faded to a frown. She stared down at her folded hands. "I canna tell ye much. But I will tell ye this: ye need not ever fear him."

Her fears forgotten, Nessa huffed in aggravation and slapped her hands on the steering wheel. "That's the same thing your mother told me. That and I just needed to look into his heart."

Aveline's pale blonde brows arched in a thoughtful look and she gave a slow nod of agreement. "Mother is right. Look into his heart. Ye will find everything there ye need to know."

Nessa banged her fist upon the steering wheel and shook her head. "I don't know how to look into his heart! I've been dreaming about him since I was eighteen years old. I didn't even know his name until your mother told me a few days ago. If I can't even figure out his name after ten years, what makes you think I'll be able to figure out what's in his heart? And answering questions is my job."

As silent giggles shook her shoulders, Aveline smiled and clapped her hands. "What fire! What passion! Trust me, Mistress Nessa, ye will find the way destiny means ye to travel. Ye must be patient and listen with your heart."

Nessa turned in the seat and glared at Aveline. "Isn't there something you can tell me about your brother? Isn't there anything else I might need to know?"

Aveline gave a wistful smile as she faded from view. "I am verra sorry. At this time, I can tell ye no more. But know there are many MacKays watching over ye, both in this world and the next."

Nessa whacked the steering wheel again as Aveline disappeared. Clenching it in a strangle hold, she grumbled out loud as she started the car. "Fat lot a good all of those MacKays are doing. So far, all they've done to help me is told me his name and I shouldn't be afraid." She thought she heard the faint sound of ethereal laughter as she squealed her way back onto the road.

CHAPTER
TWENTY

"Where have you been?" Trish met her in the driveway, yanking open the door before the car rolled to a complete stop.

"What's the matter, Mom? Did I break curfew?" Nessa taunted as she gathered her things from the car. The last thing she wanted to hear right now was one of Trish's lectures about how she should live her life. She wasn't in the mood. If Trish had any survival instincts at all, she'd back off and leave her alone.

Trish circled Nessa like a dog herding sheep, stumbling as she walked backward up the steps leading to the porch. "If you were with Gabriel Burns... You've got to listen to me. You'll just end up regretting it. I found out a thing or two about our newfound friend. He's a worthless piece of—"

"Not that it's any of your business," Nessa interrupted, shooting Trish a meaningful look she knew Trish would never take to heart. "But I went to the Wi-Fi Café to see what the Internet could tell me about the MacKays."

"Why didn't you just ask them?"

"Not those MacKays." Nessa shot Trish an impatient look as she slid her laptop onto the table in their room. "The history of the MacKay clan and all the legends surrounding them from the 1200s up until present day."

"Oh...those MacKays." Trish shrugged a shoulder. "Well, what did you find out? Anything interesting?"

Nessa chuckled as she bent to rummage through the tiny fridge. Memories of legends of time-traveling witches, cursed lairds, and Aveline's sudden appearance ran through her head. From everything she'd discovered today, her dream Highlander had once existed. As she fished her way farther into the depths of the fridge, a shiver of excitement ran up her spine. "You wouldn't believe me if I told you."

Rising with a soda in her hand, she winced as she popped the tab. "By the way, since you mentioned him, I think I also finally got rid of Gabriel Burns. There was just something weird about that guy that set my alarm bells ringing into super squall mode."

Trish's face lit up in complete agreement. "That's what I was trying to tell you. He's physically abusive. He tried to strangle Fiona and then Brodie almost killed him."

Nessa froze, holding her soda in midair as she stared over the can at Trish. "What? When did this happen? I was only gone a couple of hours."

Her eyes growing wider with every word, Trish plopped down in one of the tall wooden chairs and plunged into her tale. "Fiona and Gabriel were engaged to be married. She said he was a control freak but she didn't know just how cruel he was until he snapped on the night of the wedding rehearsal. She was thirty minutes late because she'd had a flat tire. He took her into the alley and almost killed her for what he considered shaming him in front of his friends."

Trish jumped up from her seat, waving her hands in the air. She became more animated with every word. "Brodie came along and pulled him off her. Nearly killed him from what I understand."

"Wow." Words failed Nessa as she pulled out a chair. So that explained the negativity surrounding Gabriel Burns. A stifling darkness always followed the man. He emitted a coldness that just couldn't be explained. She sent up a silent thank-you to the fates and heaved a sigh of relief.

Raising the soda to her lips, she paused, the can midair. Wait a minute. What Trish said didn't make sense. "Then why isn't our buddy Gabriel lounging in prison for trying to kill his future wife?"

"Oh, it gets better." Trish snorted, plopping back down at the table. "He blackmailed Fiona, saying the only way he wouldn't charge Brodie with assault was if she kept her mouth shut about his part of the abuse."

"What a jackass." Nessa huffed. Thank goodness she'd avoided the vicious bastard. A shiver of disgust rippled over her body. She thought back over all she'd found on the Internet and her conversation with Aveline. Nessa drummed her fingers on the table and studied Trish's still-flushed face. She wondered just how open Trish would be if she told her everything she knew.

She and Trish had been friends for years. She understood Trish's intense hatred for Gabriel because of his treatment of Fiona, and she would bet his abuse of countless other women. Trish had only been twenty years old when she'd been beaten and mutilated by a college acquaintance. That was how she and Nessa had met, their friendship forged by that traumatic event.

Nessa had decided to take a shortcut back to her apartment that evening long ago. She'd just finished one of her kickboxing classes on campus and was on her way home from the session. She'd heard a muffled shriek come from a darkened outbuilding and had recognized it as a call for help.

The adrenaline pumping through her veins had made her forget she was barely five feet tall and on a good day pushed the scale to within a shadow of a hundred pounds. Nessa had kicked her way into the building and followed the sound of the weakening cries. She'd rushed to find Trish cringing in a bloody huddle, her assailant looming over her with an upraised knife. Nessa had grabbed a broken board off the floor, not noticing the jagged roofing nail sticking out of the end. She'd connected the board with the base of the attacker's skull with all the might her adrenaline fueled.

The man had died a few days later. He'd never awakened from the coma. There weren't any charges because Trish had mumbled through a broken jaw that Nessa had saved her life.

"I really hate it when your eyes glaze over like that, especially when you're staring at me as though I'm a rare and exotic beast." Trish banged her soda can on the table in front of Nessa.

"Sorry. I was just thinking," Nessa mumbled, tracing her fingertip around the top of her soda can. With an arched brow at Trish, she leaned forward and dropped her voice to an excited whisper. "How would you like to hear something so weird you're going to think I've finally gone over the edge?"

With a grin, Trish leaned forward to meet Nessa halfway across the table and propped her chin in her hand. "Try me."

Nessa took a deep breath and prepared to tell her tale. She spread her hands on the table in front of her. Leaning forward just a bit, she struggled to control the tremble in her voice as she glanced at the door joining their room to the MacKays' private residence.

"I met Rachel MacKay in the woods by a spring. Or should I say...I met her ghost, even though I didn't realize who or what she was at the time."

Nessa waited for Trish's reaction. Nothing. Trish just sat there and stared at her. Nessa frowned. She raised her voice and leaned in closer, her fingertips curled into her palms. Trish would react when she told her the rest of the story. "She told me the Highlander in my dreams is Latharn MacKay and that I should never fear him. I didn't find out until today that Latharn MacKay is her son."

Trish frowned just a bit. She rubbed her chin, tapping her bottom lip as she spoke. "How exactly did you find out that Latharn MacKay is her son if you didn't know who she was when you were talking to her?"

Nessa leaned in closer, propping her chin in both hands. She paused to build the suspense, watching Trish's face. Her friend was taking this information entirely too well. "Her immortal daughter, Aveline, told me who she was when she appeared in the car with me on the way home."

Trish continued rubbing her chin. "Let me see if I've got this straight. The ghost of Rachel MacKay appeared to tell you the man in your dreams is her son, Latharn MacKay, but you didn't know who she was or that he was her son until you talked to...did you say the immortal daughter, Aveline?"

Nessa struggled against the sly smile tickling at her lips and waited for Trish to demand she quit joking around. Any minute now Trish would explode. She knew Trish would think she was crazy. It was a good thing she'd never had a history of alcohol or Trish would accuse her of tying one on. She gave Trish two thumbs up and a wink as she replied, "I'm impressed. It took me a couple of times to get it figured out but it sounds like you've connected the dots the first time around."

Nessa leaned back in her seat and waited for what she was positive would be Trish's traditional reply of, "Bullshit!"

Trish took a deep breath and stared at her hands as she chewed on her lower lip. "Well what else did Rachel and Aveline tell you?"

Nessa couldn't believe it. Why was Trish acting so weird? She wasn't even reacting! "They both told me even though Latharn is forbidden to speak to me in my dreams, if I'll look into his heart, I'll know the truth."

Nessa folded her hands on the table and tilted her head to one side. "Pretty unbelievable, huh? What do you think?" If Trish didn't give her a reaction pretty soon, she was going to reach across the table and smack her. She wasn't being any fun at all.

Trish rubbed her nose. She drummed her fingers on the table. "Oh, hell. I give up. It's time to tell you." Trish slammed her hands on the table. "They couldn't tell you anything else because they were forbidden. If they broke the rules, Latharn's soul would burn in the eternal abyss. The curse says that any person of MacKay blood or marriage must not help you in your quest." Trish buried her face in her hands.

"My quest?" Nessa repeated. She waited for Trish to look her dead in the eye so she could figure out if she was pulling some sort of practical joke. This was not the reaction she'd anticipated from her flamboyant friend. "My quest for what?"

Trish rose from the table and motioned for Nessa to follow as she headed for the MacKays' adjoining door. "Follow me and I'll show you. Since I'm in no way related to the MacKays, I'm pretty sure it's safe for me to tell you what you need to know."

Nessa's heart fluttered and her mouth went dry. What was Trish talking about? Nessa reminded herself to breathe. She followed Trish into the MacKays' drawing room.

There sat Brodie and Fiona as though they'd been waiting for her arrival. On the table between them sat the violet sphere. The orb bathed the entire room in an eerie light.

"Have ye told her?" Brodie searched their faces as he rose from his chair.

"Not yet." Trish pointed to a chair on the other side of the table and motioned for Nessa to sit. "Latharn MacKay lived in the year 1410 until he was cursed by an evil sorceress from a neighboring clan. It appears he was quite talented at pleasing the ladies but when he didn't fall in love with the witch, she decided to make him pay."

Nessa glanced around the room at the anticipation shining on everyone's faces. Trish's words played right along with everything else she'd learned today. Nessa had an uneasy feeling about where Trish might be headed with her tale.

"And just exactly how did she curse him? Did she send him to some mystical plane where he can only wander through people's dreams?"

Trish shook her head. She slid the crystal orb across the table until it was sitting mere inches from Nessa's face.

"No. She cursed him into this witch's ball until such time as the spell is broken."

Nessa's heart pounded up into her throat. She felt the rhythmic beats synchronize with the pulsating light of the orb. Her mouth grew even drier. She lost the ability to breathe as she glanced into the depths of the ball. "Latharn's soul is trapped in there?"

Trish nodded.

Nessa remembered all the tales she'd found about the MacKays' loves and their losses. Hands pressed against her cheeks, Nessa's heart swelled in her chest, sympathizing with Latharn's pain.

As she realized all Latharn must have witnessed, everything he knew and loved torn away. Nessa's throat ached with unshed tears. She couldn't imagine the misery he'd suffered, trapped in the crystal as he watched his world die away.

She splayed her fingers on either side of the globe. Nessa drew even closer to the swirling surface.

"Oh, Latharn, I'm so very sorry," she whispered. Her heart clenched with the sorrow he must have known. She couldn't imagine her gentle Highlander trapped inside the tiny glass tomb for nearly six hundred years. Her eyes overflowed with tears of compassion; she didn't bother to wipe them away. She just watched as they rolled down the sides of the shimmering witch's ball.

"Latharn, you've taken such good care of me all these years. You've made me what I am today." Her tears came faster. Nessa closed her eyes. Her lips trembled as she whispered, "I want you to know I have always loved you and I would give anything to be able to set you free."

As soon as the words fell from her trembling lips, thunder, and lightning split through the room. Wild energy spun around in a cyclone of blinding light, ripping everything from the shelves.

Furniture crashed against the walls as chairs and tables lifted off the floor. Nessa dove under the table, joined by Trish and the MacKays. They shielded their heads with their arms and whatever cushions they could grab. Then all went silent. The storm died just as soon as it had risen. Not an object in the room was untouched by the fierce energy that had ripped through the house.

Nessa remained motionless under the table; afraid something would fall on her head. She just knew the building must be about ready to collapse from the violent attack it had just endured. Strong hands closed around her arms and lifted her from the rubble. Opening her eyes, she found herself staring into the set of deep green eyes she'd only seen before in her dreams.

As he tenderly stroked the curve of her cheek, Latharn groaned with satisfaction. "'Tis about time ye said the words for me, lass. I'd begun to think I'd never be free of that hell."

Nessa's jaw dropped; her lips moved but no words came out. Speechless, she stared up into his face. She'd never imagined how his voice would sound.

His deep Scot's burr, the way his words rolled off his tongue— the sound set fire to her blood. The richness of his voice stroked her body, making her ache for more. Running her fingertips across the stubbled whiskers of his jaw, Nessa finally whispered, "It's really you."

Latharn lowered his mouth to hers. He savored his first true taste of her lips. When her trembling hands slid up his chest, his heart swelled to near bursting. He deepened his kiss of possession. He tightened his embrace. He'd waited for this moment for centuries. To hold her, the one woman he ever loved, to feel her breathless against his chest.

The one way he'd maintained his sanity all these years was by searching for her with his mind. He'd used his powers. He'd traveled the mists until he'd finally located her soul in the energy of eternity. Once she was born, he'd waited for her to become a woman so he could be with her in her dreams. He'd watched Nessa since her soul first came into being now, at last, he held her in his arms.

Latharn raised his head and smiled down into her eyes. "I've waited for centuries to hold ye like this. Now that I have ye, I'll never let you go."

Nessa lost herself in the strength of his arms as she heard the others rustling through the shattered room. She could stay in the loving warmth of his embrace forever and ignore the rest of the world. However, the others might be hurt from the energy storm that had released Latharn from the crystal orb. Her conscience nudged her. She couldn't enjoy her flesh and blood lover until she was sure her friends were okay. "Maybe we should unearth Trish and your cousins, since the two of us have caused a bit of a mess."

With an arched brow, Latharn tore his gaze away from Nessa and looked about the room. Flexing the corded muscles of his right arm, he stretched his hand out over the carnage of broken furniture and shattered glass. An aura of purple light surrounded his body and culminated into a solid beam flowing from his extended hand. As he guided the energy beam around the room, everything returned to its undestroyed state.

"Damn. Can you teach me how to do that?" Trish gazed around the room.

"He's more powerful than all the others," Fiona whispered, huddling against Brodie's side.

"I am the highest trained master of the ancient ones still physically walking upon this plane." Latharn's voice rang with sorrow as he faced the present-day MacKays. "When all the others passed to the next level of existence, they willed their powers to me."

Brodie stretched out his arm and waited to grasp Latharn's forearm in the ancient greeting of another member of the clan. "I'm proud we were the ones to finally see ye free, Cousin Latharn. Welcome back to our world."

Latharn nodded and his smile returned as he accepted Brodie's proffered arm. "Aye, I canna thank all of ye enough for the role ye played in helping Nessa break the curse."

With a fiery spark in his eyes, Latharn turned and swept Nessa up into his arms. "Now I must ask ye to forgive me but I'm sure ye'll understand that I've quite a bit of...catching up to do with my future bride." Then he turned and strode through the doorway to the bedroom, kicking the door shut with a purposeful slam.

TWENTY-ONE

With a sultry smile, he lowered her to the bed, his eyes never leaving her face. He claimed her mouth and nuzzled at her lips. He whispered his love to her in husky Gaelic phrases. Latharn grabbed her blouse by the front and ripped it aside, buttons popping across the room. With one quick motion, his mouth never leaving hers, he slid her pants to the floor.

Nessa pulled his plaid from about his shoulders and tossed it to the floor. She wanted her body melded against every inch of his skin. She wanted his hardened muscles playing beneath her fingertips. She wanted to memorize him with her touch, his velvety hardness pressed against her belly. Pulling him closer, she raked her hands down his back.

"Latharn, please," Nessa panted. Arching her back, she pressed against him. Why didn't he just dive in?

Nipping a blazing trail of kisses down her jaw, Latharn's voice grew hoarse as he nuzzled at her ear. "We need to slow down, Nessa. I mean to pleasure ye well. I've been waiting for this moment for centuries."

Nessa moaned as his mouth trailed down her throat, then

worked its way even lower. She bucked against him, pressing even tighter, nudging impatiently against his erection. She gasped when he took her nipple into his mouth and cupped her breasts with his delightful hands. His thumb teased at her other nipple until it peaked, hard with need. He nipped and suckled at them both until she writhed beneath his touch. She tickled her fingers down his chest, encircling his shaft until he shuddered within her stroking hand.

She moaned when he left her breasts, his tongue burning a teasing trail down her stomach. She caught her breath as he cupped her buttocks in his hands and lifted her to his mouth. He traced the valley of her inner thigh with his fingertips and teased his breath against the dark curls of her inviting center.

A satisfied laugh rumbling from deep within his chest, he smiled as his eyes locked with hers. With his eyes never leaving hers, Latharn lowered his mouth to suckle her awaiting folds. As he tongued her aching nub deep into his mouth, he buried a rapturous finger into her depths.

"Latharn!" Nessa moaned in ecstasy and buried her hands in his hair. She clutched his head against her body and wriggled beneath his mouth. Head thrown back, back arched in delight, Nessa lost the ability to do anything but feel. She screamed as she exploded with delicious rapture, not caring if her cries shook the house.

Latharn raised his head. He used his tongue to tickle delicious circles on the skin running up her side. He turned her. He took his time and licked his way up her back, reaching around to cup her breasts in each of his hands. He pulled her back against him, nuzzling her neck as his hands once more tantalized her nipples into aching peaks. His inviting erection prodded against the back of her thighs, a promise of what was to come.

As she turned in his arms, Nessa nibbled at his throat, her voice a husky whisper. "Now it's my turn." She ran her fingers down his chest joining them with her tongue. She nipped and teased until Latharn groaned and struggled to catch his breath.

She worked her way down to his straining shaft. She cupped him with one hand while circling his tip with her tongue. She glanced up at the tortured look of pure bliss on his face. Nessa purred with satisfaction. She licked and teased the length of his erection, then swallowed him down to the hilt. Latharn clutched the sheets of the bed as he gave himself over to the delicious magic of her mouth.

It was time. Latharn grabbed Nessa and rolled her beneath him.

"Now, Nessa. 'Tis time for us to be truly joined as we were always meant to be."

He slid into her welcoming depths; her wet folds guided him to her heated center. As Latharn slid his arms beneath her, he settled his hips and groaned, "By the goddess, I've waited for this moment forever. I love ye, Nessa, with all of my soul."

Her breath coming quicker, Nessa smiled into his eyes as she wrapped her legs around his body. "I love you, Latharn, my Highlander of my dreams. I've loved you since the first time you came to me."

Nessa arched her back and matched Latharn's slow grind, thrust for delicious thrust. The rhythm quickened; they drove into the dance. The bliss heightened into a luscious frenzy.

His head thrown back, Latharn's throaty roar mingled with Nessa's ecstatic cries. His release found, he poured into Nessa, shouting out her name.

All mine. Latharn raked his gaze over her shuddering body. *Forever, all mine.* The connection he'd sought, the elusive joining he'd needed, Latharn felt a melding of his soul. He groaned with the contentment he'd never hoped to find and curled his arms tighter about her. Taking care to stay deep inside her, Latharn rolled and pulled her to lie atop him. Collapsing back against the pillows, he ran his fingers through her short curls, as she lay snuggled against his chest.

"I love you." Nessa exhaled with a contented purr, wriggling even closer against his body.

"Love doesna begin to describe this feeling," Latharn murmured, kissing the top of her head. "Holding ye in my arms is tonic to my verra being. Finally joining with ye has healed the rift in my soul."

Nessa propped her chin on his chest and traced a finger across his lips. "I never thought something like this would ever be possible. I thought you'd only be in my dreams."

A contented smile tickled at the corners of his mouth as Latharn exhaled in pure satisfaction. "It has taken quite some time to make it to this point. There were times when I thought madness would surely take hold, especially after I found your melody dancing in the mists of time. It seemed an eternity for your soul to decide to join me upon this plane."

He captured her hand and placed a kiss in her palm, pausing to add a seductive tickle with the tip of his tongue.

Nessa gasped as his passion returned to an inviting hardness inside her. Her own heat answered in more than willing reply and she slid up to straddle him. She moaned with abandon, blissfully gyrating as Latharn continued to grow.

"I'm glad I found the way to you. If I'd known about this, I think I would've tried harder to find you before now."

Latharn wrapped his hands around her waist and stroked her body with his heated gaze. "We've only just begun, my dear, sweet Nessa. I'm about to show ye all that ye've been missing."

Nessa didn't hear anything else he said after that, she was too busy groaning in mindless release.

TWENTY-TWO

Coffee. The rich aroma of a freshly brewed pot wafted across her nose. Nessa inhaled; her stomach growled. "Latharn. We have to surface. I need coffee."

Latharn pulled her closer against him, spooning his knees into the back of hers as he nuzzled the back of her neck. "We've only been in here for three days, Nessa. Have ye tired of me so soon?"

Three days. Nessa couldn't resist his lips against the nape of her neck and snuggled tighter against him. "The others must think we're dead."

Latharn chuckled and cupped her breast as he suckled at her earlobe. "I think we've been loud enough for them to know we're still verra much alive."

Oh, great. She'd never hear the end of that from Trish. She did seem to remember a few times when she'd gotten a little loud. Nessa groaned and unwound herself from Latharn's arms. "I need coffee. And if this is day three, we need to emerge because there's no telling what's being said about us."

Pulling her back down into the bed, Latharn kissed the end of her nose. "First of all, I dinna give a damn what anyone says about us and neither should you. Second, I know exactly what they're saying. I can hear them and I can allow ye to see and hear them as well. Watch."

With a wave of his hand the bedroom wall wavered, then became clear as crystal. He and Nessa had front row seats of everything going on in the other room.

"They've been in there for three days. Ye'd think they'd surface by now for a bit of food and drink." Fiona fussed about the table to set the steaming scones on the trivet and turned to fetch the pot of coffee off the warming plate sitting on the back of the buffet.

"You put a fully stocked refrigerator in there, remember?" Trish shot her a knowing look above the rim of her coffee cup as she tried working the kinks from her neck. "By the way, I think it's somebody else's turn to take the couch in the drawing room. That thing's just for looks. It's definitely not for sleeping."

Brodie winked at Fiona as he held out his cup for a refill. "Have ye already forgotten our honeymoon, dear wife? The only time we saw the lobby of the hotel was when we arrived and when we were checking out."

Fiona clucked her tongue as she filled her husband's cup. "Aye, my love. Don't be distressed. I promise ye, I'll ne'er forget those days. But we had room service, full meals at our beck and call, in order to keep up our strength."

"This isn't right, Latharn." Nessa waved at the wall as though she were shooing flies. "Make it go away." There was just something weird about watching your friends as though they were in a fishbowl.

"As ye wish." Latharn waved his hand and the wall darkened, resuming its inherent state. "Then we'd best be joining them to get your coffee. I'm a bit hungry now myself."

Latharn emerged first, his arm curled around Nessa's waist, nodding a solemn greeting to the trio at the table.

"Good morning," Nessa murmured with a yawn. "Is it okay if we join you for breakfast? The coffee and scones smell fabulous."

"I'm surprised you're able to walk to the table," Trish retorted under her breath. With a wicked grin, she slid the plate of scones down the table to Nessa.

"Trish!" Nessa scolded. A surge of heat flushed to color her cheeks as she accepted a cup of coffee from Fiona.

"Trish," Latharn intoned, with a nod of his head. "I apologize for keeping ye from your bed." Then with a steaming look his gaze slid back to Nessa as he reached over to caress her cheek. "But I'm sure ye understand Nessa and I had a calling we couldna possibly ignore."

With a giggle, Trish lifted her cup in silent salute and gave Nessa a saucy wink. "Oh, I'm not angry, Latharn. I'm just jealous. She's topped any record I ever held."

"Record?" Latharn gave Nessa a questioning look.

"Never mind." Nessa handed him a well-buttered scone and kicked Trish under the table. "Don't you want me to fix you some eggs or something?" Maybe if she plied him with food, he'd ignore Trish's banter.

"No thank ye. Fiona's scones are fine," Latharn responded with a perplexed frown. "Brodie, I'll be needing the paperwork for the trust. I'm anxious to return to my home."

Setting his coffee aside, Brodie rose from the table to access the safe on the wall. Within moments, he'd returned with a worn leather envelope bound with a cord of shimmering gold.

Latharn accepted it and pulled out a weathered parchment clipped to a sheaf of more recent-looking papers. His eyes scanned the pages and he turned each one, checking to ensure nothing was amiss.

"You can read?" Without thinking, Nessa said the words, regretting them as soon as they left her mouth.

Latharn slowly raised his head from the papers he held in his hands as though struggling to control his choice of words. "Ye will discover that I am not an uneducated man, Nessa. I'm quite learned in a great many things."

Regret swelled in her throat like a lump of rising dough. She'd unintentionally wounded his Highlander pride. "Latharn, I didn't mean that I thought you weren't smart. It's just that most men from your era, most lairds, didn't know how to read." Nessa tapped on the thick sheaf of papers. "Especially not legal documents like those."

"My mother ensured we all knew how to read. She understood the power of the written word." Latharn flipped back another page, his shoulders still held stiff as he resumed his reading.

"What sort of trust?" Nessa asked. She had to change the subject. Men were so sensitive. She'd never hurt him for anything in the world. Leaning over his shoulder, she looked over the papers in his hand. They appeared to include the deed to some land.

Fiona emerged from the kitchen with a fresh pot of coffee and inclined her head toward the papers Latharn held. "MacKay Castle and all the surrounding lands have been kept ready for Latharn's return. His father proclaimed it so centuries ago, when his mother found the way to break the curse."

Fiona made her way around the table and refilled everyone's cups. With a proud smile, she gave Latharn a gracious nod of her head and hastened to add. "Latharn will now be the first real laird of clan MacKay since the Battle of Culloden."

"These look to be in order. Ye've done well, Brodie. Surely, you and Fiona will come and live with us at the keep?" Latharn grimaced as he tasted the coffee. He preferred mulled wine or ale.

"Us?" Nessa repeated. "As in you and me?"

Latharn's smile disappeared and he pulled her closer, hugging her to his side. Cradling her chin in the palm of his hand, he held her in his gaze. "Aye, us. We'll be married with the next full moon, and we'll move into the castle as man and wife."

"Married on the next full moon? Now wait just a minute. What are you talking about? I can't think...could you please stop touching me for just a minute. I can't think when you're touching me! I need some space." She pulled her face out of his hand and backed a few feet away. "You haven't even asked me, and all we really know about each other is that we're good together in...there." Nessa waved in the direction of the bedroom. "Why do we have to talk about this now? Why don't we clear this up, um, later?" Married? She hadn't thought anything about married. She hadn't thought past the mindless bliss of his arms. She wasn't ready for reality. *Breathe, Nessa. Got to remember. Breathe.*

Latharn rose from his seat so fast, he knocked the chair halfway across the room. He closed the space between them and grabbed her by the shoulders. He searched her face as he spoke. "That we're good in there, as ye call it, barely begins to scratch the surface of the bond you and I share. I've been walking your dreams for ten long years. I searched for your soul eons longer. Now that the curse has been broken, it's time for us to live as one. And as for me asking ye to be my wife, have ye not been listening to me for the past three days, for the past six hundred years?"

Nessa shrugged his hands off her shoulders. The more he talked, the wilder her emotions churned. "We haven't done much talking these past three days. Maybe I just didn't hear what you were saying."

Latharn stared at Nessa in open-mouthed amazement, then rolled his eyes to the ceiling. With an exasperated growl, he threw his hands in the air and turned to shout at Brodie. "Are all the women of this century so stubborn? How do ye ever get anything done?"

Brodie risked a glance at the threatening look on Fiona's face and backed away with a shake of his head. "I am not saying a word. Trish already has the only couch we have. If I lose my bed, I'm out on the floor."

Latharn scrubbed his face with a rumbling groan. He'd waited nearly six hundred years for this woman. He'd traveled the hallways of her mind, soothing her in her dreams. He thought she loved him. She had freed him with her love. What held the woman back? He dropped to one knee and spread his hands, searching her eyes for the love and commitment he knew she held in her heart.

"Nessa Buchanan, I am asking ye now. I am begging ye to make my life complete. Would ye do me the honor of becoming my wife and spend the rest of your days by my side?"

Nessa bit her lip, hand to her throat, staring down into his eyes.

"Say yes for heaven's sake!" Trish shouted from across the room.

Nessa ignored Trish and with a hesitating touch, reached out to cup Latharn's face between her trembling hands. "Latharn. You have to know how much I love you."

Latharn sensed a hint of uncertainty in her voice. His hands tightened about her waist. "I don't like the tone ye've suddenly taken, Nessa. Surely, ye canna mean to refuse me?"

Nessa shook her head. She glanced around the room at all the shocked faces turned in her direction. "I'm not refusing. I'm just not saying yes. At least, not right now."

Latharn took a deep breath as he rose from his knees to clutch her by the shoulders. Searching her face for some kind of explanation for her reasoning, Latharn struggled to keep from shouting in her face. "Why? I've waited forever to be with ye. Ye say ye love me and yet ye willna agree to be my wife? Give me one good reason why ye will not join with me! Help me to understand why ye cast me aside, Nessa."

Nessa's hands fluttered upon his chest as she tried to explain. "I know you've been in my dreams since I was barely eighteen. But you never spoke to me. We never talked to each other. Don't you think it would be better if we waited a few months and got to know each other before we do something as serious as getting married?"

"Get to know each other better?" Latharn roared. Releasing Nessa's shoulders, Latharn whirled to stomp about the room. Had she gone mad? Was he going to have to lock her in the bedroom until she'd listen to reason? "We will have plenty of time to get to know each other once we're man and wife."

He stormed about the room as though he were a caged animal. Latharn's frustration crackled like electricity in the air. "If we were wed in the year 1410, we might not have even met until our wedding day."

160

Nessa shouted to be heard above the rising wind and rumbling thunder rattling the parlor windows. "This isn't the year 1410, and I'm not going to marry someone first and get to know them later. I grew up in a household where my parents hated each other before they died and they dated for years before they married. Neither of them would give in and ask the other for a divorce. Their marriage turned into some sort of sick contest to see which one of them could make the other more miserable."

Latharn stopped his pacing and grabbed Trish by the arm. He pulled her across the room until she stood nose to nose with Nessa. Jerking his head toward Nessa, he looked at Trish and pleaded, "Would ye be so kind as to talk some sense into her? There is no reasoning with this woman. Tell her that she and I are not going to end up like her miserable parents. Those two misbegotten human beings wouldn't know what love was if it bit them on the arse."

Before Trish could speak, Nessa pushed around her; she locked on Latharn with a challenging glare. "You've proven my point, you see? Any time we don't agree, then I'm the one who's being unreasonable. Did it ever occur to you to try to understand what I'm saying? Don't you realize how much the world has changed since 1410?"

Latharn clenched his fists and ground his teeth in frustration. He stood silent as every fiber of his being raged. He had never imagined she'd refuse him; he never dreamed she'd deny their bond. "I would ask that ye spend six hundred years imprisoned, locked away from all ye've ever known and loved. I would ask ye to watch while the one ye love is held by another and there's nothing ye can do but close your eyes and try to block the memory that's seared upon your mind."

His breath ragged, heart hammering, Latharn took a step closer. He yanked Nessa into his arms and his voice dropped to a pain-filled whisper as he searched her face. "Nay. I've loved ye for an eternity, so I could never ask ye to suffer such a fate. All I ask of ye now is that ye love me, and I plead with ye to be my wife."

"Handfasting!" Fiona shouted from across the room. "Pledge your love for a year and a day, turn to the auld ways to settle this discord."

Brodie shook his head as he pulled Fiona closer, his voice hushed with disappointment. "Handfasting is no longer legal in Scotland. They abolished the ritual a few years ago."

Fiona pulled away from Brodie and grabbed Latharn and Nessa by each of their arms. "What does it matter what the laws of today say? Ye will perform the rite at midnight in the light of the full moon, before the Auld One to witness. Then if after the allotted time of a year and a day, ye should find the match was ill-advised, each of ye can go your separate ways, with no legal ties to bind ye. But if ye find your love has grown even stronger, then ye can bind yourselves with a ceremony sanctified by man."

Latharn still held Nessa crushed to his chest. His voice a hoarse whisper, the pain in his eyes begged her to listen to the possibilities the solution held. "Would ye be willing to do this, my love? What Fiona suggests?" He held his breath, waiting for Nessa's answer.

Latharn's heart pounded against Nessa's chest as he waited for her reply. With a sudden jolt of clarity, she gasped when she realized his heart pumped in complete sync with her own. It was a sign. Although she'd never been a believer in such things, a lot had happened over the past few weeks to turn her mind around. The synchronized beating of both their hearts convinced her they were already one.

"Yes," she whispered. "We'll start out with a year and a day." His warm chest rumbled beneath her cheek, and the beat of his heart hammered a bit faster. "But I've got a sneaking suspicion we'll end up being together quite a bit longer."

With a shaking breath, Latharn lowered his head and sought her mouth with his. Raising his head, he glanced back in the direction of the bedroom, with a meaningful glint in his eye.

"Oh, no you don't! I need to get some clothes out of there. You two can just cool it for a little while." Trish smacked her hand on Latharn's shoulder and pulled Nessa into a hug of her own.

Brodie clapped Latharn on the back as Fiona scurried back into the kitchen praising the saints in the heavens. "Thank the heavens I married a woman who never knows when to keep quiet. Fiona always speaks her mind."

Latharn agreed as he grasped Brodie's arm. "Aye, cousin. I was beginning to fear my chance at a future was about to become another curse."

A smug look on her face as she returned through the swinging kitchen doors, Fiona passed out tumblers of scotch to toast the joining of the two. "I think we should all go out to dinner tonight to celebrate the couple's happy decision."

Nessa curled her toes as she whiffed the strong spirits. Eying Latharn over the rim of her glass, the reality of his bare-chested attire suddenly struck her. "First, I think we'd better concentrate on getting Latharn a wardrobe that will help him blend into this century."

With the drink tray balanced on one hip, Fiona turned, her eyes skimming over Latharn's muscular chest barely covered with his plaid. "Aye. Ye're right. The problem is that Brodie's not as large as Cousin Latharn and canna even loan him anything to wear to the shops."

Brodie circled Latharn and looked him up and down. "One of Da's kilts might fit him. We might even still have one of his tunics in one of the chests in the attic. Da was a mountain of a man as well, although he wasna nearly so tall."

Crossing his arms over his chest, Latharn yawned in apparent boredom with the current conversation. He sported a mischievous grin as he slowly spun around. "How is this?" he asked, spreading his hands wide. He had clad his body in a skintight black T-shirt, a crotch-hugging pair of designer jeans, and a pair of fine Italian leather boots.

Trish whistled at the way Latharn filled said jeans and nudged

Nessa in the ribs. "I can't believe you came out of that bedroom at all. Who needs food with that around?"

Brodie cleared his throat and coughed a bit. "Ye might want to choose something a bit more conservative when we go out tonight to dine. At least something that doesna make the rest of us look quite so dumpy. Eh, give us a break, Cousin?"

With a grin at Brodie's irritation, Latharn once more waved his hands. His clothing changed to a less-fitted fisherman's sweater and a pair of crisp khaki pants.

Nessa pinpointed Latharn's problem. Her lust engines kicked into overdrive as he paraded around the room. No matter the style of dress Latharn chose, it was a certainty he was going to turn heads. He exuded power, pure unadulterated strength, and an undeniable charm. He was the type of man women followed with their eyes, then plotted to find a way to meet. And he belonged to her.

"Go back to the jeans. Nessa and I really liked the jeans," Trish instructed with a decisive nod.

"Trish! He's not a Barbie doll," Nessa retorted, elbowing her friend in the ribs.

"Well, he's damn sure no Ken." Trish cast a ribald wink at Nessa as she tossed down the rest of her scotch.

"Do ye always have this effect on women?" Brodie heaved a great sigh as he steered Latharn toward the outer door.

"How do ye think I ended up in that ball?" Latharn replied with a jerk of his head.

CHAPTER

TWENTY-THREE

All the people who mattered gathered around the table. Her friends and future family surrounded her. Finally betrothed to the man of her dreams, Nessa sighed with contentment. Life just didn't get any better than this. She'd been drawn to Scotland, some would say obsessed, for the better part of her life. Now she knew why. The land of her heart and the birthplace of her love, she'd been drawn here because she belonged. She'd never dreamed she'd ever be this happy.

With a disappointed jolt, Nessa decided her happiness was too tempting for the demons of discord to ignore. Their icy fingers tightened around her throat as trouble walked through the door. Nessa elbowed Trish and nodded to the archway where the hostess chatted to none other than Gabriel Burns. Cowering at his side trembled a mere slip of a woman stealing glances about the room.

"Just ignore him, Nessa. Maybe he won't see you," Trish instructed under her breath. Trish smiled and talked behind her glass as Latharn cast a curious glance at her and Nessa in the middle of his conversation with Brodie. No sooner had the words left Trish's lips then Nessa heard Gabriel's voice boom across the room.

"Nessa! Trish! It's good to see ye. Ye've not been back to the pub in ages." Gabriel ignored the meek woman scurrying behind him and headed straight for their table.

Latharn dropped his conversation to Brodie and rested a possessive hand across Nessa's wrist. His eyes narrowed to piercing slits as he homed in on his prey.

"Hello, Gabriel." Attempting to keep her tone as cool as possible, Nessa forced her politest smile across her face. Surely, he'd take the hint and leave. No one could be that dense. "Who's your friend?" Nessa leaned around and softened her smile in the direction of the quiet woman's downcast face. Her heart went out to Gabriel's latest victim.

Gabriel's eyes never left Nessa's face as he shrugged a shoulder in the woman's direction. "Oh, that's just Maery. We're old friends, she and I. Maery, this is Nessa Buchanan."

A shadow of a smile flickered across Maery's face as she cast a curt nod to each person at the table. She held her chin slightly tucked, as though afraid to speak.

Nessa clenched her hands in her lap. Poor Maery. Nessa knew exactly why.

Latharn rose, flexing his muscles to ensure Gabriel received the full effect. He looked at Maery with one of his warmest smiles and bent his head in her direction.

"'Tis good to meet ye, Maery. My name is Latharn MacKay. I am Nessa's betrothed."

"Betrothed?" Gabriel spit out the word as though it tasted bad in his mouth. "Did you just say you are Nessa's betrothed?"

"I did. Nessa and I are to be joined upon the next full moon. She has gifted me with the rest of her life. A gift I am most grateful to accept. I will also be most happy to accept your congratulations." With a triumphant leer, Latharn waited, as if praying for Gabriel to make a stupid move. Latharn's hands clenched, and Nessa reached out and touched his arm, afraid of what ran through her beloved's mind.

Gabriel's face purpled; his lips trembled as he shook beneath Latharn's stare. Gabriel flexed his fists, swallowed hard, and with a jerk, finally extended his hand. With a curt nod of his head, he growled his words through gritted teeth. "Then I must congratulate ye, Latharn MacKay. It would seem the MacKays always get the finest women in the end."

Latharn held off long enough for everyone at the table to start shifting in their seats. Then he reached out and crushed Gabriel's hand in his own, squeezing his own unspoken fury into his grasp. "Thank ye. Now if ye'll excuse us, we'll be getting back to our private celebration. Don't let us keep ye from your own plans."

Gabriel's face darkened further at the obvious dismissal. He bared his teeth in a parody of a smile. He grabbed Maery's arm and spun on his heel, but not before looking Nessa square in the eye. "Good luck to ye, Nessa. If ye should ever need me, ye know where I can be found. I promise ye, I willna forget what could've been between the two of us, you and I."

His words laced with unspoken meaning; Gabriel pulled the stumbling Maery from the room. Nessa shivered, rubbing the tingling skin at the back of her neck as Gabriel stormed out between the tables.

"There is a darkness about that one." Latharn leaned closer to Brodie. "Did ye notice? Can ye sense it?"

Brodie's hand tightened around his glass. "I've always sensed evil around that one."

"No." Latharn shook his head. "Now ye're feeling your hatred. Ye must concentrate, Brodie, and listen with your senses, not your rage."

Nessa flinched as Gabriel's roar and slamming doors echoed from the outer cloakroom. Chill bumps rippled down her spine.

"You didn't have to provoke him," Nessa scolded as Latharn settled back into his chair. She didn't like all this talk about darkness or evil. All she knew for certain was Gabriel was a jerk. "Now poor

Maery will catch the brunt of his anger. It's pretty obvious she's been abused by him before."

Latharn shrugged and picked up his knife, slicing into his steak with an unconcerned nod in the direction they'd left. "The meek lass will be safe. If he touches her in anger, his heart will constrict within his chest."

"You're gonna make him die of a heart attack?" Trish leaned forward in avid interest. She tapped her wineglass, eyes wide as she awaited Latharn's reply.

Latharn shook his head, brandishing his fork in the air before he brought a bit of steak to his lips. "Nay. He willna die. But he'll think he's about to meet his maker if he touches her in anger."

Brodie leaned forward; his voice lowered to a whisper as he glanced about the room. "Can ye teach me any of these fine tricks of yours? Or has all the magic been bred out of our DNA and lost with modern civilization?"

Latharn looked at Brodie with just the hint of a smile. "The magic is in all of the MacKays, Brodie. It lies dormant, just waiting to be found. 'Tis our legacy. A gift from my parent's union, and a blessing from the goddess Brid. Ye have but to learn to connect with the energies of the universe to watch the mysteries unfold."

Fiona squirmed to the edge of her seat and rested a hand across her middle. "Are ye saying all the MacKays will be gifted with powers passed down from the mists of time?"

With a knowing wink, Latharn answered, "Aye, Fiona. Your twins will also be blessed with all the gifts running through the bloodline of our clan." He lifted his glass and sipped.

"Our twins? Fiona?" Brodie stared at his wife and dropped his fork to the table.

"Aye, Brodie. I've been trying to find the right time to tell ye. Things have been in such an uproar of late. I wanted to wait to give ye the news at the perfect time. But even I didn't know I was carrying twins. I just knew I was carrying our child." Fiona giggled as Brodie swept her into his arms, laughing as he spun her around the table.

Nessa laughed and clapped her hands. "That's wonderful! Then this is a double celebration. I wondered why you toasted us with water earlier and tonight you weren't drinking any wine." Twins. Gabriel's poison left her mind, wiped away by Brodie and Fiona's happy news.

"This day just keeps getting better," Trish added with a smile. "Things are finally falling into place and I'm proud to say...it's about damn well time!"

Brodie pounded the table in complete agreement. "The MacKay castle will soon be filled with little MacKays running about the halls."

"Aye," Latharn agreed, pulling Nessa into his arms. "Ye had best be thinking of a few names yourself," he whispered next to her ear.

Trish's jaw dropped as she read Latharn's lips. "Are you saying you want Nessa to get pregnant or is this something you already know has happened?"

Latharn rubbed his jaw, gazing off across the restaurant. "I've had six hundred years to hone my skills. Ye would be surprised at what I'm able to do."

Nessa almost choked. Her hands flew to her stomach as she realized she hadn't refilled her birth control pills. But she couldn't be pregnant already. She had been taking them for years.

Her gaze swiveled to Latharn's knowing look and her heart nearly stopped as the smile widened upon his face. "Are you serious? Are you telling me I'm already pregnant?" Nessa had never dreamed of having children. What would she do if she was pregnant?

"Ye don't carry my child just yet. But if the future plays out as I have seen it, we will be blessed with many gifted bairns." Latharn almost hummed in satisfaction as he held out a glass of ice water to her to help her manage the rising knot in her throat.

"I...I cannot be a mother. I've n-never been around children. I won't know what t-to do," Nessa stammered as the hysteria sucked the air out of her lungs. She didn't like not being in control. Then his words took root just as she'd taken a sip of the water, and she almost spewed the mouthful over everyone at the table. "And just how many gifted bairns are we talking about here? And how close together?"

Latharn's jubilant expression slowly faded from his face. "I fail to understand why ye are no excited about the possibilities the future holds. I am one of triplets. Multiple births run in the MacKay family. Brodie himself is a twin."

Trish leaned closer, rubbed Nessa's shoulder, and gave her a reassuring smile. "It's going to be all right, Nessa. You'll be fine. You told me you've been in love with Latharn since he appeared when you were eighteen years old. Didn't you ever dream about having his baby any of those times you sat around with that dazed look on your face?"

Nessa's voice cracked with her rising sense of panic; her mouth dried up as though filled with cotton. "No! My parents were so lousy. I didn't want to become like them. Why would I want to take the chance of warping some innocent child the way they screwed me up?"

Latharn exhaled explosively. "Now I understand. I promise ye, Nessa. Ye are nothing like your parents. I watched what they did to ye with their cruel, spiteful words. Our bairns will be happy and they will love ye deeply. Maybe as much as I do."

Nessa's lower lip trembled as a tiny tendril of hope sprouted deep within her heart. The churning in her stomach lessened as she searched Latharn's face. Knotting her napkin between her damp palms, she heaved a shaking breath. "So, you promise you'll help me when it comes time for us to start a family? You'll make sure I don't turn into some kind of wicked beast and end up scarring our babies for life?"

Leaning forward, Latharn planted a kiss on her forehead and placed a loving hand across her womb. "Ye won't need my help when it comes to kindness. Ye've not got a cruel shadow in your soul."

Nessa hugged his arm close and ducked her head with an embarrassed glance around the table. Her cheeks warmed when she realized she'd dampened the mood by bringing up her troubled past. "Please forgive me, Brodie and Fiona. I didn't mean to spoil your news."

Fiona waved her words away and reached across the table to squeeze her hand. "There's nothing to forgive. But there's a great deal to be done if we're to have a handfasting upon the next full moon. Since Latharn appears to be all-knowing, exactly how much time do we have to prepare?"

A rich chuckle rumbled from deep within his chest as Latharn hugged Nessa close to his side. "We've got but two weeks before the moon is fully waxed. Our ritual shall be at midnight on that night."

Fiona propped her arms on the edge of the cluttered table, tracing a finger across the top of an empty glass. "Midnight? Are ye sure Latharn? This time of year 'twill be quite cold standing beneath the stars."

With a mysterious smile, Latharn raised his glass to his lips. "Midnight upon the night of the autumnal equinox, the full moon shining in the sky. 'Twill allow all of our guests as well as the Auld One to gather with us to witness the joining of our souls."

"Wouldn't ye have more guests during the early evening, before the midnight hour?" Brodie motioned for the waitress to return to the table and refill their empty glasses.

Latharn drained his glass and settled it in the midst of the rest of the empties before fixing Brodie with a reproving look. "Before that night, we must start your training, Brodie. Ye must stop thinking as though nothing else exists other than the physical aspect of this world."

Remaining silent, Nessa eased back in her chair, too much wine and too much news taking its toll on her mind and body. Her head pounded and her stomach rolled. She thought she understood what Latharn meant but decided to wait until another time to find out for sure. She'd had enough surprises sprung on her during dinner. Swallowing uneasily, she still grappled with the news of her possible future as the matriarch of the next MacKay herd.

Gnawing nervously on her lower lip, Nessa groaned as another problem sprouted to mind. "Who are we going to ask to perform the ceremony? Illegal handfasting isn't exactly a job for the local priest." With a worried look into Latharn's green-eyed gaze, Nessa fidgeted in her seat. She didn't feel well at all.

Raising her hand to his lips, Latharn winked as he kissed her palm. "Brodie and I have found a practicing druid who also happens to be a MacKay. In fact, he is a very special MacKay."

Brodie piped up in agreement. "And one of our more, shall we say, infamous relatives is providing identification documents to ensure that once the year and a day have passed everything can be legally registered and filed for the official ceremony." Leaning back in his chair, Brodie waggled a mischievous brow. "Lucky for us, he was paroled just last week and will be in town tomorrow."

"Excuse me." Standing, Trish rummaged through the silverware scattered on the table, found a spoon, and ting-tinged the edge of several glasses. "Since apparently you can't swing a cat around here without hitting a member of the MacKay clan. I think it's high time somebody introduced me to the one who finds redheads irresistible."

Amidst the erupting laughter from everyone at the table, Latharn raised his glass high in the air. His rumbling chuckles drowned out them all as he toasted Trish's health. "To irresistible redheads and their loyalty to their friends! If not for Trish's persistence, I might still be trapped in that crystal hell."

"*Sláinte!*"

Laughing as she raised her glass, Nessa happened to glance toward the window across the room. There was a face reflected through the dimpled panes.

Was that Gabriel standing outside the restaurant? Downing her drink, Nessa looked again once she'd lowered her glass but the scowling face was gone.

CHAPTER
TWENTY-FOUR

N essa gnawed at her lower lip as she gripped the edges of the seat. She had her fingers clenched so deep in the cushions she knew her nails were going to shred the upholstery.

"Latharn, don't you think it would be better if Brodie taught you how to drive?"

"'Tis no' a matter of being taught, Nessa. I but need ye to tell me the basic functions of the gadgets and knobs. I assure ye, I am not some foolish young pup who has to practice until he gets it right." Latharn sat in the driver's seat of the car, his brow creased with a frown as he examined the gauges and knobs. He twisted to peer down around the wheel, studying the pedals she'd pointed out at his feet.

Nessa inhaled a deep, nerve calming breath, attempting to swallow her rising anxiety. She closed her eyes and searched for something positive about Latharn trying to learn to drive. At least this thing was an automatic. She would end up with whiplash trying to teach him to use a clutch.

Latharn sat bolt upright in the seat and swiveled to fix her with an icy glare. "My love, I would like to remind ye I have been reading your mind since ye were but a lass of eighteen years of age. I am now trying to withdraw and give ye your privacy. But when ye find yourself feeling particularly sarcastic, your thoughts are much louder than your words."

Nessa's cheeks heated up with this latest revelation. She narrowed her eyes and returned his glare. Her temper flared as she arched one brow and boldly spoke her mind. "Can you hear what I am thinking now, my love?"

His eyes widened. Latharn cocked his head and smirked. "Now why would I want to do that to myself when it's much more satisfying to do it with you?"

Her teeth clenched; Nessa pointed to the keys. "Just start the car."

Latharn stomped the gas pedal to the floor, turned the keys as far as the ignition would allow— and held them there. His face locked into a mask of concentration, he stared at the road ahead. The starter whined in painful protest as the engine roared with the fury of the wide-open gas.

"Now let them go! As soon as you hear the engine start, you're supposed to let go of the keys." Nessa slapped at his hand and tapped at his right knee currently locked in the straight position, the gas pedal pushed to the floorboard. "Let up on the pedal! You're giving it too much gas. You're going to burn up all the fuel before you even put it into gear."

"Stop scolding me as though I'm an empty-headed bairn! Ye didna tell me that part when ye went through what each of these damn things do." Latharn white-knuckled the steering wheel until it almost bent between his hands as he shifted in the seat.

Flattening her hands on the dashboard, Nessa tried to swallow her frustration. "I'm sorry, I'm sorry! I didn't mean to yell. I told you it would be better if Brodie did this. Now put your foot on the brake and ease the gearshift into drive. Right, the one with the D." Scrubbing her face with her hands, Nessa glanced at the street, thankful that it appeared to be deserted. "Now before you pull out..."

The car squealed out of the parking lot. He kept his right leg locked at the knee. His massive hands swallowed the tiny tubing of the steering wheel, sawing it back and forth. Thanks to Nessa's adamant refusal to teach him unless they were on a deserted stretch of road, all he had to do was keep the car between the ditches as he barreled down the lane.

"Latharn, slow down!" Nessa squeezed his right leg to get him to relax off the gas pedal at least a notch or two. Latharn appeared to have only two speeds: dead stop or screaming, wide-ass open.

Latharn glared at the road and his leg began to relax. As the car slowed down from its breakneck speed, his hands unclenched from the wheel. "Ye see, Nessa? I told ye 'twould be no chore at all. Ye must learn to trust in what I say."

"Just because you're able to drive down a deserted stretch of road doesn't mean you've mastered this thing just yet." As she snugged her seat belt across her body, Nessa pointed up the roadway a bit. "Why don't you turn here and take us back to Brodie's and we'll see if you can park this thing."

Latharn took the corner so fast the car almost skidded on two wheels. He fixed Nessa with a chilling glare when she bellowed for him to slow the damn thing down.

He growled. "I am not deaf, Nessa. Just because I can hear your thoughts doesn't mean I can't hear you speak."

As they neared the graveled drive, Nessa pointed to a spot beneath an ancient oak. "Why don't you just pull up to that tree? I think it best if we stay away from the building."

Tearing his gaze away from the road, Latharn reprimanded her with a jerk of his head. "I will thank ye to keep the jests to yourself and might I also add I have never met a woman with such a broad knowledge of profanity in my life." He wasn't sure what some of those words meant, but there were others he sure did.

"I haven't cursed you a single time," Nessa retorted. "At least not out loud...much."

"Aye. Well, ye have done a verra fine job of it in your head." He returned his attention to the targeted spot in front of the tree. As he lifted his foot from the gas pedal, he stomped on the brake and threw them both forward into their locking seat belts.

"Ow! Didn't I tell you not to stomp on the pedals? You're supposed to lightly step on them...roll onto them with the ball of your foot." Nessa twisted her body and rubbed her shoulder where the seat belt had tried to behead her.

Latharn threw the gearshift into park, shut off the engine, and yanked the keys from the ignition. He exploded from the vehicle and threw the keys to the ground. He didn't even acknowledge Trish as she walked across the drive when he stormed off across the field.

Trish bent, peered into the car, and raised her brows at Nessa. "First driving lesson went well, I see."

"The man is impossible! He won't listen to a word I say. He acts like he's so superior. He thinks he's some kind of god!" Nessa slammed the car door and massaged her neck where the seat belt had rubbed the skin raw.

Trish leaned back against the side of the car, examining her manicure as she spoke in a reproving tone. "Do you think maybe you're being a little hard on him? After all, he hasn't walked among the living, so to speak, in nearly six hundred years."

Nessa paced in a frustrated circle back and forth beside the car. "Hard on him? I'm trying to help him adapt. This is no longer the year 1410. He can't ride around the countryside swinging his claymore and expect everyone to bow and scrape to his mighty name."

Trish pulled a nail file out of her back pocket, pursing her lips as she started filing. "So, when you got your Ph.D. in Archeology, I guess you didn't review any of the history of the clans and what was expected of their lairds and their behavior?"

Nessa stopped halfway through her second lap around the car and whirled to shoot Trish with a fiery look. "Out with it, Trish. If you've got something to say then just say it. Leave the smart-ass remarks at the door."

Trish raised her brows and clucked at Nessa. "Fine. I'll tell you what you don't want to hear but you already know what I'm going to say. I think you're scared and you're trying to find a way to keep Latharn at a safe distance without having to tell him to get lost. You've finally got the real thing and it's scaring the living hell out of you."

Trish flourished her nail file in the air as she continued. "Always before, you got rid of any guy you dated because there's no way he compared to the Highlander of your dreams. Now you're scared to death because you've got your benchmark right in your hands and you're going to have to either commit or quit."

"Bullshit!" Nessa snorted with a stomp of her foot in the gravel.

Trish gave her a wink and her smile widened as she moved closer. "Why else would you be having so much trouble understanding how hard it's going to be for Latharn to adapt to the twenty-first century? You're the expert in history around here. If anyone understands what he's used to dealing with, it ought to be you. How do you think he feels finding himself in a world where he has even less control than he had in that witch's ball?"

Nessa's gaze shifted to the ground as she bit her bottom lip. "You know I hate you, right?"

"Don't you mean you hate it when I'm right?" With a devilish grin, Trish pushed her in the direction Latharn had headed in his blind fury across the field. "Why don't you go find him? Talk to him, Nessa. And stop being so damned afraid to start living the life you deserve."

Nessa scooped the keys up off the ground and lobbed them at Trish's head. "One of these days, you're going to meet your match and I'm going to sit back and laugh."

"It'll never happen!" Trish replied with a laugh and headed for the doorway.

Nessa made her way through the tall, waving grass. She followed the path Latharn had pounded down in his fury. She didn't know what she was going to say when she found him, but she had to find a way to make it right.

Trish was right. Damn her to hell. That redhead should've been a shrink. Since he'd become flesh and blood, Latharn's presence in Nessa's life scared the living hell out of her. With his freedom from the crystal, he could be lost. What if he decided to leave her? What if he found that, after all this time of pining for her, she wasn't what he wanted after at all? It was kind of like shopping. The biggest thrill is trying to find what you want. It's kind of a letdown once the rush of adrenaline passes and you have what you've searched for all along.

Nessa reached the top of a small knoll and paused to scan the area. The grass thinned out making Latharn's path less apparent, the packed dirt hard and covered with scattered clumps of thistles and good-sized stones. Looking around, Nessa recognized the clustered trees up ahead as the copse of pines that surrounded the goddess well.

Nessa hesitated, wondering if Latharn had gone to the spring. If his mother had chosen to appear to Nessa at the well, then what would prevent her from appearing to Latharn? Taking care to ease into the trees, Nessa thrilled as the murmur of voices met her ears. Peeping through the bushes, Nessa spotted Latharn with his mother beside the well.

Latharn sat upon a stone, his hands clenched in front of him, his head sagging as he scowled into the shimmering waters below. "Has love between a man and a woman changed so much, Mother? Has it become a mere diversion or a passing thought? I couldna even convince her to say she would marry me. We're only to be hand-fasted with the next full moon. It's as though the lass thinks we've just met. She thinks we need to get to know one another, when I know her better then she knows herself." Latharn dropped his head into his hands, covering his face and heaved a dismal sigh. "She's mine, Mother! I'll always keep her safe. Why can she no' trust that I'll never leave her?"

Too busy eavesdropping to watch where she stepped, Nessa didn't see the brittle stick lying like a guardian across her path. The snap echoed throughout the wood. The birds flushed from the trees to announce Nessa's presence to all.

Both turned in unison; Latharn and Rachel visibly relaxed when they saw it was Nessa in their wood. Rachel whispered something in Latharn's ear, then smiled at Nessa before she disappeared. Her image evaporated into a mist as though she'd been nothing more than a passing shadow.

Latharn rose from his seat upon the stone. He stood silent, watching as Nessa drew near. His gaze smoldering. Smile gone. His hands flexed at his sides.

Guilt weighed heavily on her mind. Nessa knew she had put the sorrow in his eyes. She swallowed hard against her storming emotions and struggled to slow the drumming of her heart. What a fool she had been, avoiding the truth because she was so afraid that he'd slip out of her life. "I am so sorry, Latharn. I didn't mean to be such a..." She searched for the words, the words to make it right. She gave up, no words would ever do. Crying out, she rushed headlong into his arms.

She leapt on his chest, claimed his mouth, and poured her apologies into her kiss. Wrapping her legs around his waist, she buried her fingers into his hair and molded her body against his.

Latharn wrapped his arms around her, carrying her to the moss-covered bank beside the mouth of the spring. He lowered them both to the ground and leaned them back against a fallen log. Nessa straddled his body, fueling her kisses with her deepest emotions. He had to forgive her. He had to know how she truly felt.

Slipping his hand up the front of her shirt, Latharn pushed her bra aside. He let out a muffled groan of pleasure as she shivered beneath his touch. Cupping her breast, he circled her nipple with his thumb and slipped his other hand down the front of her pants.

Latharn teased his way into her folds, swirling his fingers deep inside her. "I ache for ye, Nessa," he breathed into her mouth as she moaned against his lips.

Breathless, she raised her head from his mouth, slipped her shirt down her shoulders, and tossed her bra aside. Nessa writhed and moaned as his talented fingers danced inside her. Gripping his shoulders, she closed her eyes, her head thrown back in pure bliss. She ground her hips hard into his hand, taking full advantage of his expert touch. His teasing thumb tantalized her nub until she cried out and shuddered on his hand.

Breathing hard, she held him locked in her gaze as she rose and shed the rest of her clothes. Nessa stretched before him, bare as the day she was born, still tingling from his touch.

With a wave of his hand, Latharn's clothing disappeared and he knelt before her. He traced his hands up her thigh, his tongue tickling and nipping close behind. He spread her legs and held her body steady as he buried his face between them. Suckling and teasing, he licked and nipped, until Nessa felt sure she risked bursting into flames. Moaning, gasping, Nessa raked her nails across Latharn's shoulders and pulled his head hard against her. Just when she thought she'd surely die, he slid his finger deep inside and pushed her over the edge.

With a shudder, Nessa fell across his shoulders as Latharn carried her to the pond. She gasped as the icy water of the spring washed over her heated flesh. As Latharn walked, he slid Nessa down around his waist and buried himself inside her. As he moved toward the headstone with the goddess's face, he clutched her tight against his chest. With each step he took, he slid deeper still, burying himself to the hilt by the time he'd reached the stone.

Latharn balanced Nessa against the hollowed-out ledge. It was as though the seat had been made for just such a joining. Leaning back against the rock, her arms rested along the sides of the bank, Nessa reveled in Latharn's thrusts. The icy water rushed in with each of his delicious thrusts as he pounded deeper into her body. Neither of them spoke, just stared into each other's eyes, hypnotized by the dance.

The rhythm increased; the world reeled; Nessa drowned in Latharn's fathomless gaze. Her body suckled him, begged for his essence, and enveloped him with her timeless needs. She shattered, unable to take anymore, her screams of ecstasy echoed out across the wood. His shoulders knotting as he clutched her tighter, Latharn roared his possession, his growls echoing with her cries as he filled her with his seed.

Shuddering as he emptied, Latharn claimed her mouth, burying his moans in her throat. She spasmed around him and continued to climax; he hardened again and resumed the dance. Her eyes half-closed as her passion stoked again, Nessa barely noticed how the waters shimmered with a strange glow around their bodies. Arm in arm, they finally emerged from the water. With a tired wave of his hand, Latharn materialized a tartan around them. He wrapped them in a heavy winter plaid, the softest wool his magic conjured protected their bodies from the evening chill. As they lay together upon the mossy bank, Latharn squinted and a roaring campfire appeared. Nessa stirred in a feeble attempt to prop her chin on his chest.

"Latharn."

"Aye?" He didn't open his eyes.

"I have changed my mind about the handfasting ceremony," she whispered, watching his face.

His eyes flew open in alarm and his arm tightened around her shoulders. "What are ye trying to tell me, my love? Nessa, what are ye saying?"

As she snuggled deeper into the crook of his arm, Nessa yawned before she replied. "I want a wedding. I want us to be married when the child we just made is born."

Latharn's arm relaxed around her and his deep chuckle rumbled beneath her head. "Ye mean when our children are born."

CHAPTER

TWENTY-FIVE

"Did he say exactly how many children?" Hands buried in the makeshift filing cabinet; Trish glanced at Nessa. Pencil clenched between her teeth; she paused in her filing.

Studiously ignoring Trish's probing gaze, Nessa trained her eyes on the screen of her laptop and shrugged her shoulders. "He won't tell me. Just gives me that smug know-it-all grin that says he's proud of the fact he's successfully sired the first of his brood."

Trish chuckled as she pushed the drawer shut and tucked the folders under her arm. "I'd bet a paycheck you're at least carrying triplets. You know he's not going to let himself be outdone by Brodie. That would be unbecoming of the laird!"

Nessa felt a bit faint at the prospect of triplets. Swallowing hard, her breath hitched as she remembered the strange effects of the well and the wonderfully erotic afternoon. "Oh, don't even joke about that. What if it is triplets? Are you going to move in with us to help me maintain control of the herd?"

Trish fixed Nessa with a wistful gaze as she nodded. "I wouldn't miss it for anything in the world. But you know I can't sponge off you guys forever. Once this project is over and our grant money is gone, I'll eventually have to go back to the States. My work visa won't be good forever." Trish's voice quivered as she turned away.

Nessa caught the earpiece of her reading glasses between her teeth and spun around in her chair.

"Obviously, we're going to have to get you hitched to a MacKay. If you're family, you'll have to stay."

"I think we need to concentrate on your ceremony first. After all, it's only three days until Latharn makes an honest woman of you." Trish nodded toward the desk, dropped the folders on the chair, and frowned at an oddly carved stone lying in the middle of the blotter. "What's this? I thought we'd crated up this week's artifacts. Whose head are you gonna have on a plate for leaving this one behind? And it's not even properly labeled."

Nessa rose from behind her desk, brow furrowed as she leaned closer to the ancient rock. "I've not seen this one before. Maybe they just found it this morning. But they know better than to bring it in here. I can't imagine any of them being this careless. Every one of them has been more professional than I could have ever hoped."

Nessa opened the drawer, fished out a pair of gloves, and snapped them on her wrists. She cupped the football-sized stone between her hands. Turning the stone, her eyes widened as a surge of energy jolted up her arms. She grimaced and tried to set the stone back down on the desk. She panicked when she realized she couldn't pull her fingers away from its surface. "Trish, I can't put it down! This thing won't let me let it go!"

Trish rushed to her side, trying to grab the stone. Whenever she reached for the artifact in Nessa's hands, the stone yanked itself, as well as Nessa, out of her reach. "This isn't an artifact from the site, Nessa. That thing's carrying some kind of a curse meant for you alone. You've got to find a way to put it down. You've got to concentrate on letting it go!"

Nessa struggled, pulling against the invisible force, her body trembling as she fought to break free. Terror overtook her with the realization that nothing she tried worked.

Nessa cried out, battling against her rising hysteria. "Get Latharn! He'll know what to do. Hurry, Trish. Before it's too late. Trish!" A roaring wind drowned out her words. The inside of the tent. Trish's face. She couldn't hear, couldn't see the words Trish's lips formed. Spinning. If she closed her eyes, she might be able to stand but she feared she'd never see Trish again. She stumbled, the spinning increased, and the out- of-focus whiteness snapped to black.

LATHARN TRIED to get through Trish's panic as she grabbed her keys and stumbled for the door. "Latharn," she bellowed again at the top of her lungs. "Latharn! You've got to hear me. Nessa's gone!"

He felt her attention focused on him. Latharn shushed her. *"I am with ye, Trish. I can hear ye. Ye must calm down. We will save her. Just get here as quick and as safe as ye can."*

"She just disappeared. She just vanished!" Trish sobbed as she pounded on the steering wheel.

Latharn let her anger play itself out before speaking again.

Trish moaned. "Who the hell could've done this to her? Where could she be?"

"I swear to ye, Trish. We will find her. I did not wait six hundred years to be with my love only to have her torn away. And I will not forfeit my children either. Now, calm down and get here as soon as ye can."

Alerted by the horn as Trish roared into the driveway, Latharn yanked open the door and pulled her from the seat almost before the tires had stopped turning. "Ye must tell me every detail of what happened at the site. Ye must leave nothing out if we are to find where Nessa has been sent."

Trish blinked at him in confusion. "Where Nessa has been sent? You sound as though you expected this to happen. Are you telling me you knew she was in danger all along?"

How could he explain it? There wasn't time. Raking his hands through his hair, Latharn struggled to make Trish understand.

Brodie rushed to his side. "Brodie and I have been watching increasing darkness, a growing disturbance among the mists and the ripples of time. We felt sure it was the evil of Gabriel Burns and his negativity disturbing the energies with his rage. But with this kind of magic, the strength of this kind of curse...I just don't know for sure. We can take nothing for granted."

Out of the corner of his eye, he caught sight of Fiona emerging from the outer shed. She was dusty from head to toe from searching through storage shelves. Pale, her eyes shadowed with shock, she brushed her hair back with a trembling hand. With a nod from Latharn, Fiona clutched at Trish's hand. "I saw the vicious devil practicing the darkest of magic. I saw his altar once when he didn't know I was around. But always before, his spells failed. That was part of the reason for all his anger."

Latharn steadied Fiona's shoulders as she shifted a box filled with jars labeled in an ancient script higher on her hip. Her dazed look deepened as she recalled Gabriel's dark habits aloud. "As far as I knew, Gabriel was only capable of physical evil against women. Not once did any of his curses come to pass. I once found the journal he kept where he tried to discover what he did wrong. I just assumed he didna have the gift."

Brodie growled and fisted his hands. "This time he will die if he's the one to blame for this evil. We will send him to meet his master of darkness in the very pits of hell."

Taking the box from Fiona and settling it in the back of the jeep, Latharn turned to find Trish glaring at all their faces.

"If he's the one to blame?" she said. "You mean you're not even sure Gabriel's the one we're after? If not, Gabriel, then who? Or what could be to blame for Nessa being zapped out of existence into thin air? Latharn, what's going on? You promised me Nessa would be safe!"

His rage drummed the call to battle; his body tensed, ready to attack. Latharn jerked his head in Trish's direction. He didn't have time to explain, especially not to a novice such as Trish. Growling, he yanked open the back of the jeep. All this chatter solved nothing. They must get organized, plan their attack. They had to move. "Enough. There is no time for this banter. We must get to the castle. A hidden library is there that will aid us in our search. If we are unable to find her before the full moon, she may be lost to us forever. The autumnal equinox could realign the stars and hide her away from this reality for an untold number of years."

Spurred into action by Latharn's words, Fiona set the dusty carton down and held out her hand to Trish. "Come help me, Trish. We must gather the rest of the bottles and books that we've kept hidden here over the years." Fiona pulled Trish by the arm and led the way to a hidden room behind the storeroom walls.

Latharn directed the two women as they filled every box until nothing remained in the room. He selected vials and bottles of morbid-looking objects, wrapping them to ensure they survived the journey. He packed ancient texts that would make any archeologist tremble in excitement. Latharn double-checked everything they packed, nodding his approval before each box was sealed.

He turned one last time to scan the now bare room, to ensure they'd left nothing behind. Latharn wouldn't entertain the thought that they'd not get to Nessa in time.

They reached the castle just as the edge of the fiery orange sun had dipped below the horizon and the glowing white moon had begun to rise. The promising light shimmered upon the rippling waves of the ocean, oblivious to the malevolence in the air.

Latharn's gaze settled on the home of his birth for the first time in hundreds of years. His chest tightened as memories of his childhood flooded his mind.

Shadows of children at play, of women as they bustled about the castle grounds danced before his eyes. Images of ancestors laughed, slapping each other on their backs as they walked their horses in from the courtyard gate. His emotions squeezed the wind from his chest as he watched three brothers laugh and wrestle in the mud.

Latharn shook himself free of the ghosts of the past and made his way into the great hall. Once Nessa was safely back at his side, the memories could surface then. He led the others to the northernmost tower and up the spiral steps. Yanking down on the iron sconce on the farthest wall, he waited for the timeworn stones to obey the forgotten command. An eternity passed before the answering grind of the stone gears rumbled from far beneath the floor.

At a snail's pace, the dingy passage appeared. Within it was a small landing bearing two sets of stairs. One staircase descended into the musty darkness, the other rose in the direction of a shaft of shimmering moonlight. At Latharn's nod, they took the staircase leading to the stars. Latharn held the torch high over their heads, its flickering light doing little to beat back the shadows of the narrow stone hall.

His heart drummed harder the higher he climbed. This was Mother's tower. A gifted witch from the twenty-first century, she'd traveled back in time to join with his father. The portals of time had strengthened her powers; her mystical abilities had grown with the energy within the veil. Inhaling a great breath, Latharn held the torch higher. He didn't fear the unknown the darkness held; he feared the emotions of the past.

Mother had combined her knowledge with that of the chief druid of the clan and the two of them had recorded everything they had ever learned. Usually, rituals were committed to memory by repetition and practice. Ancient Druidry wasn't recorded on parchment or stone. But neither Latharn's mother nor the wise druid of the clan wanted to risk the knowledge ever being lost. Death was an ever-threatening thief of knowledge. It could strike down a gifted teacher at any moment.

With a shudder, Latharn recalled the day his mother had told him of her plans to hide the gathered knowledge after his father's murder. She'd seen to the concealment of the library of the mysteries before she'd jumped to her death. Although it had been several centuries ago, the memory still pained him, as though the wound was still fresh. It was a dark time for the clan MacKay; several members had been falsely accused of spell craft by rival families. The avaricious witch hunters had gone so far as to torture one poor woman to death. This death had sparked a bloody clan war. A war that had sent his father's lifeless body home, his shield laid upon his cold, still chest. His mother had then ordered all the clan records of the mysteries hidden within the castle walls.

Defending magic and his people had killed her husband. Never again would she allow magic practiced among the clan. Then she'd gone to the cliffs overlooking the ocean to fling her body down upon the jagged rocks below.

Latharn shook himself back to the present as they arrived at a heavy door with a single iron circlet hung in its center. Handing the torch to Brodie, he gritted his teeth, set his shoulder against the barrier and shoved. Dust and dirt sifted out of the crevices that hadn't been disturbed in hundreds of years. The ancient portal groaned its way open and revealed a suffocating darkness within.

Brodie raised the torch, the glowing circle of light struggling against the shadows of the room. Latharn instructed him to light the additional sconces hammered along the wall. Lights blazed about the room, revealing a high-ceilinged chamber. Mouths agape in amazement, Trish, Brodie, and Fiona all spun around to gaze at the sheer number of books lining the walls.

Trish groaned as she wandered around the room, staring at all the shelves. "We'll never find the answer in three days' time. This place is as big as the Library of Congress!"

Snapping around, Latharn grabbed her by the shoulders and gave her an irritated shake. "Never speak such negativity again! Ye attract whatever ye send out. I willna listen to words of defeat. In three days' time, my Nessa will be back at my side."

Trish fended him off, twisting out of his grasp as she backed her way across the room. "I'm sorry, Latharn. It's just there are so many books, so many scrolls, so much...stuff. Tell me where to start and I'll help any way I can. Just tell me what I'm looking for."

So many shelves. So many books. How had Mother managed them all? *Damn it, Mother. Did ye have to write down every thought?* Scrubbing his jaw, Latharn turned and eyed the crowded shelves covering the walls. "I wish the mirrors of time hadna been destroyed. I could've traced her soul across all of the planes with one simple incantation."

"Mirrors of time?" Trish arched a brow as she turned the pages of a dusty tome she'd pulled from one of the shelves.

"Aye, the mirrors of time. I remember reading about them." Brodie nodded in complete agreement. "There were three of them. Past, present, and future portals. Ye could scry with them, ask them to find ye anything, and if ye had the gift, they would tell ye the answer ye sought."

Trish emitted a low whistle of admiration. "Well, that would've definitely made our search a lot easier. What happened to them?" She turned to Latharn after she replaced the book she'd been studying back on the shelf. "You said they were destroyed? Who would do such a thing to something so rare?"

"My mother." Latharn heaved a heavy sigh as he remembered the incident as though it happened yesterday. Rachel had thrown a fit of uncontrollable rage when Caelan's body had returned lifeless and cold. "She cursed them with a shattering spell for not warning her of the danger to my father's life."

Her mouth formed into a silent O. Trish cringed and turned back to search the shelves. "So what subject am I supposed to be searching for? Curses? Autumnal equinox? Full moon? Disappearing into thin air? What?"

"Scrying," Brodie shouted from across the room where he pawed through the lowest shelf in the corner. "What about scrying? I know ye don't have the mirrors, but there are other tools that can be used to see into the mists."

With a wave of his hand, Latharn lit the thick stubs of the many candles scattered across the table and motioned for Brodie to bring the book he'd found. Brodie grunted, pulling the three-foot-wide wedge from the shelf and wrestled it to the table. Worn leather sandwiched yellowed parchment. The ancient tome was huge.

Reverently, Latharn opened the weathered cover. The leather crackled in protest at being disturbed. With a ginger touch, Latharn turned one page at a time, his fingers spread as they traced the text he scanned. The mustiness of the pages smelled of time forever lost and the faintest hint of his mother's favorite scent, heather. His mother must have pressed a flower somewhere in the book's pages. Latharn frowned and tried to shake free of the fragrance and concentrate on the spell. Since his parents' funeral, he hated that smell. It had even permeated into his crystal prison. His lips moved with a whisper as he absorbed the words. "Do ye know if the chapel is still intact?" Latharn asked without looking up from the ancient grimoire.

Emerging from a set of bookshelves across the room, Fiona nodded, paging carefully through a book she held in her hand. "Aye, I visited it myself a few months ago to lay some heather upon the altar. The stonework is worn but it still stands whole and has survived the tests of man and time. Why do ye ask, Latharn?"

Latharn eased the delicate parchment over to the next page to finish reading the passage. This gave him his answer. This spell would guide him to Nessa. He stroked his chin, leaning closer as he peered at an elaborate equation scribbled off in one of the margins. "I need holy water that's been charged by the waxing moon to have the most power o'er seeing into the mists."

Trish pushed up her sleeves and stepped up to the table. "Give me a bucket and point me toward the chapel. I'll tote all the holy water you need. I have to do something besides just stand here."

Latharn moved to the farthest wall and spread his fingers across the stones. Scowling, he searched his hands over the rocks, closing his eyes as though listening to the wall's silent instruction. Arms widespread, he placed his right hand high, the left lowered to his knees. Latharn leaned hard against the wall and pushed into it with all his might. He gripped and clutched the oddly carved stones, twisting and turning to shove them deeper into an unseen passage. As the stones receded, the wall ground its way out and revealed a breathtaking vista of the sea. Moonlight flooded the room, illuminating it with an ethereal blue-white glow.

Latharn gazed into the sky and drew a shuddering breath. He sent up a silent plea to the goddess and every mystically blessed ancestor in his past. He bowed his head and turned from his supplication to the moon. The eerie glow of the beacon of the night energized him for his task ahead. "Fiona, you and Trish must find the divining bowl. It should be somewhere amidst these many shelves. It must be filled with holy water from the baptistery, then set upon this pedestal to absorb the power of the moon. At daybreak, we will bring it back into the darkness. There must be no other light in the room. Then through the power of the mists, we will find our way to Nessa and how to bring her back."

CHAPTER
TWENTY-SIX

Her head pounded. Blood roared in her ears. Nessa swallowed hard at the bile burning in the back of her throat. Whatever she did, she couldn't allow herself to vomit. The gag in her mouth would cause her to choke to death if she did. Her shoulders ached from the odd positioning of her bound hands Her feet throbbed from the over-tight ropes at the ankles. A blindfold covered her eyes, the material thin and pulled tight as though made of a silk scarf. Trussed up like this, she felt trapped in a box.

She fought against visions of live burials, of dirt thrown on the tops of screaming victims. She struggled against the hysteria of claustrophobia, fighting to convince herself she could still breathe.

I am getting air. I am breathing.

She forced away the feeling of suffocation and the rising panic it fueled. She concentrated on the fact that she could breathe. She reminded herself she was getting air.

I am breathing. I'm going to be okay.

Instinctively, she knew in order to survive, she couldn't show her captor any sign of weakness. If she did, that weakness would become a tool of torture for them to use.

She forced herself to lie still even though her body ached. Her muscles screamed out for relief. Nessa strained, listening to the room around her. There wasn't a sound. She'd never witnessed such silence. It was almost as suffocating as the darkness. The one other sense available to her was her heightened sense of smell.

Mildew. Damp stones. Centuries-old decay. Her nose transmitted this information to her brain. From the scent of things, she was either in the bowels of some sort of stone structure, or worse yet, deep in some underground tomb. She forced that out of her mind. Inhaling a careful breath, Nessa reminded herself she still had plenty of air. She wanted to ensure the rise and fall of her chest gave nothing away about her level of consciousness. She didn't know if she was watched or not but she wasn't ready for them to know she was awake.

"I know ye're awake. I can tell by the color on your cheeks. The fair-skinned can keep no secrets." Gabriel shoved the blindfold up onto her forehead and leered down into Nessa's face.

The sudden light blinded her. She blinked up into his face as her pupils adjusted to the abrupt absence of darkness. Gabriel? She'd believed Fiona's stories of Gabriel's violent nature, but she'd never thought him capable of this.

Gabriel traced a fingertip along the edge of her jaw, his leering scowl growing even darker. "Ye see, Nessa? Ye underestimated me. Ye should've given me a chance." His face relaxed, grew thoughtful as he cupped her cheek in his hand. He licked his lips as he turned and scanned the rest of her body. As his gaze traveled across her breasts and then lower, he flinched and clutched a hand to his chest.

Nessa swallowed hard, almost gagging, and forced herself not to react. He'd only feed on her fear. She just continued staring up into his face and blinked when she absolutely had to.

Gabriel returned his hand to trace his thumb across her bottom lip and brought his face closer to hers. "But now we'll ne'er know what it could have been like, thanks to that bastard ye've decided to wed. I don't know how he's done it, but whenever I even think about giving ye what ye deserve, my heart almost explodes in my chest."

His sneer grew wider. Gabriel's eyes took on a maniacal gleam as he jerked his head. "I can't even obey what the voice tells me to do. Just binding ye nearly stopped my breathing."

Voice? Nessa almost shuddered, her skin crawling beneath his touch. Great. Not only was Gabriel violent, but he wasn't the only one inside his head.

Yanking his hands through his hair until it stood on end, Nessa saw clearly that Gabriel had left sanity in the dust. He jumped up to circle about the room while he scowled and batted at something only he could see. His voice became shrill as he shook his fist at his mysterious tormentor. "The powers? The powers ye promised to me are useless if ye refuse to allow me to use them! What good is control over another if I must keep it hidden?"

As Nessa watched him, she realized Gabriel argued with a voice only he could hear. While Gabriel ranted to his invisible friend, she flexed her hands and tested the ropes at her wrists. If he'd leave her blindfold up where she could watch him, she was almost positive she could wiggle her hands free.

"I don't give a damn about that bastard! I told ye I'd kill him but ye would not allow it, even when I promised to make the son of a bitch suffer, even when I swore ye would enjoy what I would to do to him. Ye said wanted him for yourself. That he was yours to save or destroy. What do ye want from me? When do I get something out of this?" Gabriel growled, stomping a path back and forth across the room. He jerked his head and flailed his arms as he shouted into the air.

Nessa glanced around the room while she kept watch on Gabriel out of the corner of her eye. Her heart fell as she discovered the room had just one way out. The walls consisted of rough-hewn blocks. The ancient stones glistened with condensation. As far as she could tell, no windows existed, at least not in her current line of vision. She dare not move much for fear of interrupting Gabriel's argument with whoever resided in his head. There was the one door, a solid piece of some sort of metal, blackened as though oiled to protect it from rusting. From the size of the hinges holding it in place, the weight of the door had to be immense.

She could tell she was lying upon a raised block of some sort; it appeared altar-like in its position. Stationed between two tall candelabra against the back of the room, Nessa wondered if this was where bodies had once been prepared for burial. From the chill settling into her bones, she was positive the slab consisted of some sort of stone.

She flinched as Gabriel swung his arms in the air. Nessa sent up a silent plea for help. She remembered what Latharn had told her about the connection between their minds. She prayed he would somehow hear her silent cries and come crashing through that door to her rescue.

"Fine! I will keep her from him until the equinox has passed. But ye must promise me something in return. Once ye've cast him into the abyss, Nessa only exists for my amusement." His eyes glittered with total madness. Gabriel shoved the blindfold back down across her eyes.

"Go to sleep," he barked. "Ye're going to need your rest for what I've got in store for ye once your protector is gone."

Then he slammed the heavy door and left her trembling in the darkness of the blindfold. With only the hiss of the burning candles for company, she concentrated on calling out to Latharn for help.

Nessa cried out with every fiber of her being. She visualized Latharn's face in her mind. He had to be able to hear her call. It was her only hope. She wouldn't allow herself to believe otherwise.

"He canna hear ye, Nessa. There's a spell around this room as strong as the protective love aura Latharn's placed around you."

Nessa knew that voice. Light and airy, like a Highland breeze when it riffled through the leaves, somehow Aveline had managed to find her. But if there was a spell around the room, how could Aveline's voice be so clear in her mind?

The immortal woman's laughter tinkled like chimes in the wind as Aveline sent a breeze to brush across Nessa's cheek. "The spell is against Latharn, against any mortals who would dare try to find ye. Gabriel Burns doesn't realize I exist. I am immortal. I'm not so easily stopped by a few magical wards placed at the corners of stone walls."

Nessa swallowed hard against the bitter gag in her mouth. Her tears soaked into the blindfold covering her eyes. She took a deep breath and struggled to remain calm. She concentrated on projecting her thoughts to Aveline's consoling image. Nessa formed the words clearly in her head. *"When is Latharn going to come and get me? No, let me rephrase that. Tell Latharn to come and get me right now. Gabriel is insane."*

With a breathless sigh, Aveline's voice grew soft, more solemn in its tone. "Latharn must pass one final test. He canna come to ye until sunrise on the day of the equinox, and he must use his powers to find ye for himself. I canna save ye nor can I tell him where ye lie."

Nessa's heart pounded as the meaning of Aveline's words sunk in. She couldn't mean she was just going to leave? Nessa shook her head, sank her teeth hard into the gag. *"No! He has to come and get me now. Aveline, you can't just leave me here alone. I'll never be able to survive until then. You saw Gabriel. He's out of his mind. Who knows what he's going to try to do?"*

"I'm sorry, Nessa. 'Tis only a little while longer. And 'tis the only way to free Latharn permanently from his past. When all the pieces fall into place, ye will understand. Trust me." Aveline brushed an ethereal kiss across Nessa's forehead before her spirit disappeared into the darkness.

Nessa strained to hear something other than the hiss of the burning wax of the candles. She groaned when she realized she was all alone. How could Aveline desert her like this? She didn't care what pieces Latharn needed to free him from his past. She wanted out of here and she wanted out now. They'd take care of Latharn's past—later.

"I'll be damned if I lay here and wait to be sacrificed," Nessa fumed.

She twisted her wrists until they burned, raw and bloody from the ropes. She wrenched them free of the tortuous knots. She pushed off the blindfold, ripping the gag out of her mouth, then sat up to work on the ropes at her feet.

She kept one ear cocked toward the door as she clawed at the stubborn bindings until her fingernails bled. She almost panicked, as the knotwork at her feet tightened with every frustrated yank. Losing what little patience she'd ever had; she scooted to the end of the stone altar and held her ankles up to the candles until the ropes caught fire.

Nessa pulled her feet apart as the ropes burned in two, then slapped out the flames. As she rubbed the tingling, hot skin of her legs, she glanced around the remainder of the room she hadn't been able to see before.

Adrenaline surged through her veins as the promising spikes of the iron candelabra caught her eye. Her heart rate picked up as she noted the sharpness of the long metal prongs. Her breath came quick, excitement fluttered through her chest; hope tingled like electricity through her body. Testing the sharp tip of one prong with her finger, an escape plan rooted in her mind. When Gabriel decided to return to her room, the iron stand would be the perfect weapon.

Nessa realized the first strike was her only chance. With the madness she'd seen reflected in Gabriel's eyes, negotiation would be senseless. Years ago, she'd killed a man while defending Trish. If needed, she would kill Gabriel to save her own.

She formed all the burning candles into a blazing pillar on the floor, wincing as she brushed against the raw flesh on her wrists. With a hissing gasp, Nessa cringed as one of the wounds cracked open to bleed. There wasn't time now. She had to plan her attack. She'd deal with her wounds later.

Nessa picked up the spiked candelabra, hefting the weight of it in her hands and nodded in satisfaction. She was lucky. It stood even with her shoulders. If the stand had been any taller, she'd never be able to balance it when she thrust. Taking a deep breath, a strange calm settled over her. She intended to surprise Gabriel just as soon as he walked through the door. Surprise was a better weapon then the candelabra.

A muffled scrape sounded on the other side of the door, a thudding sound echoing closer with a rhythm of footsteps. It was the sound of hard-heeled boots hitting stone as they approached from down the hall.

Nessa clutched the candelabra to her side like a javelin, bracing her feet as she pressed her back against the wall. She held her breath as the key turned in the lock, the rusty tumblers grumbling in protest at being disturbed.

Pushing the door open, Gabriel left his chest exposed. His left arm held back the heavy door, while his right relaxed at his side.

Now. Sensing her opportunity, Nessa lunged with the shaft, aiming for the underbelly of the beast. Propelling forward, she shoved the spike upward with as much force as she could thrust. She grunted as the rod sank deep into its mark. She planted her feet and held fast.

Gabriel's mouth fell open. His shocked eyes blinked, and his clutching hands trembled at the shaft of iron shoved up beneath his ribcage. He staggered back against the opened door, gawking at the blood as it poured out over his hands. He gasped for air as his lungs collapsed. He stared at Nessa in disbelief, then slid to the ground, blood bubbling from his lips.

"Ye stupid bitch," he gurgled through dying lips. His eyes glazed over into an eerie stare as Nessa watched him shudder and then relax, deathly still.

She hugged herself to stop her shaking and stared down at his paling form. She almost felt sorry for him lying there, now helpless in a pool of his own blood. It seemed suddenly ironic. Just a few weeks ago, she'd been horrified by the nightmare of his beheading. Now he'd died by her own hands, and she felt nothing as she wiped the blood off her arms where he'd spit on her with his dying breath.

Nessa stepped over his outstretched legs, never taking her eyes from him as she eased toward the opened door. Did something just move? Surely, it was just a death twitch. Holding her breath, she peered closer, a peculiar chill gripping her body.

Inky fog circled and rose out of the center of Gabriel's chest. Hypnotized by the strange, curling black mist, Nessa wondered if his wicked soul sought to escape to the other side. But as she stood frozen in horrified fascination, the mist rose and grew until it formed a column just a little taller than Nessa.

Swirling and roiling, the heavy mist swelled and receded until it sculpted itself into the voluptuous shape of a curvaceous woman.

"Surely ye didna think I would ever allow Latharn to find happiness when he refused to give contentment to me?" Bloodred lips curved into a malicious smile, the mysterious woman smoothed her ebony hair away from her face. "I was positive once the fool's mother took her life, the madness would have him begging me to save his soul. Had he done that, I would have brought ye back through time to release him from the bauble. I might have even let ye live in the past with some sheep herder or some other smelly Highlander of your own." With a wicked laugh, the seductress added, "Contrary to what ye might have heard, there have been times when Deardha has been merciful."

Smoothing her hands down her waspish waist, she drummed her ivory fingertips atop her generous hips. Her pouting lips pulled into a venomous sneer as Deardha eyed Nessa up and down. "The man must be insane to think himself in love with a little chit such as you. Do ye think perhaps he's gone blind from his isolation? Perhaps I left him to the crystal too long. Some of my other pets lost their sight while in captivity." She stopped as if pondering a great mystery. "Some of them even withered and died."

Nessa returned the witch's glare, her body shaking with rage. So, she was the one. This bitch was the source of Latharn's pain. Nessa clenched her fists at her sides. She wasn't giving Latharn up without a fight. She didn't care what kind of powers this so-called sorceress possessed. She'd had enough of this twisted fairy tale. She was tired, cold, sore, and hungry and she wasn't taking any more of this crap. "I think his eyesight is absolutely perfect. After all, he saw you for what you really are."

Her heart pounded as her nails dug into her palms. Nessa felt no fear, just pure, unadulterated fury pounding through her veins. She knew there was no way this woman was going to kill her. After all, Deardha needed bait for her trap.

Deardha moved closer. Her form grew and shifted until she towered over Nessa's tiny frame. "Ye would be well advised to fear me, little girl. I can send ye to a plane of existence so terrible, your worst nightmares would be a welcomed escape."

Nessa remembered what Aveline had told her about Latharn's protection and decided to put it to the test. If she was going to strike, the time was now while the element of surprise was on her side.

Nessa whirled with her favorite kickboxing move and her foot connected with Deardha's jaw. Caught off guard by the force of the impact to her face, Deardha fell hard against the stone wall. As Deardha rubbed her already purpling chin, she rebounded up from the floor. Her eyes glowed with the fury of an enraged beast focusing on its prey. A blue-white fireball appeared, swirling in her trembling hand. Her eyes narrowed as she took aim. The sorceress screeched with the wail of a banshee as she lobbed the fireball at Nessa's head.

Nessa dropped to the floor, dodging the explosive missile. She rose and shifted her center of balance from foot to foot. Nessa moved in and landed another blow. She might not have magic, but by the frustration on Deardha's face, her courage was a force the *bana-buidhseach* hadn't expected.

Another fireball whizzed by her head, so close the room filled with the acrid scent of Nessa's scorched hair. Nessa grabbed the flaming candles and lobbed them at Deardha's head. Hot tallow splattered across the crone's ivory skin. Nessa didn't know how long they were going to keep up this dance. All she knew was she wasn't going to be the one to go cowering into the corner.

"I'm going to kill ye and go after Latharn m'self. I've had enough of this insolence." Deardha rushed at Nessa, her claw-like hands outstretched, features reverting to those of an eon-shriveled creature. As she tried settling her talons into Nessa's neck, a powerful energy field lifted her off the ground and crashed her against the wall.

As her beady eyes widened in disbelief, the crone's snaggled teeth lengthened into snarling fangs. The witch's face transformed into a hideous beast of rage, her form more repulsive as her fury grew. "This canna be possible. He canna have grown so strong. He was never a master of the Ways."

Breathing hard, heart hammering in her chest, Nessa edged her way to the door. She taunted Deardha with her words. "Don't ever underestimate Latharn's power. You gave him six hundred years to perfect it. Remember?"

The crone's scowl deepened as she rushed the door, her black robes lifting her into the air. Once out in the hall, she passed her hands across the threshold. A pulsating energy field sealed off the portal trapping Nessa inside.

Her voice deteriorated to the croak of a raven as the she-devil sneered at Nessa from the other side. "Ye shall be the bait for my trap, bitch! I will have Latharn. He will come."

Deardha's dark eyes glistened and her head tilted to the side as she clutched her gnarled hands in front of her. "When I've tired of toying with him and cast him into the abyss, then I'll return to enjoy tormenting you. Ye will find that once your precious Latharn is dead, his protection of ye will be no more."

Nessa pounded her fists on the table as Deardha disappeared into an evaporating mist. She heaved the iron candelabra into the energy field, ducking as crackling sparks filled the air.

Backing into a corner, Nessa slid down to hug her knees. She rested her cheek on her arms.

All she could do now was conserve her energy, wait for Latharn, and hope he could beat the witch at her own vicious game.

CHAPTER

TWENTY-SEVEN

L atharn sat and watched for the first blinding rim of the sun to edge its way over the distant horizon. The holy waters of the prophecy bowl shimmered before him. The glowing moonlight had charged the liquid for hours. All he needed now was for the arc of the breaking sun to banish the stars from the sky. Then he could ask the waters the way to Nessa and he'd have his answer. The goddess moon never lied. It always gave the answers to those who asked...those faithful to the Ways.

Fiona dozed in Brodie's protective embrace. As midnight had passed, they'd settled on a heavy bench on the other side of the room. Brodie hadn't slept. He'd kept silent vigil. Latharn had found comfort in his presence and his loyalty.

Trish had collapsed into a pitiful ball curled against the base of Latharn's chair. Tears of guilt streamed down her face. She'd paced about the room for hours. While she'd paced and apologized to Latharn for allowing Nessa to touch the stone, Latharn had quieted her with a subtle wave of his hand. The tranquility spell would cloud her mind long enough for her to get some much-needed rest. He needed all of them at their sharpest for what lay ahead.

His gaze found Brodie. Latharn alerted him with a single nod as the sun crested over the hills. He reached down to rest his hand upon Trish's shoulder and squeezed until she opened her eyes.

He helped Trish from the floor and motioned her deeper into the room. As he rose from his chair, he nodded toward the bowl where it shimmered upon the pedestal opened to the sky. His voice calm with determination, he said, "'Tis time."

Brodie shook Fiona, pressing his lips to her ear and whispered her awake. She stretched like a cat, rose from his arms, and tied her hair back from her eyes. "Do ye need for us to gather anything else? Have we all the tools needed for the spell?"

Latharn flexed his hands as though warming up for battle and inhaled a cleansing breath. His gaze settling upon Fiona, he spoke in a thoughtful voice as he nodded toward her waist. "Aye, we have everything listed to complete the spell. In fact, we have an added boon. Fiona, since ye carry new life within your body, it will strengthen the vision of the bowl. I want you to be the only one to touch the bowl now that the water has been magically charged."

At Trish's wide-eyed look of confusion, Latharn pointed toward the sky at the fading vision of the almost fully waxed moon. The bright blue brilliance of the early morning was already washing it from the sky.

"The goddess cherishes all stages of womanhood, but she truly blesses those who lovingly carry within them a child. Fiona carries twins of the MacKay line. The magic already flows in their veins."

Fiona lifted the bowl from the pedestal, cradling it between her forearms. She eased her way across the stone floor, gasping as the water slopped dangerously close to the edge.

One step and then another, she edged her way across the room. She glanced to Latharn for direction. He didn't say a word, just bestowed a reassuring smile upon her and gestured toward the table.

Following behind her, Latharn joined Fiona at the table as she lowered the bowl. With his hands on her shoulders and a gentle nod for her to sit, Latharn covered her hands with his own. Her hands trembled beneath Latharn's strong grasp; her fingers spread upon the stone of the ancient bowl.

As he trailed his fingers up her arms, he circled around behind her. Hands settling upon her shoulders, Latharn closed his eyes. He'd connect with every power and every force to be found to reclaim his Nessa. The charged water pulsated in the ancient bowl and transmitted power to him through Fiona's impregnated body. As the magnified energy focused within his body, Latharn opened his eyes. With a nod to Trish and Brodie, he took a deep breath. He was ready to find his Nessa.

"Close the portal, Brodie. We must have complete darkness. Trish, please extinguish all the flames and then join your hands to Fiona's."

Brodie raised his hands to the sky and closed the room like a giant eyelid. As Trish extinguished every flame, an electrified darkness crackled through the room. The holy water trembled in the scrying bowl on the table and took on an eerie glow.

His hands still resting on Fiona's shoulders, Latharn stared unblinking into the shimmering water. Concentrating his powers, his hands warmed as his energy flowed through Fiona's body into the awaiting bowl.

"Blessed goddess, I call upon ye to open the veil to my sight. Remove the barriers. Part the mists. Guide us to the one I love. Blessed goddess, I call upon ye to show me who has stolen she who is mine." As Latharn's words stirred the waters, the prophecy bowl began to spin between Fiona's hands. Fiona gasped as it broke free of her hold and rose from the surface of the table. It levitated into the air until it floated a few inches above their heads. As the waters swirled, the energy from within the basin emerged into the total darkness just above the bowl's surface. An image of Nessa appeared in the hovering aura.

Latharn tensed as Nessa's bound and blindfolded form shimmered into view. He fought against the rage surging inside him. If his fury took hold of his consciousness, the visions would disappear. He

204

wanted to cry out as he witnessed Nessa tear the flesh on her wrists and wrench her hands free of the cutting ropes. He clenched his fists until his palms bled as Nessa burned her ankles free of the restraints.

Pride and satisfaction filled him to bursting as Nessa impaled Gabriel with the candelabra spear. His woman's passion was only rivaled by her courage. He was truly blessed by the goddess to have been matched with such a wondrous soul.

His elation was short-lived. Bile rose in his throat as he watched the dark *bana-buidhseach* emerge from Gabriel's lifeless body. He bit through his lip to stifle a shout as Nessa attacked the sorceress. He marveled at his beloved's strength and speed. He flinched as Nessa successfully dodged each of the destructive swirling balls of energy the crone lobbed at her head.

As Deardha disappeared and Nessa sank to the floor in exhaustion, Latharn shuddered and drew a ragged breath. "Show me how to find the one I love. Show me how to bring her home."

At first, the aura that had risen from the bowl flickered and hesitated as though about to fade away. The silver mist shimmered as though the veil of magic struggled against some unseen force and was unable to grant Latharn's request.

"Show me the way to the one I love. She carries my sons. She carries innocence within her womb. Ye must show me the way to make her safe. Ye must show me the way to bring her home!"

No sooner had Latharn bellowed the words did the mist strengthen and refocus. It showed the ancient stone mausoleum squatting behind the family chapel residing on the MacKay grounds. Nessa had been right under their very noses, mere yards from where they were currently sequestered in the library of mysteries high within the castle walls.

Jumping up from the table, Trish headed toward the door, only to be barred by Brodie's strong, restraining hands. As she tried squirming her way loose, Trish shouted in his face. "Let me go! You saw where she is. Fiona and I walked right past her when we went to get the holy water."

With a firm shake of his head, Brodie held her arms tighter, and led her back to sit at the table. "Ye saw the dark witch holding her captive. Ye saw the immense power of the crone and her ability to control the energies. We must carefully form a battle plan before we go rushing into the tomb."

Latharn raked his hands through his hair and locked his fingers behind his head as he paced about the room. "Aye, this time, it will definitely be a battle to the end. And not one I intend to lose."

Latharn turned to plunge his hands into the holy water. He flung the droplets into the air and bellowed into the darkness. "Ancestors, I call upon ye to join me! My goddess, hear the call of your son. Grant me my rights as brother to an immortal. Help me destroy this one from the shadows."

The droplets of holy water hung suspended and shimmered with a power all their own. Fueled by the authority of Latharn's summons, they splintered and spun through the air. Whirling above the heads of all in the room, the flowing field of moonlit energy sparkled as it gained momentum. As the hurtling vortex heightened in its intensity, the murmur of many voices rippled through the air. Thunder rumbled deeply; a rising battle cry sounded by all the gathering MacKays as they returned from centuries past.

All the voices melded into one strong and echoing mantra rumbling clearly throughout the room. "We stand ready, Laird MacKay. 'Tis time for vengeance against this evil foe. The *dhubh bana-buidhseach* brought down many of this clan. Ye have the power and the right to lead us. Summon us when ready. We will heed your call to send this abomination to the eternal abyss."

The storm of energy surrounded Latharn's body and melded itself into his being. The essence of his ancestors coursed through his body. His mind pulsed with the memories of thousands. His thoughts churned with the knowledge of eons, his ancestors' strengths now his own. His voice echoed with the voices of his kin as he gestured toward the horizon. "At dawn, we will not only take back what is ours, we shall also right a great many wrongs. As soon as the sun rises, we shall rip the *bana-buidhseach's* black soul from this existence and send it deep into the abyss."

Trish took a step back and addressed Latharn. "Latharn, once it's over. Once Nessa is safe...will all the rest of those MacKays...umm...go back where they belong?"

Latharn spread his hands to encase the entire castle and shook his head with a look of pride. "They belong here, Trish. This is the only place where they can find true peace and this is where they shall return. Ye needn't fear them. They're guardians to watch over and protect us. They honor us with their presence."

Fiona squeezed Trish on the shoulder and whispered her agreement. "We'll need their help in overcoming the Dark One. And 'tis also their natural right. She tortured many of them for centuries and suspended their souls from the peace promised beyond the grave."

Trish chewed her lower lip and glanced back over at the table at the now lifeless prophecy bowl. "I just wish there was a way we could somehow warn Nessa. I wish we could give her some hope that help is on the way."

Tinkling laughter trickled out of the darkness as two shimmering women materialized into the room. Each of them rested a hand upon Latharn's arms as they gazed up at him with pure adoration.

The youngest one affectionately snuggled her cheek to his shoulder and smiled to all in the room. "Have no worry, Trish. Our Nessa may be tiny but she is fearless. Did ye no see how the lass killed the gutless cur and then stood against the Dark One without batting an eye? Her bloodline does the MacKays proud. She is full of fire, that one is."

The older woman nodded her agreement. "Aye. Those sons she carries in her womb will inherit her fire as well. Latharn, you are going to finally pay for your raising. I'll have my revenge for all the gray hairs you placed on my head! I'm going to truly enjoy watching these grandsons add their stories to the MacKay legends."

At the shocked looks on Brodie, Trish, and Fiona's faces, Latharn spread his arms to encircle the two transparent women clinging to his sides. Nodding to the younger of the two, he inclined his head as he began the introductions. "This is my sister, Aveline, immortal consort to the sea god Mannanan mac Lir. How is your husband, my fine little sister? 'Twould be nice if he'd lend his help."

Aveline waved a glimmering finger in her brother's face as she gave a pert lift of her chin. "The ancestors and I are all the help ye'll be needing, my brother. We dinna want to take the joy of vengeance out of the hands of the MacKays."

Latharn turned to smile into the motherly gaze of the woman at his right and bent to press a kiss against her misty cheek. "This is my mother, Rachel MacKay. Why did ye not join the others inside my body?"

Her eyes flared with six centuries of rage as she hissed her reply. "Your father is within you, along with the others. I choose to stand apart and land a few strikes of my own. Hell hath no wrath like that of a mother avenging her son's life of pain."

"Well then." Trish threw up her hands. "I guess there's nothing to worry about. But how exactly do you go about yanking a soul out of a witch? From what we saw in the vision, she can change her form. Isn't it kind of useless to stab a hole in a shifting bank of mist?"

Brodie frowned as he turned the pages of the journal and scanned along the passages. As he glanced up, he locked eyes with Latharn's watchful gaze. "Nessa willna understand what is happening at first. But once it's over, hopefully, she'll see why it was done."

Trish tiptoed to peer over his shoulder. Her eyes widened as she read the instructions on the yellowed page. "You're right. If this is what you're going to do and the witch doesn't kill you, Nessa might be the one you need to fear."

CHAPTER

TWENTY-EIGHT

Curled up in a shivering ball on the floor, Nessa drifted in and out of sleep. There wasn't a square inch of her body not aching from the damp chill seeping up through the stones. She was starving and the brackish water in the bowl on the table had only made her thirst worse.

She'd reduced herself to licking the moisture off the stones in the corner. She'd gagged at the taste of the mildewed droplets, but at least it had helped moisten her dry, cracked lips. As near as she could figure, she had to survive maybe one more day.

Aveline had said Latharn would arrive on the dawn of the autumnal equinox. But with no windows, Nessa had to guess how much time had passed since she'd been locked away in the room. She also didn't know how long she'd been unconscious when Gabriel had spelled her into the place. All she knew was she was determined to survive. She'd be damned if that witch would win without a fight.

She felt a presence on the other side of the energy field. Nessa called out as she shielded her eyes. "Who's there?" she croaked. She tried a futile swallow to clear her throat and ran her dry tongue over her lips. "I know you're standing there watching me. I can feel your beady little eyes."

"It's beyond me what Latharn sees in such a rude little bitch. And one who's so plain and tiny as well. Ye have no tits. Ye have no curves. Ye are so small the man would split ye in two if he tried to give ye a good pounding. What did ye do to him while he walked in your dreams? How did ye trap his heart in your spell?"

Deardha had once again reverted to her beguiling form of pale ivory skin, voluptuous curves, and red, pouting lips. She cupped her hands under her heavy breasts and pushed them high as she arched her back. The creamy swells of tempting flesh threatened to overflow the deep vee of her low-cut gown. "I remember how I rode him well and drew his seed many a time with any part of my body he cared to explore. I made him hard with the slightest glance, and yet not once did he offer his heart to be joined with mine."

Nessa rolled her eyes and took a deep breath to control her seething emotions. How stupid did Deardha think she was? She knew Deardha baited her. The hag was trying to make her fly into a rage and waste what little strength she had left. Besides, even if Latharn had slept with the woman, it had been over six hundred years ago. Nessa shrugged a shoulder and pretended to stifle a bored yawn before she took the time to reply. "I could really care less about your technique. Obviously, it wasn't good enough to keep him or he never would've come looking for me."

Deardha's lips curled into a vengeful sneer. "Once I'm finished destroying the insolent MacKay, I'm going to take a great deal of pleasure in torturing you. The hour will be upon us soon when he makes his presence known. The sun has but to rise a wee bit higher above the horizon, then my revenge will truly be sweet."

Nessa rubbed her eyes to hide her surge of elation. Finding out that Latharn would be arriving soon was just the shot of adrenaline her waning strength needed. With newfound determination fueling her, Nessa pushed herself up from the floor. Shoving her hair out of her eyes, she took a deep breath and edged her way closer to the electrified door.

With a bounce in her step from her newfound hope, Nessa goaded Deardha. "Since you're so positive you're going to win, take down the barricades. Unless you're afraid?"

Deardha bared her teeth and opened the portal with a hissing wave of her hand. But the witch was prepared. As soon as the field disappeared, she lobbed an energy ball at Nessa's face.

Nessa dodged and slipped through the doorway. She scurried into the main chamber of the mausoleum before Deardha resealed the door. She glanced around the room, her heart in her throat. She needed a place to hide and catch her breath. There. Behind a reclining stone effigy.

She rolled behind it and pressed her back against the cold, damp stone, struggling to slow her pounding heart and figure out her next move. A shaft of sunlight pouring across the floor caught her eye. The door to the mausoleum had to be open. She was almost free. Just as she was about to bolt for the outer door, Latharn strode into the room.

His eyes flashed with eerie fire. Flexing his hands, the sheen of his well-muscled body glowed bronze in the light of the torches. Scowling around the room with a fearsome sneer on his face, Latharn exuded confidence for a battle.

Nessa vaulted herself at his body. Wrapping her arms around his neck, she planted tearful kisses all over his face. "It's about time you got here! Now fry that bitch with a lightning bolt or something so this nightmare will be over."

Latharn fought the urge to sweep her up into his arms and carry her off to the keep. He had to finish this or their family would never know any peace. He sucked in a deep breath as he heard the inner souls remind him of what needed to be done.

With a groan, he settled her to the floor and gently cupped her face in his hand. He peered intently into her eyes, silently placing his words in her mind. *No matter what happens ye must trust what I do and remember that I love ye with every bit of my soul. Can ye do that, Nessa? Make your promise to me within your mind. Ye will trust me in what I am about to do?*

A look of confusion replaced Nessa's relief as she clenched her fists. She'd heard his words even though he'd not spoken aloud, so silently, she replied, *I'm not so sure I like the sound of that, but... I promise, I trust you with all my heart.*

His thumb caressed the curve of her cheek. Latharn ached to crush her to his chest. But that was for later. He dare not overplay his hand. He must wage the war as they'd planned or lose everything to the darkness of the eternal abyss.

Lifting his head, Latharn put Nessa aside and raised his hands high. His deep voice echoed with the legions of all the MacKays, the walls trembled as he bellowed the MacKay battle cry. "*Bi Tren! Bi Treun!*"

"No need to shout, my dearest love. I may be eons old but I can still hear ye perfectly well." The enchantress floated her way out of the shadows and glided across the floor. The barest black silk gown clung to her body. The seductive shimmer accentuated each and every curve. Her ivory breasts swelled above the plunging neckline; her rose-tinted nipples strained through the edging of lace. The dress sank into the cleft of her thighs, hinting at the pleasure lying between.

"Tell me, Latharn. Ye havena seen me in hundreds of years. Compare me with that little milksop sniveling at your side. Remember how I pleasured ye in every way ye ever dreamed. Ye could have that again. We were good together, you and I."

Latharn eased toward her. He kept his back to Nessa and fixed Deardha with a heated glare. "If ye were willing to give me a second chance, why did ye ignore me in the crystal until a mere mortal set me free? Why did ye not come to me after the first hundred years, knowing how I'd do anything to be free of that crystal hell?"

Deardha's eyes flickered from Latharn and then to Nessa. She tossed her head at Nessa and spit in her direction. "Mere mortal, eh?

Ye know the Ways, my dearest love. Once a curse is set in motion, it must be allowed to play its course. But how do I know ye truly want me now? Ye could be but toying with me to gain the little bitch's freedom and once again toss me aside."

Latharn dropped his voice to a seductive tone and curled his lips into a beguiling smile. He stalked closer to the doubting woman, unwound his plaid, and dropped it to the floor. "Does it look like I don't remember what we did together? Tell me, my sweet seductress, do ye still like what ye see?"

The shaft of sunlight sculpted his muscled body, his enormous erection testament to the sincerity of his words. Latharn ignored Nessa's gasp at the sight of his state of arousal.

The crone's garment of shimmering black silk disappeared from her body. She floated to Latharn and stroked her hands up his chest. Turning, Deardha leered at Nessa then pulled Latharn's mouth down to cover hers.

"No!" Nessa cried out.

"Trust me, my love," he sent his voice to echo in her mind. *"This is all a part of the trap."*

Latharn pulled Deardha tighter into his arms, crushing her against his chest. He sank his hands into her hair, claiming her mouth roughly as if he meant to possess her. He devoured her lips. He dove his tongue deep into her throat. He ravaged her mouth until she melted against him. Finally, Latharn raised his head and clutched her by the nape of her neck.

"Pledge yourself to me, Deardha. Then I shall seed your womb while the mortal watches from the corner. Pledge your soul to me now so I can bury my cock into your delicious depths."

Molding her curves against Latharn's body, the seductress shot Nessa a gloating sneer. She shouted to the witness of the dawning equinox and threw her head back with a malicious laugh. "I pledge my oath to Laird Latharn MacKay. I open my soul and my womb to his seed. I lay myself bare and wait to accept whatever he gives. I pledge my soul to fill his every need."

Latharn carried her clinging body to the stone slab centered in the room and spread her upon the table. As he loomed over her between her thighs, he paused for just a moment. Stroking his fingertips along her ivory throat, Latharn dropped his voice to a husky whisper. He mesmerized her with his touch.

"By the power of your pledge, by the power of all the MacKays, I hold ye to your oath. I now give ye the gift of the eternal abyss and my need is that ye cease to exist."

As soon as Latharn uttered the curse, his mother, Rachel, appeared at the head of the stone. A vengeful smile curled her ghostly lips as she placed her hands on each side of Deardha's head.

Rachel leaned close, peered deep into the dark witch's eyes, and added her curse to her son's. "I join my powers to those of my son's. I condemn you to suffer well. I condemn you to see the pleasures outside the abyss. I condemn you to a window from hell."

Deardha's eyes filled with panic as their joined curses echoed over her head. Baring her teeth in a viperous hiss, she sputtered as Latharn's fingers crushed her throat. Clawing at his arm, her form changed as her powers diminished into the powerful aura surrounding them. The ivory of her skin faded to ash. Her enticing curves decayed to rotting flesh. Latharn clenched his teeth. He held his breath to avoid the rising stench as he maintained his stranglehold on Deardha's throat.

Shrieking and thrashing, her body deteriorated and putrefied beneath his powerful body. At last, she disintegrated into obsidian dust, leaving Latharn atop the tomb on all fours.

He climbed down from the stone, brushing off his hands as he bent to retrieve his plaid. As he wound it about his body, he took a deep breath and turned to face Nessa's accusing glare.

She smacked her fists upon his chest and pummeled the sculpted mountain of his abs. "You could've at least warned me you were going to have to seduce her to get her to let down her defenses!"

Latharn grabbed her wrists, enclosing her in his arms as he buried his face in the crook of her neck. "I did warn ye and told ye to trust me. Do ye not remember? There wasna any time to go into specifics. There was no other way for me to get to her soul. She had nearly made herself immortal with all her protection spells. I had to convince her to pledge her soul to me. I swear to ye, Nessa, it was the only way."

Nessa folded her arms and scowled up at him through a haze of jealous tears. "Well, a certain part of you sure seemed to enjoy it entirely too much. And it's not like it was the first time you'd ever been with her."

"Nessa." Latharn's voice dropped to a chiding whisper as he nuzzled at her cheek. "A man's cock can grow hard by a slight rub of his plaid. When I made the mistake of lying with that woman hundreds of years ago, it left me feeling as though I needed a verra hot bath. I felt tainted for days just from a few moments by her side. Her heart was as cold as a Highland winter and my body deadened to her touch. She couldna even give me a good hard rising back then much less bring me to spill my seed. How do ye think I figured out how to take down her defenses? She thought she had been able to capture my heart when I promised to seed her womb."

"So, she was lying about how she'd been able to please you? The fact that she couldn't make you...come...was why she'd cursed you to the witch's ball?" Nessa sniffed back her tears as the realization of his words sank in. She trembled a smile as it all made sense. She snuggled deeper into his arms, a contented warmth seeping through her body.

Latharn scooped her up into his arms and arched a quizzical brow. "Apparently, the fact that she couldna successfully start or finish the task didna set well with her pride. But enough of her, she will bother us no more. We need to get ye back to the castle. Food and a warm bed are waiting in our room. I fear ye will become ill from all ye have suffered."

Nessa yawned and cradled her head against his shoulder. She rubbed her nose with the back of her grimy hand. "Food and bed sound really great, but a hot bath would be so much better. I think I smell like a filthy goat."

His laughter rumbled beneath her head as Latharn cuddled her even closer against his chest. "I canna remember when ye have ever smelled better. Ye are as sweet in my arms as a meadow after a fresh spring rain."

Latharn passed the relieved faces of Trish, Brodie, and Fiona as he walked into the hall with Nessa in his arms. He didn't pause but continued toward the winding staircase that led to the laird's private rooms. "If ye'll excuse us, Nessa desires a hot bath, food, and bed. We shall be back down in a little while."

"In a little while, my ass," Trish observed with a snort. "We'll be lucky if we see them in a week."

TWENTY-NINE

"Mmm." Nessa hummed with contentment as she leaned back into his cradling embrace. The steaming water relieved her aching bones like a tonic easing the chill from her body. The lavender-scented vapor soothed her weary mind, while the heat from the pulsating jets relaxed her knotted muscles. Her eyes closed, and she smiled with a sigh as Latharn soaped her breasts. He nibbled at the tip of her ear as his hands circled to more enticing parts below.

"Feeling better?" he breathed into her hair as he lathered and massaged her body.

"This is heaven," Nessa purred, turning to float against his chest. His hardened body nudged against her belly as she wriggled her soapy torso against his most inviting feature.

"I never imagined a Jacuzzi tub this big in a castle as old as MacKay keep." As she slid her slippery body against his, Nessa hummed and nibbled against his throat.

"Aye," Latharn groaned, guiding her body over his and burying himself into her welcoming depths. "The clan did well to keep the place up with the times. I'll try to remember to tell them how well they've done."

Nessa ground her hips to settle him well and arched her back as she moaned with pleasure. She relished in his satisfying ability to fill her so nicely and hit all the right spots along the way.

Latharn ran his hands up her body to cup her slippery breasts. He thumbed and teased her dusky nipples until they perked in demanding pebbles. Rising to suckle these tempting treats, he ground his hips to delve even deeper. He groaned in satisfaction as her body clutched around him and he brought her to her peak.

He moved to her mouth and restoked her passions. Beneath the water, he cupped her hips. Latharn spread her legs with his hands and with tantalizing slowness, slid his body in and out. The jets of water surged in with him, vibrating his body with every slow and deliberate thrust.

Rising out of the water, his body still buried in her depths, Latharn carried her to the rug in front of the hearth. He spread her out among the piles of inviting pillows, growling as he pounded into her delicious heat. It was time. He could wait no more. He needed to take her with every emotion he'd ever felt. He'd come too close to losing her.

She was his. They were finally where they belonged. Nothing would ever separate them again. As Nessa shuddered with release, she called out to him, Latharn's husky growl echoed with her cries. Their heat flowed together. He gave and she took as their essences combined.

They snuggled together before the crackling fire, a warm throw pulled around their bodies. Latharn smiled down into Nessa's satisfied gaze and kissed the tip of her nose.

"Now ye know ye're about to marry a verra selfish man. I shouldha let ye eat and rest before I claimed your pleasures once more."

His face growing serious, Latharn brushed a kiss across her forehead. "But I needed to be inside ye. I needed to fill ye again, to mark ye as my own. We were meant to be this way, Nessa. We're a single soul, and when I thought I'd lost ye, I couldna stand it."

Nessa snuggled deeper into his arms. She sighed. Her heart swelled with emotions too deep for words. "I needed you to take me. I needed to feel you, to know you're still real and I'm not just having another dream. When I thought I'd never see you again I nearly gave up. I can't imagine life without you."

She traced a fingertip across his chest and stared into the flames. Then Nessa remembered this day was supposed to be the night of her rather unorthodox wedding. She released a shuddering sigh as she worried with the hair on his chest.

"We've missed the autumnal equinox. Is there any way your ancestors and the Auld One can attend our wedding if we have it on a regular full moon?"

Latharn stretched and lifted a cup of rich steaming broth down, from the table, holding it to Nessa's lips. "This day is not done. The sun is just now setting and the moon has yet to reach its zenith. If ye have the strength, we could still speak our vows to each other upon this very night."

Nessa grew quiet and avoided Latharn's gaze as she peered down into the steaming mug. "It's just...I wanted tonight to be special. I wanted to dress up for you. Now it'll just be plain old me."

"Nessa," Latharn chided as he cupped her chin in his palm and lifted her face to his. "There is no such thing as 'plain old you.' All I see before me is my beautiful bride. Ye shine in body as well as in soul."

He waved his hand over her body as he grazed her lips with his mouth. Latharn raised his head and watched her. He waited for her reaction as she became aware of the gown, he'd summoned for her.

The color of perfect sapphires sparkling in the sunlight. Nessa caught her breath as she ran her hands over the satiny folds. She moved to stand in front of the floor-length mirror, gasping at her reflection. The deep blue of the velvet collar, just off her shoulders, framed her ivory skin and mirrored her sparkling eyes.

Walking up behind her, Latharn placed his hand on the pulse beating at the base of her throat and his eyes became remote once again. With a satisfied smile, a teardrop-shaped sapphire harkened to his call and sparkled at the end of a golden chain around Nessa's neck. "This is my gift to you upon our wedding night. But its beauty pales in comparison with yours."

Nessa blinked against unshed tears, sniffing as she cradled the precious gem in her hands. She caught her lower lip between her teeth and took a slight step back. As Latharn moved beside her, the jewel glistening in her hands was forgotten. Running her gaze up and down his well-sculpted body, she couldn't resist licking her lips. "I'm ready to go up to the rooftop and say our vows, but don't you think you're slightly underdressed?"

Latharn glanced down at his naked body. With a grin, he waved his hands across his powerful torso. As soon as his hands lifted, he appeared in his family's colors. He hadn't worn his dress kilt since before Deardha's curse. He stood taller and squared his shoulders with pride.

His full Highland dress brought a gasp of pleasure from Nessa. His finest kilt hugged his narrow hips. He stood as though ready for battle. The whitest of tunics stretched taut across his broad chest, his plaid pinned to one shoulder with the original MacKay crest. His sporran and his father's claymore finished the vision of fierce Highlander 'til death.

With a bow, Latharn extended his arm, smiling as Nessa laid a trembling hand on his own. "Let us go to the rooftop. Our family waits to hear us speak our vows beneath the autumn moon."

As Latharn and Nessa emerged from the tower of the laird's private rooms, Fiona clapped her hands and cried, "I told ye they'd be here! I knew they'd still wed." She elbowed Brodie and fixed him with a superior glare.

"I never said they wouldn't be." Brodie snorted.

"It's about time." Trish raised her wine glass in a toast.

A cloudless night blessed the couple's gathering. The battlements were awash with the blue-white glow of the swollen autumnal moon. The cold, crisp air attested to the endless turn of the seasonal wheel. Winter was not far away. The kiss of frost bit the air.

Arm in arm, the couple wound their way across the stone walkway surrounding the top of the keep. A shimmering table bearing a golden braid materialized against the farthest wall facing the ocean.

Dozens of MacKay ancestors appeared along the inner wall of the castle. Everywhere, clansmen from ages past materialized out of thin air. It was as if they'd all been biding their time for the appropriate moment to make their presence known. Many of them had been victims of the evil sorceress. Some had once been starving children, grown to healthy warriors thanks to Latharn's rescuing hand. All were proud to make their presence known at the wedding of their newly freed laird.

Latharn's mother, Rachel, stood close beside the altar with a tall, striking man holding her close to his side. Inseparable in life, they were joined in death. Nothing would ever keep Caelan and Rachel apart.

Aveline stood beside her parents. She greeted Nessa with a glowing smile. With a wave of her hands, she adorned the walls and the altar with white roses tipped in silver. She smiled once more at Nessa and gave a regal tilt of her head. A circlet of white roses appeared in Nessa's hair with silver ribbons flowing down her back.

Thank you, Nessa mouthed, clutching Latharn's arm tighter. There were so many of them. So many MacKays. She had to remember to breathe.

Latharn squeezed her hand in the crook of his arm. "'Twill be all right, Nessa. Just feel the love that surrounds us."

Both of Latharn's brothers were also in attendance. They stood with their wives and many children that Latharn had only seen as he'd looked out of his crystal tomb.

Nessa caught her breath when she saw the man waiting to hear their vows. He seemed so very old. Latharn had told her he was the ancient MacKay, the original Auld One. Brought forth by the goddess, his magic strengthened by the addition of Rachel's talents to the bloodline, it was he who fathered all MacKay magic. He had been the first.

His waist-length hair and beard took on an eerie glow in the energy of the autumnal moon. His eyes burned with the knowledge of eons; his face as weathered as a sheet of ancient papyrus. He nodded once and glanced around at all the souls of the gathering, his authority commanded silence.

"Latharn. Nessa. Come forward to be joined. Ye have been patient in your quest." He extended his hand and held his upturned palm toward the couple, waiting for them to place their hands within his.

The ancient MacKay glanced down at the golden braid upon the table and then returned his eyes pointedly to the couple's hands. The rope obeyed the ancient one's silent command and wound its way around Nessa and Latharn's wrists.

With a satisfied nod, the Auld One looked to the moon, then down upon the couple's loosely bound hands. His booming voice echoed into the velvety night and traveled through space and time. "Joined in this life. Joined in the next. These two are now one. From this moment on, they are eternally bound. Through this life and beyond."

A shaft of pure energy shot down from the moon. It exploded as it hit the metallic loops encircling their hands. A surge of heat flashed through Nessa's body. A sense of elation fluttered through her heart as Latharn's hand tightened over hers. She'd never be alone again.

When the blinding light cleared, the rope had disappeared and left a glowing ring on each of their hands. Without a word, Latharn pulled Nessa into his arms and sealed the joining with a kiss. When he raised his head, he smiled down into Nessa's misting eyes.

"I love ye more than ye will ever know. Ye have always been my own. Now and forever. Through this life and into the next. Now that we have found each other and performed the joining rite, we will never be separated again."

Nessa caught her breath, holding his face between her hands as tears threatened to overflow. "I never thought as long as I lived that I would ever find this much happiness. I'm so glad you found my soul."

EPILOGUE

With a contended sigh, Nessa settled deeper into the pillows and watched Latharn silhouetted against the window. "I hope you're proud of yourself, my dearest husband."

He stood with his head bowed, mesmerized by the squirming bundle squeaking in his arms. "I am verra proud, my love. Proud of my wondrous wife—and I am truly humbled." He walked back to the bed, settled the wriggling bundle back in the pillows beside her, and brushed a kiss across her forehead.

"Are ye ready for me to go down and get the others? I am sure they heard them. I'm afraid our sons have verra strong lungs." Latharn grinned across the bed at the little bundles as they kicked and squirmed beside their mother.

"Not yet. Wait just a little longer. Right now...they're still just ours." Nessa reached over and touched a tiny pink fist waving in the air. Her emotions swelled, flooding her with a serene glow. She never dreamed she'd be this happy.

"We havena decided on their names." Latharn eased down on the bed beside her to cup a tiny head in his massive hand. "I rather liked Trish's suggestion. She said we should go out to the loch and the name that bellows the best across the water is the name we should choose. She seems to think a son of mine will be having his name constantly shouted. Can ye imagine a son of mine getting into a bit of mischief? Why would she say such a thing?"

Nessa rolled her eyes. "Oh, I can't imagine. Not a son of Latharn MacKay." She pushed herself higher on the piles of pillows and added, "And what's this I hear from Fiona and Brodie about catching you in the nursery giving lessons to the twins?"

Latharn arched a brow, a twinkle in his eye as he gave Nessa a sideways glance. "Lessons, you say?"

"Yes, lessons," Nessa repeated. "It appears that although the twins can't even sit up by themselves, they're getting quite good at making objects appear out of thin air."

"Truly?" Latharn fixed Nessa with a look of wide-eyed innocence. "Such magic is verra good for one's so young."

"Latharn!" Nessa scolded. Then she couldn't hold back a smile. He enjoyed his time with his family so much. He'd been imprisoned from those he loved for so long. He embraced his loved ones and cherished every moment to the fullest. Latharn never let an opportunity slip by.

The bundle at the farthest side of the bed yowled, starting a chain reaction with his brothers. With a resigned sigh, Nessa shook her head. "I guess we might as well introduce them now. It doesn't sound as though we're going to keep our secret any longer."

Latharn grinned and pecked a kiss on the end of her nose. "I love ye, Nessa."

"And I love you, Latharn."

Pausing at the top of the staircase, Latharn grinned, reveling in the strength of his sons making their displeasure known. Fine strapping lads! Every one of them. He and Nessa were truly blessed.

Trish held up her fingers. "One, two, three...three of them. I knew it! I win the pot! I knew Latharn wouldn't let Brodie beat him with twins." Running across the room, Trish reached up on the mantel to retrieve the money out of an earthen jar.

Latharn shouted down from the top of the stair, roaring the MacKay battle cry until the dust shook loose from the rafters. His laugh rumbled across the room as he waved them all up the stairs.

"Brodie! Fiona! Trish! Come and greet my sons! And Trish, put back the money jar. Ye canna count your winnings just yet. Come and see. Ye canna tell anything by counting the number of cries."

Curiosity registering on all their faces, they scrambled up the stairs. As he ushered them inside, Latharn clapped Brodie on the back and hugged the women until their faces turned red.

Nessa greeted them all with a tired smile. She sat propped up among the piles of pillows, two sons on one side and two sons on the other. Four wriggling little bundles surrounded her on the bed, their faces still red and angry from emerging from their mother's warm comfortable womb.

Nessa smiled down at her sons and caressed each of their downy heads. "I think we're going to need some more help in the nursery. The twins and now these four are a little much for one nurse."

As she stroked the velvety softness of the nearest baby's cheek, she felt her weary smile widen. "By the way, Trish...didn't you say you were taking Dugan MacKay on a picnic today to show him the goddess well?"

Trish nodded as she bent to pick up one of the babies. Pressing a kiss to his tiny fist, she looked up and smiled. "Yep. We're going there this afternoon. Why do you ask?"

With a knowing wink, Nessa fixed Latharn with a meaningful glance, then pointedly looked at each of their sons. She shook her head then snuggled down into the pillows as she pulled the rest of her babies close.

"You might want to take care about getting close to that water in the presence of a MacKay."

READ ON FOR AN EXCITING EXCERPT FROM:

The Highlander's Fury
A MacKay Clan Legend
Faolan's Story
Book 3

CHAPTER 1

Ciara leaned against the doorpost in front of the preoccupied man, shifting her awareness as easily as a sigh. She ensured she didn't cast the slightest shadow across the pristine office floor. She held her breath to suppress a giggle. The fool hadn't the slightest inkling of her presence. With a lazy blink, she kept herself invisible to her prey hunched behind the gleaming desk.

Repositioning against the door facing, Ciara allowed herself a languid stretch. The man ignored her, intent on his computer screens. After all these years, the sheer ease of it almost filled her with boredom. Bending particles came as simple as drawing breath. Blinding mortals to her presence was second nature. She *so* enjoyed stalking her victims before moving in for the kill. Once she punished her chosen sinners, the thrill of the hunt disappeared.

And there he sat in his cold, stark office, her latest offender, totally oblivious to the silent blast of his personal judgment horn. Ciara had struggled with indecision before settling on this particular man. There had been so many from which to choose. The twenty-first century was rife with black-hearted mortals consumed by insatiable greed and cruelty. She'd grown so weary of all the horrors she'd seen. Their continued creativity at torturing each other sickened her beyond reason.

This one had infuriated her for hours. She'd fumed and shifted between the dimensions while he'd thoroughly enjoyed watching the people he'd fired make their final trip out the door. She'd nearly revealed herself when he laughed aloud as they stumbled with their pitiful cardboard boxes holding their personal belongings. He had snickered and clinked his coffee cup against the glass of the window in a toast as the cabs had passed them by.

Yes. He was the one. She would punish this mortal tonight. Her rage had seethed into vindictive surety when she'd overheard his latest phone conversation. He'd cinched a deal with another corrupt soul to store barrels of hazardous chemicals in an adjoining state's closed landfill. He'd save the company millions by disposing of chemicals illegally in an abandoned dump. Transporting the chemicals wasn't a problem either. He had the transportation cabinet of his home state splitting the kickback with the transportation cabinet on the receiving end.

Ciara decided this mortal deserved a most painful death. She would terrorize him first, build the suspense, and then end it with a slow and agonizing finale. She hadn't decided how she would finish him off. She'd just play that one by ear. She would wait until the last office worker had left for the day and then playtime would begin.

Keeping her essence suspended between the dimensions, Ciara hovered through the halls until the only sound heard through the sterile building was the clicking echo of a single computer keyboard. The *tick tick tick* came from the lush corner office at the farthest end of the hall. The hour had grown late and her excitement had built as all the worker bees from the rows of identical gray cubes slogged their way through the elevator doors.

Now Ciara studied her prey as he leaned back in the squeaking depths of his plush leather chair. His eyes narrowed and the light of the monitors lit up his face as he scanned the reports flashing across the three computer screens lined across the gleaming black desk. With a cynical curl of his lip and a click of the mouse, he smiled and leaned closer to the screen on the right. From the gleam in his eye, Ciara knew the greedy bastard had found another set of victims.

"Let's see what you're up to now, my fool," Ciara purred as she entered his mind.

In the annals of his thoughts, she read his plan to drain his employees' retirement accounts. Ciara's rage boiled through her veins when she saw his plot of funneling the income into an overseas resource where the shareholders would be none the wiser. Then he would shut down another division and pocket more millions by laying off hundreds of workers.

Ciara recoiled from the CEO's mind as though she'd just touched a piece of rotted flesh. This mortal sickened her. He was just as evil as a serial killer. He had made his execution even easier. It was time she made her presence known.

She materialized in the doorway, still leaning against the frame, drumming her fingertips atop her folded arms. "The levels of greed to which you humans rise never cease to amaze me."

Startled, the man jerked, his eyes squeezing closed as though she had struck him. Choking on the mouthful of coffee he'd just gulped; he spewed a shower of the amber liquid as he threw the cup across the room. "Who the hell are you?" he sputtered and coughed. "How did you get in here?"

Ciara slipped out of the doorway and sauntered into the room. She adored the sound of fear in her victim's voice. It played sweeter than the softest aria to her ears. Shrugging her long braid over one shoulder, she smoothed a hand down her hip as she purred, "I am known by many names. But for the purpose of our little meeting, why don't you just call me 'Vengeance'?"

With a shaking hand, he fumbled at the receiver of the phone. The man's face whitened when he held it to his ear.

"What's wrong, baby? No dial tone?" Ciara stretched across the desk, plucked the receiver out of his hand, and swung it like a pendulum in front of his face. Oh, she loved it when their eyes rolled back in their heads and their faces paled to that lovely shade of pasty gray.

He ripped his cell phone out of his pocket; his eyes widened as the words *No Service* lit up across the readout on the screen.

Yanking open the side drawer on his desk, he glanced first at Ciara then looked down. He withdrew a pistol with a shaking hand and pointed it at her chest. "You take one more step and they'll write any name you want on a toe tag for the morgue."

Oh, this one played the cat-and-mouse game better than the time she had tortured that serial rapist. Ciara smiled her most wicked smile. She loved it when they got cocky! Tossing her head back, she spread her arms wide, then released her best chilling laughter to echo off the wall to wall windows as she gave a teasing wiggle of her hips. "Take your best shot, baby. Do you think you can hit me from here or do you need me to take a few steps closer?"

Beads of sweat appeared across the man's face then rolled down his heavy jowls as he shook the muzzle of the gun in her face. "Don't think I won't kill you. I own the mayor of this city and every cop in the surrounding precincts. With my money, I don't have to worry about prison. I can do anything I want."

With a bored roll of her eyes, Ciara leaned forward and rested her hands on his desk. Wriggling her nose, she brought her face so close she almost touched the tip of his nose and crooned, "Go ahead, sweetheart. Do whatever you like. After all, you should get the most out of your last few moments on earth. Consider it your last wish before your execution. Kind of like having your last meal before you fry."

The man jerked as though trapped in an uncontrollable seizure. He emptied the chamber of the gun. As he fired the last round, his jaw fell to his chest, and he let the pistol crash to the floor.

Ciara waited, tapping her red, manicured nails atop the computer monitor. With a bored yawn, she stretched and smoothed the dents from the bullets out of her shirt then bestowed a wicked smile upon him. "Okay. My turn! Now let's figure out the best way to punish you for all your naughty little deeds. Where shall we start this evening? There are so many fun things to choose from."

Scooting back from his desk, he back-pedaled his chair into the farthest corner against the darkened window. The wild-eyed man stared up into her face, his hands white-knuckled into fists on the chair. "Who the hell are you? What do you want? You want money? I've got a ton of cash over in the safe. You want drugs? I can get them too. Just tell me what you want. Whatever you want it's yours. Just leave me the hell alone!"

Ciara couldn't resist a sadistic laugh as she circled her way around the desk. Good. The fool finally understood he should fear her. Let the games begin. "I already told you what I want, baby. You really should pay attention when your executioner is speaking. You can call me Vengeance. I am here to administer justice. I want nothing from you but pain and a great deal of suffering. You've not only raped the earth with the illegal chemicals you've dumped but you've robbed and cheated your own kind. You've stolen the meager wages your employees have slaved for and you've left them in complete ruin and disgrace. Many have suffered pain, starvation, and even death by your hand. Tonight, it's *your* turn to pay up."

She held the shaking man transfixed in her gaze as she rested her hands on the arms of his chair. "Tonight, we're going to discover your greatest fears and then we're going to see how well *you* face them."

The man lunged at her throat. His beefy hands shook as he grabbed her by the neck; his eyes widened as he crashed back against the wall.

Ciara loved it when they looked so surprised. Just another perk of being an immortal Fury. They never realized how powerful she was until it was much too late. Dragging him up from the floor, she settled him back into his chair then took his fleshy chin in her hand. She lifted his face, turned him first one way, then the other, studying him as though she held the jowls of the prize pig at the fair. Her eyes narrowed as she gazed into his watery little eyes. "So, you fear losing your money. Well, no big surprise there. What else? I know a man like you must have many fears."

Ciara grabbed his tie and wheeled him like a pull toy back to the front of his desk. With a flick of her hand at the computers, she brought up his accounts on all three wide screens. With a laugh, she zeroed them all out.

"Watch this." She winked at him and brought the screens up again one at a time. She pointed to each of the monitors and yanked his face closer to the desk as she explained, "Pay attention, now. Okay, that account has now transferred all funds to the World Wildlife Fund. This account has transferred all funds to Feed the Children and last but not least, this account has replenished your employees' 401k's with an added bonus to a new healthcare package."

The man sputtered as the tie tightened around his neck, his face turned a reddish purple and a vein in his forehead visibly throbbed.

Ciara grinned and yanked again.

The man clawed at the choking knot at his throat. "Fine. Now just let me go. You've paid me back, now just let me go and get the hell out of my life."

"Oh, I think not." Ciara clucked her tongue and forced a chiding frown across her face as she spun him back and forth in the chair. She pulled the tie even tighter, perched on the edge of the desk, and crossed her legs in his face. "We're not done. You see, I discovered one more fear while slumming around in your mind."

After kissing the tips of her fingers, she slowly traced them down the side of his face. In the wake of her touch, a trail of blistering pustules festered across his skin.

"You see, I discovered your greatest fear next to losing your money is the fact you seem to be deathly afraid of the toxic chemicals your company dumps into the earth. You're afraid you're going to end up with cancer and your flesh will rot off your bones."

The CEO paled even further, to an ashen, unhealthy gray. His breath came in quick, uneven gasps and his eyes whitened as they rolled back in his head. As he fell over limp, the only thing keeping him in his chair was Ciara's relentless grip on his tie.

"Dammit! Don't you dare die until I give you permission." Ciara yanked on the man's body and pushed him back in the chair. She pounded on his chest. The color drained even further out of his skin. His lifeless body slumped over to one side.

"Ye seem to be losing your touch, Vengeance. Ye used to keep them terrified for hours before ye allowed them to die." Alec's sarcasm floated down from the rafters where he sat preening the pinfeathers beneath one of his out-stretched wings.

With a disgruntled huff, Ciara didn't bother looking up at the raven. Alec always had impeccable timing. "Don't start with me, Alec. I'm in a black mood since I've just been robbed of my night's entertainment."

Brushing her hands together, she stared down at the man. He lay twisted in a pitiful lump, hunched over sideways in his chair. Ciara scowled as she circled his body. With a growl, she kicked at his foot. It would take just a twitch of her brow to rip his limbs from his body, just one tiny twitch. But he'd robbed her of any satisfaction in the act since he'd taken the coward's way out. "Why have they evolved into such piteous creatures, Alec? Why have they become so ruined with greed and cruelty?"

Alec hopped down from his perch on the rafter and onto the desk. He stared at the man slumped over in the chair. "It's just their nature to be greedy. I can't believe ye would even bother asking after all these centuries of punishing them for their wicked ways."

Alec jerked his glossy black head, then cast a nervous glance around the room. He resettled his wings across his back and strutted his way across the desk. "Some of them, I mean. Only some of them are born to be greedy. Ye have also met a good many of them through the years that ye have found to be pure of heart. Remember there were plenty of good ones too."

Alec hopped closer. He stretched and flapped his great, dark wings their full span. His ebony feathers shone beneath the fluorescent lights. "By the way, I have a message for ye. The mothers bid ye come to them before the next new moon." He swaggered along the edge of the desk, speared a paperclip in his beak, and tossed it across the room.

Ciara smoothed an escaped curl away from her face as she turned to study Alec where he rummaged through the shiny objects scattered across the desk.

The news of a summons from the keep of the goddesses did not bode well at all. And why was he acting so nervous? The bird weighed each of his words before he spoke as though fearing he might be overheard. Something was up. There was no way this summons could be good news. Ciara slid her hands into the back pockets of her jeans and sauntered closer to the fidgeting raven.

"Why do they want me to return to the keep? What did they tell you, Alec?"

Pecking at the keys on the computer keyboard, Alec paused in his rifling to fix her with a beady eyed glare. "All I know is they want to speak with ye, and they ask that ye come to them with all due haste. Ye know they are not in the habit of taking me into their confidence. I'm no' exactly their favorite being."

"That's never stopped you from finding out the truth before. Remember the Stones?" Ciara gave him an encouraging wink as she nudged the great black bird. Alec had stolen the secret of bending time and space from Brid and shared it with the mortals. Ciara shivered when she remembered Brid's anger. It was a wonder Alec had survived.

"Aye. I remember the Stones. It's a wonder I am standing here talking to ye at all. I'm surprised they didna curse me into some sort of recurring wart on the crack of some Highlander's arse. At least all they did was ban my ability to return to human form."

Ciara glanced down at her clothing and groaned. She'd have to discard her favorite twenty-first century clothes. The silky black T-shirt, the curve hugging jeans...the enlightened plane would literally shudder if she didn't change her apparel. Once she'd shown up donned in skintight leather and the veils of the keep had frozen into solid sheets of the blackest ice. The coldness of the goddesses' combined disapproval had frosted everything over within the enlightened plane for eons.

"Alec, I know you. There is no way you would just blindly follow their commands. You've never been able to mind your own business. Your inability to adhere to complete obedience is what stripped you of your powers to return to human form in the first place. I can see the wheels turning in that wicked little mind of yours. Now tell me what you know."

Alec shifted from the shape of a raven into the form of a peaceful snowy owl. With an innocent blink of his wide owl eyes, he swiveled his head away. "Ciara—I mean, Vengeance—I am truly hurt that ye've taken such a tone with me. Haven't I served ye faithfully all these years, for more centuries than I care to recall?"

Suspicion surged through her being. *Ciara?* He'd called her Ciara. Ciara shoved her face so close it almost touched the snowy owl's hooked beak. "Ciara? No one's called me by that name in centuries! Not even Cerridwen or Brid. Out with it, Alec! Tell me what you know about this summons, or I swear to you, I will seal the veil to this world when I leave and you'll be trapped here forever in this madness."

She couldn't believe he'd called her that! She had abandoned her given name eons ago when she'd grown so frustrated with the charge she'd been given. At first, she'd felt honored when the goddesses had asked her to travel through the worlds, righting wrongs and punishing evil. However, as the ages passed, the corruption coursing through the many worlds in her care had only grown more severe.

The futility of it all ate away at her heart. She'd had to abandon most of the worlds and concentrate on saving just one. It had torn at her very being to abandon so many innocents. But the evil and greed taking over the realities was more then she could master alone.

Ciara had settled on saving Danu's mortals. She'd seen the depths of love and creativity these complex beings could attain. But as the world matured, the humans changed for the worse, and Ciara couldn't understand why.

Her prey tonight was just one example. He was just one of the millions who'd been eager to destroy and corrupt without a second thought. He'd destroyed the lives of his own as well as the lives of countless other creatures unfortunate enough to cross his path. Ciara hadn't found a shred of remorse in his heart. His soul festered black and rotten. Without hesitation, he'd reduced the lives he'd tainted to mere numbers flashing on a screen.

Ciara had grown weary; her retaliations became more futile with every passing century. She might save a few innocents with her actions, but she had begun to think her quest a waste of time. With every tyrant she felled, ten more sprang to take their place. Danu's world had become a place of darkness.

Drawing a shaking breath, Ciara extended her arm to the owl and glanced around the bleak heartlessness of the corporate office. "I'm sorry, Alec. You know I would never abandon you to this hopeless world. But please, I *need* you to tell me what they want. I know you have to have an inkling of what they've plotted. You've always been my best spy."

Alec returned to his favorite shape of a raven and hopped onto her arm. He stretched and rubbed his beak against her chin, as he chirruped in her ear. "I know ye wouldna leave me behind in this place. Ye still have a heart as big as the universe even though ye think ye buried it long ago. But truly, Ciara, all I can tell ye is they say they have a new charge for ye, and it seems much better than this sorry business ye already do. They said something about changing the course of mankind's destiny. I swear to ye that is all I truly know."

"Mankind's destiny," Ciara repeated, her gaze falling to rest on the lump of the dead man sprawled across the floor. "Mankind's destiny is to be consumed by his own greed until he destroys everything in his path."

Alec churled and crooned, rubbing his feathered head against her cheek. "Come with me, Ciara. At least hear what they have to say. They know ye need a respite from your charge. They know ye wear thin with this duty they've given ye. Perhaps they just want to ease your pain and give ye a bit of rest."

Ciara drew a heavy breath. "All right, Alec. Let us leave this place and see what they have to say. Perhaps the goddesses have thought of a better way to save this misbegotten world and all that's in it."

CIARA SHIFTED into the dimension in front of the gilt-encrusted mirror gracing the entryway wall. She examined her glamour one last time to ensure she'd not throw the fortress into another ice age. Her properly clothed reflection smiled back at her with an approving nod. Her mothers would find this attire acceptable, much better than the leather chaps and spike-heeled boots of her last visit. Brid hadn't quite appreciated the biker chick look.

Smoothing her hands through the fluttering layers, Ciara twirled in front of the mirror. The silken gown floated around her body, the deep violet veils swirling about her curves highlighting her fair, creamy skin. She'd wrestled her mane of dark curls into an intricate braid pulled away from her face. She'd seen the Goddess Brid restrain her own flaming tresses into this same complicated weave resembling the knots of the Celts. Ciara patted her hair and turned once more in front of the mirror.

Yes. She felt sure her mothers would approve of this presentation. She'd modeled her proper appearance after her mothers' attire. They might be immortals but they never changed when it came to style.

Drawing a deep breath, Ciara closed her eyes and shivered before turning to make her way out to the balcony. The scent of heather wafted through the air mixing with the briny crisp air filtering in from the sea. Ciara smiled. Visions of magical Alba danced through her mind at the very scent. Brid and her beloved Scotland. Even here in the goddesses' keep, Brid kept her favorite things close to her heart by stroking the senses.

Ciara tapped her fingertips atop the railing of the balcony and glanced around the keep. This was ridiculous. Just because immortals had an eternity, why did they always make everyone wait? She peered through the corridors, fidgeting back and forth across the balcony. They asked her to hurry and yet now they made her wait. With a sigh, Ciara paced, flipping her hands through the layers of her gown. Some things never changed. They had summoned her, said it was urgent, and now there was no sign of anyone about. Ciara huffed, drumming her fingers along the railing a bit harder. Cerridwen and Brid always had a flair for the dramatic.

She paced back and forth across the striated black-marble floor, her footfalls clicking with every step. It had been several centuries since she'd been back to the goddesses' keep but very little about the fortress had changed. Watching the three obsidian dragons holding the brazier of eternal burning coals in the center of the room, Ciara darted back and forth across the room at different speeds until she bored with taunting the beasts. Their glowing red eyes followed her every move. She'd never truly trusted those three. She'd seen Cerridwen leaning close to them once and nodding as though they'd whispered in her ear.

At the sight of the crimson veils fluttering down from the unseen ceiling, Ciara's curiosity grew. The brilliant veils rippled and billowed in the gentle breeze sifting in from the sea. The mother goddesses' mood determined the color of the veils. Whatever was going on, Mother Brid's emotions must be in a stir to color the keep in such a vivid hue.

The black marble floors, the matching columns, and wide steps sparkled with flecks of silver and gold but at least the keep itself appeared to be warm. That in itself was a good sign. If the mothers were displeased, the entire keep would be a solid sheet of ice.

Alec lit upon the banister, strutting and cocking his raven's head first one way then the other. He grumbled a low chirrup when he glanced across the room and spied Cerridwen's sow and hen. At the sight of Cerridwen's favorite creatures, Alec puffed out his chest and preened his feathers into glistening blue-black perfection.

Cerridwen's glossy black hen crooned and chortled as she pecked about the room. After much strutting about, she appeared to decide there was nothing of interest among the glittering striations of silver in the marble. With a contented churdle, she snuggled down into the nest of satiny pillows beside the softly snoring sow.

"It is beyond me what Cerridwen sees in those creatures. They have absolutely no personality whatsoever." Alec kept his coarse voice low as he pressed his beak to Ciara's ear.

Ciara leaned close, nodding in the direction of the cauldron. She turned to whisper next to the ruffled feathers of his head. "You had best mind your thoughts as well as your tongue, jealous Alec. Cerridwen doesn't need to overhear your voice to know what's in your heart."

Rich laughter danced upon the air as a hauntingly beautiful voice floated through the veils. "Ye were always wise to our ways, dearest Ciara. Alec would do well to mind your words."

Ciara and Alec turned to greet the voice's owner as the goddess Cerridwen emerged from her private chambers deeper within the keep. Black silk floated around the lissome goddess's body like dark mist swirling through a stand of trees. Her long hair flowed around her pale, delicate face, the dark tresses mirroring her sparkling black eyes.

"Mother Cerridwen, you honor me with your words. 'Tis so good to see you again." Ciara bowed her head and held out both hands to the goddess, awaiting her welcoming embrace.

"And what about me, my child? Have ye no greeting for your other mother who helped draw ye from the mists?"

Brid's coppery, bright hair also flowed free, her fiery locks lifting as though caught in a delicate breeze. Her deep green eyes shone with love and pride as she held her arms wide for Ciara's embrace.

"Mother Brid." Ciara rushed to embrace the powerful goddess and pressed an affectionate kiss on each of her ivory cheeks. "I didn't realize until I saw you both how long it had been since I'd last felt your embrace."

Brid grasped Ciara's shoulders and held her back, looking her up and down with a critical gaze. "I'm verra glad to see ye've discarded the leather attire and befitted yourself with much more appropriate wear."

A caw of laughter echoed through the chambers. Alec ducked his head as the three women spun on him with reproving glares. "Sorry, won't happen again. I'll just be over here on the balcony looking out at the lovely waves."

Ciara hid her smile behind her hand. She rubbed the tip of her nose as she turned to face Brid and Cerridwen. "Tell me, my mothers. What is so important that you would summon me here before the next new moon?"

Cerridwen inclined her head, as she floated over to her cauldron. She beckoned for Ciara and Brid to follow. "Ye never were one to dance about with words, Ciara. Ye always did get straight to the marrow."

Brid rested her hand on Ciara's shoulder, motioning toward the dark water within the massive cauldron. As all three women stared down into the inky depths, images stirred upon the surface.

A desolate world, void of any life at all, floated burned and gray upon the surface of the water. The land lay bleak, sterile, and inhospitable. Ruins of buildings, blackened spikes of trees, and nothing but barren ground appeared as far as the vision spanned.

Brid shuddered as she peered down at the image. She wilted against the rim of the cauldron as though the sight of the destroyed world below sapped the very strength from her body. "This is one possibility of mankind's future, of Danu's world, if we are unable to change the current course of events. The mortals' world and all life upon it will cease to exist. When the destruction is complete that plane of existence will be permanently removed from among the Veils of Realities."

With a heavy sigh, Ciara lifted her gaze. She hugged her body against the chilling desolation portrayed within the vision. "I don't doubt this, my mothers. And I don't think this destiny is far from where I have been battling in the year 2011."

Cerridwen reached out and stirred the waters to dispel the dire prediction. With a steady hand, she passed her palm above the cauldron as though soothing a nightmare from the mind of a child. As she did this, another image shimmered, a brighter world filled with hope. This world spawned green and full of life. Joy swelled in the colorful auras surrounding every being on this new plane. "If we can ensure the Auld Ways are never forgotten, if we can strengthen the respect for Danu's earth, we can nurture the reality ye now see and watch it come to pass upon this plane."

Ciara pressed her palms against the cool rim of the cast iron cauldron as she surveyed the peaceful world. With a sigh, she pondered the image on the waters. "I've been battling the malevolence and greed down through the centuries and haven't been able to change a thing. I've tracked them all down and destroyed them in their nests. It hasn't made a difference. It hasn't changed the course of events or swung the odds a bit in our favor."

Brid wrapped an arm around Ciara's shoulders and gave her a consoling hug. "Ye've fought valiantly against every evil in the world. No one denies ye have been loyal to your charge. But Cerridwen and I have thought of another way that we could possibly change the course of this world."

At Brid's nod of encouragement, Cerridwen passed her hand over the waters once again. A new image shimmered into view. Wild. Furious. Pure, unadulterated strength. The man's aura pulsated power and control. Sleek black brows knotted over angry flashing eyes. Hair the black of a raven's wings perfectly matched his surly demeanor. His square jaw was shadowed with a day's growth of beard. Nostrils flared on a slightly crooked nose that must have been broken at some earlier time. Full, sensuous lips curled back into a sneer. Teeth clenched in barely held rage. Ciara didn't know who this compelling human was but it was obvious he was sorely displeased.

"Who is he?" Ciara leaned closer to the waters. This mortal might be worth her interest.

Brid smiled, nodding her approval. "That is the chieftain of Clan MacKay, their powerful and well respected leader, Faolan."

Now she knew they plotted something. Brid loved dabbling with Scotland. Straightening from the cauldron's edge, Ciara crossed both arms over her chest and fixed the smiling goddesses with a suspicious glare. "Laird Faolan MacKay. And in what year exactly does Laird MacKay reside and what does he have to do with your solution for Danu's world?"

Cerridwen circled the massive black cauldron, bent to scoop her hen from the nest of pillows, and cradled the chirruping bird to her chest. "Ye are currently looking at the year 1415 in the Highlands of our beloved Scotland. As to our solution, perhaps Brid could explain the plan we've put together better than I."

Brid turned to glide across the polished floor and held out her hand for Ciara to join her at the balcony. Gazing out across the mist swirling over the dusky waves, she smiled as the whorls of sparkling fog formed into her beloved eternal spirals. "The MacKay family has been very dear to my heart now for many a year. Many of their clan are mystically blessed, and they have kept the legends and rituals alive. However, Faolan has experienced a great deal of loss in his life. Grief and heartache have turned him away from the Ways. He has abolished the workings of magic and ritual among the clan and has forbidden the practicing of the old religions."

Ciara ran her hands across the smooth surface of the railing; the velvet-like marble soothed her emotions with its cool, solid touch. The life force embedded deep in the stone called out to her, begging her to save the beloved earth and all its denizens. "So, you want me to talk to him? Convince him to turn back to the Ways? You do realize diplomacy is not one of my strongest traits? And just how exactly is getting one man to return to the old religions going to save the fate of the world?"

Ciara tapped her fingertips on the railing. She couldn't believe they'd called her back through the veils for this. She could've vanquished at least three dozen unrepentant mortals and punished who knows how many lower level immortals in the time she'd been here at the keep. Why had they called her here for this task? Cerridwen and Brid were slipping.

Cerridwen joined them at the railing after shooing the fussing black hen back through the veils into the room. Cerridwen's gaze met with Brid's and she gave a subtle nod.

"We need a child, Ciara. Fathered by the magical wolf of the MacKays and blessed with the talents of an immortal mother. Such a child could help ensure the old religions would never be forgotten and the magic would never die." With this statement, Brid faced Ciara and waited for her reaction.

They couldn't be serious. Ciara opened her mouth then closed it again. No. Surely, they had something else in mind. Her mothers couldn't possibly be suggesting what she thought they had just said. She looked to Cerridwen and then turned back to Brid. Taken aback at what she thought Brid proposed, she repeated the words to ensure she understood what Brid had in mind. "Fathered by the wolf? Born of an immortal mother? Are you actually asking me to join with that mortal from the Highlands and bear the man a child?"

"Is he not pleasing to the eye, Ciara? Any man able to hold such fury must be capable of great passion as well." With a wave of her hand, Cerridwen floated the cauldron to where they stood so they could gaze once more down upon his image.

Faolan MacKay electrified the waters. He was dark and dangerous, a delightful temptation to watch. The man towered over most in his clan, the breadth of his shoulders balancing his mountainous height. Ciara's palms itched to touch the cut of his muscles straining against the leather of his tunic. Her gaze traveled lower, appraising his fine narrow hips and his powerful, well-muscled legs. Cerridwen was right. Faolan pleased the eye and Ciara would bet her finest torque he pleased in bed as well.

Before Ciara pulled herself away from Faolan's mesmerizing image, Brid hastened to continue. "Faolan has truly grown into the meaning of his name: the loner, the ever watchful wolf. He has sworn never to love or sire children of his own due to what he has perceived as the unfair suffering of his parents and siblings. He blames love and magic for all the problems in his family's lives when these energies are actually the only salvation for what seeks to destroy his world." Brid edged closer to Ciara as she spoke and leaned over the cauldron's edge. "We are asking ye to assume the role of his betrothed. You can temporarily replace the woman selected to be his wife. Seduce him, Ciara, consummate the vows, and bear him a fine gifted son. Once this task is complete, we will return the mortal woman to his side and ye will be free of your obligation."

Ciara couldn't believe what they were asking of her. She was a warrior. A Fury. She wasn't a wife and mother! So flustered by their plan, she reverted to her comfortable T-shirt and jeans. Glancing down at her curves straining against the thinly stretched cotton, she scrubbed her face with her hands. In an instant, the airy violet gossamer veils returned to swirl about her body. "The MacKay has sworn never to love and yet you say he's betrothed? Why can't we just let human nature take its course? Let him lie with the woman, get her with child and then you can train the boy in his dreams." Ciara huffed an escaped curl out of her eyes. She waited for them to see the perfect reasoning of her easy solution. She couldn't understand why they'd interrupted her from scouring evil from the world when it was obvious this duty was not her calling.

Without a word, Cerridwen passed her hand over the cauldron and dispelled the image of the striking Scot. Her summons to the cauldron replaced Faolan MacKay's handsome scowl with the vision of a slight, wispy maid wandering through the dimly lit hall of a dreary stonewalled keep. "This is Chieftain MacKay's betrothed. Her name is Dierdra Sinclair. Look closely, Ciara. Do ye notice anything different about this frail young lass?"

With growing uneasiness at the focusing vision, Ciara leaned closer and studied the image of the girl floating before her. As the picture cleared, she understood. Her heart sank the longer she watched the girl until she finally raised her head to meet Cerridwen's gaze. "She is one of the touched. A pure innocent. What kind of man would agree to marry such a woman? Is he a brute predisposed to raping children?"

Brid raised her hands. She interceded with a firm shake of her head. "No. Ye must not think ill of Laird MacKay. He felt wedding the Sinclair lass the perfect solution for both their problems. She is the wife he can ignore, and he is the husband who will never harm her. His advisors arranged the match for the benefit of the clan. The Sinclair's bride price and their adjoining lands were far too great an enticement for the MacKay advisors to resist. Faolan agreed to the match to silence the avaricious men so they would leave off with their insistence that he must wed. He has yet to meet the sweet Dierdra but his spies assured him of her innocent state. Their first meeting is set for tomorrow eve at their betrothal feast. We know if we do not intercede, he will never consummate the vows and there will never be a child. And remember, the child we need born of this union must not only hold the MacKay magic but also the powers of an immortal mother. The responsibilities of this child will be great and the bloodline he begins must be strong. His strength and knowledge must be immense to pass down to future generations."

Ciara's irritation waned a bit at Brid's assurances of Faolan's reaction to Dierdra. Once more, she leaned over the cauldron and watched the vacant-eyed maiden bend to stroke a mewling cat. Ciara reached down and dipped her fingers across the water to bless the child with her touch. "And if he never consummates the vows, this innocent could possibly fall from his protection. There are many more men who would gladly spoil her without a thought of shattering her soul."

Ciara plunged her hand deeper into the water and erased the image from view. "Tell me this, my honored mothers. If I bear the man's child, what happens then? Once I've done this thing you've requested of me, then what will happen to this unlikely pair...not to mention what will happen to the child? I'm not worried about falling in love. This weakness called love is a human problem. And I'm not concerned about The MacKay since you tell me he's hardened his heart. I am worried about who will care for my child once I have gone from their midst. I will not leave my own innocent abandoned and unprotected in Danu's dangerous world."

Brid nodded in agreement with Ciara's words as Cerridwen returned the prophetic cauldron to its platform in the corner. "We know ye would never be in danger of falling in love with the man. Ye have reminded us quite frequently of your immunity to the mortal's weakness of love. And we also know ye would never abandon a child, especially a son of your own.

"Ye will stay with the MacKays until the child is seven years of age and nearly ready to be fostered and trained. Then we will return Dierdra back to her husband's side where she will be safe from the evils of the world. We will protect her with a glamour identical to your likeness. We will hide her delicate fae-like form. No one will doubt the lass is truly his wife since she will look just like you and will have obviously borne him a son. The union will be safe from any of the accusations of non-consummation that might have otherwise occurred. Faolan will be a bit confused at first when we return the lass to his side. However, since he has sworn never to love, he will leave the lass to herself and his sense of honor will force him to protect her. All will be in place and we will have our gifted child to ensure the safety of future generations."

Ciara paced across the balcony, warring with indecision over what she should do as she stared out across the glistening mists. She watched the dance and swirl of the silver-gray fog upon the waters as she listened to the sea below. A little over eight mortal years spent wed to the mortal MacKay. Not to mention having to seduce the man. No more judgments, no more executions, just perform the role of dutiful wife to a temperamental laird and bear the man a son.

A delicious flush surged through her body as she remembered his image in the cauldron. She hardly considered the seduction of Faolan MacKay an unpleasant possibility. From the looks of the man, she had to admit she looked forward to exploring his *merits.*

It wouldn't be the first time she'd seduced a mortal. She'd occasionally treated them to erotic dreams. The joinings had been amusing enough ways to pass a lonely night but they'd left her with an even greater wariness of the complex beings. The men had become obsessed with her immortal passions. They'd become addicted to her visits to the passages of their minds as though she were a drug. She'd finally stopped indulging in this form of amusement. She'd feared some of them would surely go mad.

Eight or so years and bear the man a child. Then return the innocent Dierdra to her untouchable husband's side. The child would be safe. By seven years of age, Ciara could have him well versed in the basics of the mystics. He'd also be old enough to be fostered out to train in the more human realities of fifteenth-century Scotland.

Dierdra would be safe from any accusations of not having consummated the union. Faolan could return to his detached scowl and this could possibly set the world's salvation in motion. With a little more guidance down through the generations, they could change the course of the world.

Her palms still rested upon the soothing marble. The call of the earth pulled at her very essence. She would do this. She would follow the wishes of her mothers. She would accept this task with honor.

She sealed her fate with a decisive nod and turned to face the awaiting goddesses. "I will do this thing you ask of me. I will bring this child into the world. All I ask is that you allow me to visit Dierdra in a dream to ease her into what will occur."

Cerridwen and Brid smiled as they nodded in unison. Brid stepped forward and took Ciara's hands between her own. "We are proud of ye, Ciara. Ye have made the right choice. Ye have our blessings to perform this task as ye will. By accepting this charge, ye not only help Danu's world in its survival but ye protect the very legends of the Auld Ways themselves. When ye are ready to set these energies in motion, call out to us across the realms. Then we shall open the portals wide to allow Alec to carry Dierdra to the Land Beyond the Mists."

CHAPTER 2

"**D**amn, the woman is out of control," Faolan muttered as he stomped through the arch. The servants had scrubbed the great hall of the MacKay keep within an inch of its life. Under the command of Mistress Sorcha, no corner or crevice was safe from scrutiny.

As overseer of the care and upkeep of the castle, Mistress Sorcha ruled with a firm and unrelenting hand. Heaven help the servant foolish enough to ignore any instruction given. If unlucky or daft enough to be caught slacking, they'd best be giving their soul to their maker, for Mistress Sorcha would surely have their arse.

Faolan groaned, giving a look at the floors, wondering if it was safe to step any farther. *God's beard.* 'Twas a sorry day when a man feared walking in his own keep.

The lads had swept the great stones free of the soiled rushes and scoured them with lye and boiling water. Wrinkling his nose, Faolan cringed; the bite of the lye nearly burnt his eyes from the sockets. His keep would never smell the same. What the hell was the woman thinking? The slabs shone in the glow of the burning torches as though the stones had just been set.

"This is such a waste of time and manpower," Faolan grumbled as he stomped his way toward the kitchens. He shook his head as he watched a serving lad scurry by with two buckets of steaming water to the other side of the room.

The servants scalded and rubbed down the tables and benches until not a drop of grease stained the boards. They had cleaned and greased the irons upon the hearths; the tools and huge swinging arms holding the black pots glistened in the flickering light. The hearths had been shoveled clear of excess ash and debris. Fresh split wood stood stacked at the ready. The maids had drawn down the tartans and banners from the rafters and beaten the dust from them before they'd been re-hung.

The surrounding hills had supplied overflowing baskets of heather. The fragrance wafted throughout the keep. Faolan rubbed the back of his hand across his nose. His stomach clenched at the scent of the sweet perfume; he preferred the acrid sting of the burning lye. The scent of the heather reminded him of his parents' funeral. The fragrance brought back the darkness of that day and the stabbing loneliness still echoing through their empty chambers.

Ivy, the symbol of eternal fidelity, wound its way into every nook and crevice. Braided boughs of the emerald leaves formed an archway at the head of the hall. Fidelity. Faolan snorted. What a mockery. There would be no question of faithfulness in this union.

Casks of wine and barrels of ale lined the farthest wall and stood in neat piles beside the stairs. More stood at the ready, stored in racks in rooms offset from the hallway. The banquet required the meat of three wild boars; a successful hunt produced the necessary pigs. They now turned on spits above open fire pits behind the kitchens. Faolan spared an approving nod at the red-faced lads stationed at the fire pits. Sweat poured in rivulets down their faces as they kept the massive sides of meat sizzling and turning over the glowing coals. Breads, cheeses, and fruits of the season piled high upon serving boards along the tables. Not a spot was empty on any of the sideboards in the kitchen. All stood ready for the start of the celebration. Faolan hoped his clan was happy. This damn betrothal was finally set. *All this food.* Faolan clenched his teeth. His clan could've survived on it for half the winter.

Faolan paused just outside the kitchen doorway and peered around the corner. He'd learned long ago if he wanted to know what was truly going on in his keep, all he had to do was listen at the doorway of his own kitchens.

Mistress Sorcha made one more round through the kitchens, her ample girth swishing her black skirts upon the floor. She hefted a long-handled ladle from its hook upon the mantel and slid the heavy lid from the pot. Her eyes narrowed as she tested a bubbling broth hissing above the fire. "Bring me the dried rosemary hanging from the farthest shelf and fetch me the crock of salt."

A spindly kitchen maid hopped from the bench where she'd sat scrubbing the skins from a pile of carrots. She returned with the herbs and the crock of salt, holding them aloft until Mistress Sorcha had taken what she needed.

With a satisfied nod, Sorcha smiled her approval at the maid and replaced the ladle upon the hook. "Everything must be perfect. The clan has long waited for the day The MacKay would take a wife."

"The clan has long waited for additional money to be added to the coffers," Faolan mumbled under his breath. At least this would silence his advisors; it was either marry or murder the bastards. Faolan's stomach growled as he shifted positions; Sorcha's stew smelled delicious.

As she returned the crock of salt to its designated shelf, the kitchen maid scurried back to the bench and the enormous heap of carrots. "Have ye seen Laird MacKay's betrothed, Mistress Sorcha? Is she a fine woman worthy of our chieftain's good name?"

Faolan leaned closer, biting back a bitter laugh to be sure he heard what Sorcha replied.

At the girl's question, Sorcha's smile faded. "Lyla, I have heard the chatter of the chambermaids and I will have none of it repeated. I havena seen the lady, myself. But I am certain she will be a perfect match for our fine laird."

Faolan's heart warmed as he overheard her words. The one bright spot in this sorry mess was Sorcha's loyalty to her laird.

With a curt nod toward a basket of vegetables sitting beside the doorway, Sorcha ended the direction of Lyla's conversation. "Now make haste, Lyla. The feast will be upon us soon and ye have yet to chop all the vegetables for the other stewpot. Once ye have finished with the carrots, be sure to brush the dirt from the mushrooms that ye spread upon the shelf in the larder yesterday eve. I will be needing them for the gravies for the meat. They must have something to sop with their bread."

As she re-tied her apron around her ample hips, Sorcha headed out of the kitchens toward the great hall. As she barreled through the archway, she nearly bumped into Faolan as he slipped away from the door. "Such a fierce look! M'laird, what appears to be amiss? What have we forgotten for your celebration?" Sorcha rushed to his side, knotting her apron between her hands as her gaze darted about the room.

Raising his hands as though to ward off her words, Faolan looked around the room at all the preparations and swallowed a groan of disgust. "Ye have done well, Sorcha. Be at peace. As usual, all is perfection."

Sorcha tightened her lips into a worried line and patted her graying hair back from her weathered face. "Forgive me, my chieftain. But for a man who's about to meet his betrothed, ye seem sorely troubled."

Faolan scrubbed the stubble of his beard as he sank to the bench and dropped his head between his hands. "Sorcha, ye have been like a mother to me ever since my own mother jumped to her death. Even before then, ye relentlessly spoiled me whenever I wandered into the kitchens. However, in this matter, ye canna help me, nor can I seek your counsel. I have agreed to this match for the good of the clan and that is all that best be said."

Sorcha knotted her hands in her apron, fixing him with a worried scowl. "Blessings to ye, m'laird. Trust that all will be well. I shall leave ye in peace. I shall be in the kitchens if ye need me. All ye need do is call."

Faolan raised his head. He glanced across the room and took in the betrothal decorations with a snort of disgust. This was such a mockery. His clan sought to celebrate the securing of lands, cattle, and possible future holdings. They didna give a damn if he took a wife.

Faolan had never met Dierdra Sinclair, but he'd received reports from his informants about her simple mind and her childlike ways. Her father had been trying to marry her off for years, but her affliction had made a desirable union difficult to obtain. An avaricious man, Gordon Sinclair not only wanted rid of his vacant-eyed child, but as chieftain of the Sinclair clan, he wanted to profit from the match by obtaining an alignment with a stronger clan. In his view, the fact that his daughter might have the mind of a child had nothing to do with her ability to breed.

When Faolan had learned of Gordon Sinclair's offer and the innocence of his only child, Faolan had agreed to the match for two very simple reasons. If he took Dierdra to wife, it would silence the incessant droning of his advisors for him to marry. It would also protect the childlike Dierdra from the dangers of a less scrupulous man, one who might not give a second thought to raping a helpless innocent.

The match with the reportedly sweet, daydreaming Dierdra would perfectly suit Faolan's needs. He'd sworn he'd never open his heart to the pain he'd see his parents suffer. Because of the passion they felt for each other, their lives had met a tragic end: his father murdered while protecting his mother and then his mother had taken her own life. Faolan had sworn he'd never bring a child into the world just to abandon it when his own life ended. Love and children brought nothing but pain and suffering. Someone else could take the lairdship.

Faolan rose from the table, rolling his weary shoulders to work out the tension knotted through his muscles. He'd much rather be in the courtyard, slicing the air with his sword as he practiced with his warriors. With a resigned sigh, he plodded to the staircase leading to his private rooms. He stopped by the stairwell and tucked a cask of ale under one arm. This one belonged to him. *Lore, I need a drink.* His mood darkened as though he headed for the gallows rather than to meet his bride. It was time he readied for his betrothal banquet and resigned himself to his fate. In but a few short hours, he promised himself to a wife, whether he wanted one or not.

THE STUMP of a sputtering candle on the splintered table beside the bed fought against the shadows of the room. The darkness reeked of damp mold-covered stones and the mustiness of mildewed cloth. A dwindling fire hissed in the neglected hearth with barely enough coals to heat the surrounding stones. A moth-eaten tapestry was wedged in the cracked masonry around one narrow window in a meager attempt at blocking the bone-chilling wind.

As Ciara swirled her energy into the room, she flared into an enraged vortex of white-hot fury. If not for fear of ruining the goddesses' well-laid plan, she would've avenged the innocent girl imprisoned in the stale, dank room. Nothing would've pleased her more than terrifying the soul who had so cruelly neglected such a helpless innocent.

Ciara trembled with anger as she formed beside the crumbling frame with a ratty sheet meant to be a pitiful bed. She forced herself to take several deep, calming breaths before she attempted to connect with Dierdra's dreaming mind.

"Dierdra," Ciara breathed to the slumbering girl shivering on her side. "Dierdra, open your mind to me, child. My name is Ciara. I want to be your friend and tell you about a wonderful adventure I have for you."

Pale eyelashes fluttered on the pink of her cheeks as Dierdra nestled her tousled head deeper into the threadbare pillow. The faintest of smiles pulled at the corners of her mouth as her mind hearkened to Ciara's call.

A shimmering mist of swirling greens and blues flowed around Ciara's body as she made her way deep into Dierdra's mind. Iridescent sparks of chaotic energy and light gained momentum in their fevered dance the farther she traveled into the innocent's dream. She found the girl at the edge of a bubbling stream. Dierdra laughed as she sat wiggling her toes in the gurgling water. Ciara smiled as she noted Dierdra's once confused gray eyes now shone clear and sparkled with happiness. The vacant haze of uncertainty appeared unable to touch her while she walked the dream plane of her chosen reality.

Dierdra waved aside her floating skirts and patted the glowing mossy ground beside her. She scooted over and made room for Ciara. With a smile up into Ciara's face, she held out a trusting hand. "In my dreams, I understand the way of things. In here, I'm not afraid I might say the wrong thing or seem quite such a simple soul as I do on the other side."

Ciara lowered herself to settle on the bank beside her and dipped her bare feet in the swirling water of the bubbling stream. "I wish you didn't have to be afraid, Dierdra. However, you know the earthly plane can be a cruel place for the touched who decide to explore that reality. There are too few there capable of understanding how special the touched truly are. Danu's world can sometimes be a cold and lonely place for special ones such as you."

Dierdra looped a silvery blonde tress behind one ear as she sadly smiled down into the gurgling water. "My mother was a witch who was determined to bring me into the reality of her physical world. She met me when she conjured me in a vision and knew I was her chosen child. She couldn't bear our separation and longed to cradle me in her arms. Our energies were as one while she traveled through the cosmos and she knew I'd be lost to her upon her awakening. She didn't realize some wouldna be able to accept me when they saw me for what I truly was. My father had her killed when she laid me in his arms and he saw I was one of the touched."

Ciara's reflexive thirst for vengeance tightened in her throat as she remembered the starkness of the innocent girl's existence. She struggled to tamp down her protective rage and her desire to strike down the cruel Sinclair. She had to concentrate on remaining in Dierdra's mind. Negative energy would only confuse Dierdra's thoughts and flush her out of the girl's consciousness. She reached out to smooth her fingers through the girl's silvery hair as she ground her teeth and steadied her temper. "I'm so sorry, Dierdra. I'm so sorry you had to suffer the loss of your mother and grow up in the household of such a cruel and vicious man."

A serene smile lit Dierdra's face as she gave Ciara a reassuring shrug and tucked a flower into Ciara's dark hair. "Don't be troubled, my brave new friend. My mother's soul is now free to travel where it will. Nothing can ever harm her again. As for my father, I feel nothing but pity for the man for he will never know true peace in his heart. His soul will soon arrive in the depths of the abyss. That place is far worse than anything he could ever do to me."

Ciara's heart caught at Dierdra's benevolence. So mistreated and yet still so pure. Ciara took a deep breath. She covered Dierdra's fragile hand with her own as Dierdra trailed a willow branch in the stream. "Dierdra, would you like to spend a little while in the Land Beyond the Mists? Would you like to visit the land known only to the immortals?"

Dierdra dropped her stick and clapped her hands as she bounced up and down beside the spring. "Oh yes! I've been longing to know more of that place since I was just a wee bairn. Before my mother's soul left me, she sang a lullaby to me of the Land Beyond the Mists. I never dreamed I'd live to see it. Only the immortals live beyond those gates. My mother's lullaby is the only song I've ever heard and I've always kept it in my heart."

Again, Ciara swallowed hard at the lump of emotions aching in her throat. How could one who had only known suffering still be at peace with such a cold cruel world? "Dierdra, I need to explain to you exactly what will be done. While you're spending a bit of time away from this world, I'll be here making people believe that you've never left. I'll be the one to marry the MacKay chieftain and I'm going to bear him a child. Then no one can ever say you're not really his wife and force you to leave the safety of the MacKay keep. When you return, they might think you're not well. However, they'll never doubt you're truly his wife. You'll never be locked away for being different or treated unfairly ever again."

Ciara watched Dierdra's face to see if she understood. She needed Dierdra to understand and remember the truth. While Dierdra appeared quite lucid in her current state, Ciara knew Dierdra would revert to her usual state of confusion as soon as she awoke from the dream.

Dierdra hummed to herself and ran her fingertips across the petals of an oversized rose she held to her nose. "Ciara, ye know it doesna matter how they treat my body. Ye know they can never touch my soul."

Ciara took a deep breath. She'd never been the patient sort but she didn't dare get flustered. She didn't have the time to argue with such philosophical logic but she wanted to be sure the information seeded somewhere in Dierdra's subconscious mind. The girl would need to have the basic knowledge of what had happened to be able to cope with life when she returned to the harsh reality of the world. It would be eight odd mortal years later. It would be difficult enough for Dierdra to adapt. Somehow, Ciara had to seed what was going to happen deep within Dierdra's mind.

With a placating nod, she eased the rose out of Dierdra's hands and leaned forward until she was almost nose-to-nose with Dierdra. "You are absolutely right. They can never touch your soul, but if we're able to outsmart them, then getting through this life won't be such a trial. Wouldn't it be much more pleasant to be physically comfortable until it's time to move on to the next plane and the newest adventure?"

Dierdra's clear gray eyes darted about the forest of her mind as though searching among the swaying trees for an answer. At last, as though a ray of sunlight settled upon her face, she gifted Ciara with a smile. "I agree with ye completely, my new friend Ciara. We will play our game of hide-and-switch to trick those who don't understand me. When do we get to start our game? When do I get to pass to the land of the immortals?"

Finally. Exhaling as though she'd been holding her breath, Ciara raised one hand to summon Alec from just beyond the other side. "My friend Alec the raven is here to guide you. He will take you through the mists and get you settled. First, could you please stand and let me have a good look at you? I need to make sure we're able to look just alike whenever it's time for us to return to our own lives.

Dierdra jumped up from her seat on the mossy bank and raised her arms in the air. As she spun around, she lifted her face so Ciara could study her appearance.

Long blonde hair the color of spun silver framed her small oval face. Spidery blue veins traced just beneath her skin, which was as translucent as the finest bone china. Her tiny frame danced as delicately as an elfin maiden. She reached just above Ciara's waist. She had nary a curve. She could barely make a shadow so slight was her tiny body. Dierdra seemed almost ethereal in her appearance so fragile and wispy was her form.

Ciara circled the tiny maid, her fingers tapping out her thoughts against her chin. She bit her lip and turned to Alec waiting on a branch in one of Dierdra's imaginary trees. "The goddesses were right. She will have to be the one hidden by a glamour. I was going to try to assume her form but I don't think I can make it work. I don't think I'd be able to contain my energy within such a fragile form for such an extended period. She is so tiny, so *airy*. Since I'm a Fury, I don't think there is any way I could maintain such a level of tight control over all my conflicting energies."

"Don't worry, Ciara. No one has seen me but Father and it's been years since he set foot in my rooms." Dierdra bent to pick a handful of flowers from a nearby bank, skipping away as she pulled the petals from the stems.

"What?" Ciara blinked at Dierdra then hurried to follow the maid deeper into her mind. "What do you mean no one's seen you? Are you telling me, he's kept you locked away your entire life? How did you receive your food? Clothing? How have you survived?"

Dierdra spun in a circle, skipping along the path. She laughed as she let the flowers flutter to the ground. "The doors to my chambers are usually kept locked from the outside. Sometimes the servants forget and I wander the hallways until someone happens to hear me. The servants always leave the food tray in an anteroom and my seamstress is a deaf-mute who lives in fear of my father's wrath. My father forbade anyone to ever look upon me or allow any around me who can speak. He told them my beauty was too great to behold but I know 'twas because I am simple. I once had a servant who could actually speak, but I havena seen her in several years."

Ciara's frustration mounted as though she were about to burst into a lightning storm. If not for the fact she'd given her mothers her word, she'd hunt down Gordon Sinclair this very night and rip his soul from his body. Ciara promised herself when this current task was over, she'd be having a word or two with the cruel Sinclair. She eased her anger by thinking of several choice ways she'd torment the man before he died.

However, that still didn't solve the problem of what form she should take since at some point in time Dierdra would have to return. As an experiment, she passed her hands over Dierdra's body, then stood back to survey the results.

With a croaking screech of approval, Alec cawed from the tree. "Well done! The lass looks just like ye." Hopping farther down the branch, he cocked his sleek black head and peered closer into Dier-dra's face. "But the eyes aren't right. Her eyes are still gray, they're no' the golden color like yours. Other than that, ye look quite the same. Wave your hand again over her eyes."

Ciara shook her head and stroked her chin as she circled the smiling Dierdra who could now pass as her twin. "I can't change the eyes. The eyes are the reflection of her soul. I can no more change her eyes then I can my own."

"Are we ready now? Can we go to the other side? Are ye ready to take my place?" Dierdra hopped up and down on each foot as though she were a child begging to go to the fair.

Ciara motioned Alec over and gently took Dierdra's hand. "If you're ready, Alec will be your guide. Take care, my innocent, we will return to fetch you soon."

Dierdra gave Ciara an affectionate peck on the cheek. "Goodbye, brave Ciara! I shall see ye soon!"

GET your copy of The Highlander's Fury to find out what happens next!

If you enjoyed this story, please consider leaving a review on the site where you purchased your copy, or a reader site such as Goodreads, or BookBub.

Visit my website at maevegreyson.com to sign up for my newsletter and stay up to date on new releases, sales, and all sorts of whatnot. (There are some freebies too!)

I would be nothing without my readers. You make it possible for me to do what I love. Thank you SO much!

Sending you big hugs and hoping you always have a great story to enjoy!

Maeve

ABOUT THE AUTHOR

maevegreyson.com

USA Today Bestselling Author. Multiple RONE Award Winner. Multiple Holt Medallion Finalist.

Maeve Greyson's mantra is this: No one has the power to shatter your dreams unless you give it to them.

She and her husband of over forty years traveled around the world while in the U.S. Air Force. Now they're settled in rural Kentucky where Maeve writes about her courageous Highlanders and the fearless women who tame them. When she's not plotting the perfect snare, she can be found herding cats, grandchildren, and her husband—not necessarily in that order.

Also by Maeve Greyson

HIGHLAND HEROES SERIES

The Chieftain - Prequel

The Guardian

The Warrior

The Judge

The Dreamer

The Bard

The Ghost

A Yuletide Yearning

Love's Charity

TIME TO LOVE A HIGHLANDER SERIES

Loving Her Highland Thief

Taming Her Highland Legend

Winning Her Highland Warrior

Capturing Her Highland Keeper

Saving Her Highland Traitor

Loving Her Lonely Highlander

Delighting Her Highland Devil

ONCE UPON A SCOT SERIES

A Scot of Her Own

A Scot to Have and to Hold

A Scot to Love and Protect